Mary S. Lippincott, Hugh Foulke

Life and letters of Mary S. Lippincott, late of Camden, New Jersey

a minister in the Society of Friends

Mary S. Lippincott, Hugh Foulke

Life and letters of Mary S. Lippincott, late of Camden, New Jersey
a minister in the Society of Friends

ISBN/EAN: 9783337017521

Printed in Europe, USA, Canada, Australia, Japan

Cover: Foto ©Raphael Reischuk / pixelio.de

More available books at **www.hansebooks.com**

LIFE AND LETTERS

OF

MARY S. LIPPINCOTT

LATE OF CAMDEN, NEW JERSEY,

A MINISTER IN THE SOCIETY OF FRIENDS.

" *I love them that love me ; and those that seek me early shall find me.*"—
Prov. viii: 17.

PHILADELPHIA:
WM. H. PILE'S SONS, PRINTERS, 422 WALNUT STREET.

1893.

PREFACE.

The reader will bear in mind that this work has been prepared for the press at the request, and by direction of some of the *relatives* of M. S. L.

These felt desirous to preserve her writings in a form more convenient and more permanent than that of manuscript, also to give to the many who had known and loved her, an opportunity to learn something of her *inner*, as well as of her outer life.

In the hope that it may prove acceptable to her friends without, as well as to those within the circle of kindred, and to some even beyond the limits of personal acquaintance, it is submitted to such as may feel inclined to peruse it.

CONTENTS.

CHAPTER IV.

CHAPTER V.

INTRODUCTION.

In preparing for publication the writings of Mary S. Lippincott, it seemed desirable to give the prominent incidents of her life in the order of their occurrence, and to make the account as nearly complete as the preserved memoranda, with some additional information, would warrant.

To do this, involved the necessity of collecting items from different sources, and of arranging them in the order of time, or of subject, as nearly as the void intervals would permit, and as the narration of the incidents seemed to require.

CHAPTER I. has been prepared on this general plan ; and since much of the information was unwritten, the phraseology could not be given, but the attempt has been made to render the thought, and to supply such details as the data would furnish.

From her tenth to her eighteenth year there is little to be found in the records of the family, and from the time of her marriage until after her removal to Moorestown, a period of thirteen years, the Diary is a blank. From the year 1842 until the close of her life, we are fairly well informed of the most important incidents connected with her personal history, and also of her impressions and religious exercises. The first entry in her Diary [that has been preserved] was made when she was in her twenty-third year : and the last one was recorded on the seventy-fourth anniversary of her birth-day. Family memoranda, oral information, and some reminiscences have furnished the information given before the former date : and her own letters, the accounts of her friends who visited her, also the testimony of members of her family, and of the physician who attended her, have been drawn upon for the remaining thirteen years of her life.

CHAPTER II. needed but little alteration, and no additions ; and as it is her own account of her trials and exercises, it will be of interest to those who can enter into sympathy with the pathetic narration of her experience. As it gives a view of her inner life, it enables us the more to appreciate her *ministry*, after we have seen the depths from which it was evolved.

CHAPTER III. is a series of extracts from a voluminous correspondence ; and it introduces the reader into her society as she was known in her middle and later life. Though few of the letters have been given in full, yet it was not deemed necessary to mark the omissions by asterisks, but simply to make *this statement* in lieu thereof. As a letter-writer she was natural and versatile ; and could her effusions, sent to her absent friends, have been published *entire*, they would have been marked by the same easy flow of expression that gave such a charm to her conversation in the social circle.

But there were many matters of interest to her correspondents, and especially so at the time of her writing them, that did not seem adapted to a wider circle of readers. As has been well said, it is a delicate matter to publish private letters without the consent of the writer.

CHAPTER IV. is a collection of papers on different subjects, each of which had made such an impression upon her mind, that she thought it worthy of record. The last four of these papers are descriptions of death-bed scenes, to three of which she was a witness and for all four of the deceased she was, in the Christian acceptation of the word, a mourner. With the exceptions of these obituaries, there was no personality requiring omission or abridgement in this chapter.

CHAPTER V. consists of metrical effusions, written at different periods of her life, but all of them between her twenty-first and her sixtieth year. Her fancy was lively, her expression free, and her love of nature as genuine, as it seemed ardent. Of the standard poets it would appear that Cowper was her favorite. In her appreciation of poetry, as in other matters, she was too sincere to affect admiration for anything merely because it was conventional.

In the Appendix will be found a number of miscellaneous items, that are directly or indirectly connected with the life of the subject ; and on account of this connection it seemed fitting to give them a place. Some of these have come to hand while the work was going through the press.

In conclusion, the editor would acknowledge his indebtedness to friends who have rendered valuable assistance in the *preparation*, the *publication* and the *distribution* of the work.

HUGH FOULKE.

PHILADELPHIA, PENNA., Second Month 28th, 1893.

MEMORIAL

OF

MARY S. LIPPINCOTT.

A Memorial of Chester Monthly Meeting, New Jersey, concerning our deceased friend, MARY S. LIPPINCOTT.

Under a sense of the loss that we have sustained by the death of this dear and valued Friend, we feel it right to make a brief record of her life, and of her religious experience, for the benefit of survivors, desiring that it may serve as an incentive, especially to those who are in the morning of life, to walk in the path of obedience to manifested duty, and to profit by the example of one, who by an early dedication of all her faculties, experienced preservation from evil, strength in weakness, and comfort in seasons of outward trial.

Mary S. Lippincott, daughter of Anthony and Jane S. Hallowell, was born on the twenty-third day of the Sixth Month, in the year 1801, in Cheltenham Township, Montgomery County, Pennsylvania, and was a birthright member of the religious Society of Friends. She was endowed with a vigorous intellect, and retentive memory,

2

and before she had concluded her tenth year, had read aloud to her grandfather, Benjamin Shoemaker, the Bible, as well as the Journal of George Fox, and portions of other Friends' works.

The influence of this early course of reading was plainly manifest throughout her life, as she was both ready and accurate in her quotations from the Scriptures, and familiar with the writings of early Friends.

Her school education was received at day schools at Hatboro and Abington, and at boarding-schools at West-town in Pennsylvania, and at Fair Hill in Maryland. When about twenty-one years of age, she engaged in teaching, a work for which she seemed to be fitted, both by nature and training, and which was not finally abandoned until she was in her eightieth year. She taught at Cheltenham, Abington and Westtown, in Pennsylvania; at Fair Hill, in Maryland; at Alexandria, in Virginia; and at Rensselaerville, in New York.

In 1829, she was married to Isaac Lippincott, a member of Chester Monthly Meeting, New Jersey, and removed to reside with him, becoming a member of the same meeting, and so continuing until her death. In 1842, she and her husband, established the Moorestown Boarding School for Girls, which was continued under her supervision for a period of thirty-eight years. The influence for good which went out from this institution has been widely felt. Her pupils not only received thorough instruction in the ordinary branches of a school education, but their moral and spiritual being was carefully nur-

tured, and the training there received was of priceless
value in after life. In the matter of school and family
discipline it may truly be said that she "ruled with
meekness,—they obeyed with joy"—and her authority
"was but the graver countenance of love." In the education of young women whose means were limited she
was almost over-generous, and in this and in other acts
of beneficence she did much that was only known to herself and to those whom she benefited. She was ever
desirous that an increased liberality might prevail in the
Society for the advancement of its schools, and encouraged Friends to improve those they had, and to use their
best endeavors in the establishment of others.

It would appear from the memoranda, that she was
early brought under the preparing Hand for service in
her Master's vineyard. She records that while a school
girl, engaged in some household duties, being in a serious
state of mind, her spiritual ear was saluted with the
language: "Simon, son of Jonas, lovest thou me?"
"Feed my sheep." This salutation seemed to foretell
the labor that would be required of her, and she alludes
to its fulfilment many years afterwards.

When about twenty-two years of age, and for some
time subsequently, she passed through many deep baptisms; of these she has left abundant notes. In the early
part of the year 1824, she records a fervent prayer, a part
of which is as follows: "Be pleased, O righteous Father!
to look down with pity on a poor frail mortal of the dust,
whose heart is ready to sink, and who is almost over-

whelmed. Suffer me not to perish, but keep me, I beseech Thee, and suffer me to abide under the shadow of
Thy wing. Cleanse me, purify me, try me, prove me, and
spare not the rod, till all within me that is offensive in
Thy sight, be purged away. Refine me, and baptize me
again and again, if consistent with Thy holy will. Create
in me a clean heart, and renew a right spirit within me.
Teach me humility, yea keep me down in the valley, that
I may not think much of myself. Lead me wheresoever
Thou desirest me to go, and make me willing to bow in
full submission to Thy holy presence."

She was then in the twenty-third year of her age,
and feeling deeply exercised, she writes that she was not
at liberty to unburden her mind to any human being,
but adds: "I believe it best for me to be sober in all my
movements, quiet and retired, that I may be more watchful over myself." The time for her to be cheerful had
not yet come, and those who tried to anticipate it, were
strangers to her inward struggles.

She lived in the desire to do good, and as she grew
older, became convinced that it was obedience to manifestations from the Most High that qualified for good
works,—even the Grace of God that maketh known the
Divine will to his children, and giveth ability to perform it.

As she followed her convictions, she was early led
to exhort others with much tenderness, to a dependence
on the same Divine Comforter, expressing the assurance
that under its guidance every human effort, however

small, when made with a sincere desire to do good, is
acceptable with the Father. By abiding in humility,
and keeping a strict watch over herself, in conduct,
conversation, and thoughts, she gradually experienced
a growth in grace, and in her ministerial gift. In her
twenty-ninth year, with the full unity of her meeting,
her gift in the ministry was acknowledged and approved.

In the year 1845 she was appointed Clerk of the
Yearly Meeting of Women Friends held in Philadelphia,
and by successive appointments, filled that position until
1867. For this service she had unusual qualifications,
—executive ability, great forbearance, and an inward cri-
terion for determining the true sense of the meeting,—
all combined with readiness and felicity of expression.
While faithfully serving the meeting as Clerk, she was
careful not to neglect her individual exercises. Sometimes she would find it necessary to lay down her pen,
get into the quiet, and find what she had to do. After
a short season of waiting, she would arise, deliver her
message with clearness and power, and then proceed
with the business of the meeting.

A concern opened by our Friend at the close of a
First-day morning meeting, was the origin of the First-
day school at Moorestown, which was one of the first
within the limits of Philadelphia Yearly Meeting. She
entered upon this important work with her usual earnest-
ness, and was Superintendent of the school for many
years. Here, as in her ministry, she did not feel called
to sound the note of controversial doctrine, but her teach-

ing was according to the new commandment given by
Jesus,—"That ye love one another." The testimonies
embraced in our first and second Queries, were to her,
vital realities, and her steadfast endeavor to maintain
them has been of lasting benefit.

Her heart ever went out in sympathy to those in
distress, affliction, or bereavement, and amid her many
engrossing cares and labors she was never too busy, or
too weary, to listen to their troubles, to give words of
advice, encouragement or consolation, and to the extent
of her ability, share their burden.

In her middle and later life, she was a bright example of the happiness to be experienced from a full sur-
render, and an early dedication of heart. In the social
circle she was a general favorite, her animated and interesting conversation being instructive and enlivening,
both to the young and the old.

About eight years before her death, she and her two
daughters removed to Camden, New Jersey, where, so
long as her health permitted, she continued to attend
meetings.

Her life as to the outward was a checkered one, and
many were her trials and bereavements. Her aged
mother, who died in 1847, was the object of her tender
care, and her faithful ministrations to promote the comfort of this revered parent, are worthy of record, as well
as imitation. The loss of her husband, in 1858, was
keenly felt. As partners in life they had been congenial and closely united, and as an elder he had sympa-

thized and traveled with her in her religious exercises. Of five [six] children, only one survived her.

But throughout all she was sustained by an unfaltering trust. One of her pupils gives expression to the feelings of many, when she says: " I have marvelled at her cheerfulness, her courage, her patience, and her unwavering faith in the goodness and protecting care of her Heavenly Father."

During her last illness, which she bore with great fortitude, she said to her friends that her sufferings were doubtless permitted for a wise, though unseen purpose, and was comforted with the firm belief that she would be accepted. That " more sure word of prophecy" to which she early gave heed, and which had been followed by the dawning of the day and the arising of the day-star in her heart, had been her faith through life ; and when her sun was about to go down in brightness, she desired that the young might have their attention called to this same more sure Word.

With full faith in the promise of a happy eternity, she made a peaceful close on the 18th of the Fourth Month, 1888, and on the 21st of the same her remains were interred in Friends' burial ground at Moorestown.

She was aged nearly eighty-seven years, sixty of which she had been a faithful and acceptable minister of the Gospel.

Read and approved in Chester Monthly Meeting of Friends, held at Moorestown, N. J., Third Month 7th, 1889, and directed to be forwarded to the Quarterly Meeting.

JOHN M. LIPPINCOTT, } *Clerks.*
RACHEL A. COLLINS,

———

Read and approved in Haddonfield Quarterly Meeting of Friends, held at Moorestown, N. J., Third Month 7th, 1889, and directed to be forwarded to the Representative Committee or Meeting for Sufferings.

CLAYTON CONROW, } *Clerks.*
ELIZABETH L. JESSUP,

LIFE AND LETTERS

OF

MARY S. LIPPINCOTT.

CHAPTER I.

A BRIEF ACCOUNT OF HER LIFE.

Mary S. Hallowell was the daughter of Anthony and Jane Hallowell, and was born in Cheltenham Township, Montgomery County, Pennsylvania, on the 23rd of Sixth Month, 1801. Her parents being members of the religious Society of Friends, she had a birthright therein, and her name was so recorded on the books of Abington Monthly Meeting.

Her grandparents were William and Mary [Williams] Hallowell, and Benjamin and Mary [Comly] Shoemaker. She was the fifth and youngest child, and only daughter of the family. Her name combines those of her two grandmothers, Mary Shoemaker Hallowell.

Her brothers were James S., Benjamin (who died in infancy,) Joseph, and Benjamin.

The place of her birth was the homestead of her grandfather Shoemaker; and the house which stood until quite recently, was near the corner of York Road and Cheltenham Avenue. The latter is sometimes

called Chelten Avenue, and was formerly known as
"Graveyard Lane." It took its early name from a small
enclosure, which was commonly called "The Shoemaker
Burying Ground," though more properly designated as
Cheltenham Friends' Burial Ground. It is situated on
Cheltenham Avenue, a short distance above where Benjamin Shoemaker's buildings stood, and on the opposite
side of the road. It has recently been ascertained that
forty-five persons named Shoemaker, besides the many
descendants of the family having other names, have
been interred in this ground.

The place is in close proximity to the village of
Ogontz, which was, until quite recently, called Shoemakertown, as most of the prominent residents, and
nearly all the property owners, were named Shoemaker.

So far as we can learn, they were (nearly, if not
quite all) members of the Society of Friends, and were
persons of good repute; being honest, industrious, thrifty,
benevolent, and some of them—for that time—quite well
educated.

Their ancestor, George Shoemaker, came with his
family from Kreisheim, near Heidelburg, in the Palatinate, to England. From London they embarked for
Pennsylvania, in the ship *Jefferies*, Thomas Arnold,
master. On the passage the small-pox broke out, and
many of the passengers died, among the number being
George Shoemaker. His family, consisting of a wife
and seven children, were thus left to establish themselves,
and found a home in the New World. They landed at

Chester, Pennsylvania, in the early part of the year 1686, and came up to Germantown, now a part of the city of Philadelphia.

The eldest son, George Shoemaker, Jr., was about twenty-three years old, and being a steady, capable young man, as well as a dutiful son, he assisted his mother in the care of the younger children.

About eight years after their arrival in America, George married Sarah Wall, the granddaughter and only descendant of Richard Wall, an English Friend who had settled in Cheltenham.

It would appear from the records that Richard took much interest in the maintenance of Cheltenham Friends' Meeting [which afterwards became Abington Meeting], and in his will he bequeathed to said meeting the burial ground already referred to.

It was in the early part of the year 1801 that Jane Hallowell and her two sons, James and Benjamin, came to live with her father. The other son, Joseph, went to live with an uncle named Brumfield, at Columbia, Pennsylvania.

Benjamin Shoemaker was about seventy-four years of age, and had been a widower nine years, when his daughter and her boys came to live with him, and to add so much to the comfort and enjoyment of his home. After the birth of Mary he had an added source of joy to cheer him in his declining years.

As Benjamin was a farmer, and had the work of planting and gathering the crops carried on by hired laborers, his daughter was much occupied with household duties, such as providing for the men, attending to the dairy, spinning, &c. From the memoranda that we have of the domestic arrangements, it would appear that Benjamin passed much of his time in his arm-chair, with his little granddaughter near him. Which was the entertainer, and which the entertained, we need not inquire, for we may suppose that the care was reciprocal and the enjoyment mutual. He taught her to knit, to spin, and most probably to read, as there is no mention made of her having attended any school until after his death ; but we are informed that she had read aloud to him the whole of the Bible, and of George Fox's Journal. While these two books had been read in their entirety, portions of others had also received attention ; but there is no account of anything light or frivolous— only the Holy Scriptures and the writings of Friends being chosen.

But the time was approaching when this close companionship must cease ; when the affectionate grandparent and his devoted little attendant must be separated, he going to his long home, and she mourning on her way for the loss of one whom she had revered, trusted and loved.

Benjamin Shoemaker died on the 16th of Third Month, 1811, aged eighty-four years. His death lacked but one day of being eighteen years after that of his wife. Of their fourteen children twelve had lived to adult age, but only three survived their father. These three were Nathan, Comly, and Jane.

On the day following his death, the remains of Benjamin Shoemaker were interred in the Cheltenham Friends' Burial Ground, near which he had lived and died.

Of the Hallowell, Williams, and Comly ancestors, we are not so fully informed, but it appears that they, also, were Friends, and that Mary Williams (grandmother of M. S. L.) was a descendant of George Shoemaker, Jr., though not of his first wife Sarah, but of his second, who was named Katharine.

About two years before the decease of her father, Jane Hallowell had passed through a sore affliction in the death of her son Joseph. Though only about twelve years of age, he assisted in the store of his uncle, with whom he lived. One evening, while he was weighing some gunpowder for a customer, two boys who were in the store were playing, and when one threw something at the other, a spark, either from a candle or from a cigar, fell into the powder and caused a terrific explosion, after which Joseph was found in the cellar, the floor under him having given away. When found he was unconscious, but soon after became sensible, and told the family how the accident had occurred. He lived until next morning in great agony, but fully aware of his situation, and made some remarks suitable for one of his age, and his innocent life. His mother was expecting him home on his first visit, and when the sad

tidings of his death came, her inward grief was no doubt
very great. Her son Benjamin, in his "Autobiogra-
phy," says, "All the reference mother ever made to it
afterwards, was to say, ' Poor Joseph,' and weep."

Soon after the death of Benjamin Shoemaker, his
estate was settled by selling the homestead, and thus
the family had to be broken up. It now consisted of
Jane Hallowell and her two children, Benjamin and
Mary; the eldest son, James, having previously gone
into the store and the family of his uncle William Hallowell, in Philadelphia. Jane and her daughter went to
her uncle, Samuel Shoemaker's, near Hatboro, Montgomery County, Penna. Both mother and daughter
found it to be a pleasant home, and as it was near the
Lollar Academy, Mary was entered as a pupil in that
institution. It was under Presbyterian management,
and was in high repute for being a good school.

Benjamin went to live with his uncle, Comly Shoemaker and wife, on their farm, called Pleasant Valley,
adjacent to the old homestead.

Subsequently, Jane Hallowell and her daughter went
to live with their relative George Williams, whose home
being near Abington Meeting House, was probably a
resort for traveling Friends. While there, most likely,
Mary was a pupil in the Abington Friends' School.

In 1819, after she had entered her nineteenth year,
she went to Westtown Boarding School, in Chester
County, Pennsylvania, and continued there as a pupil
about one year.

In Ninth Month, 1820, came another family affliction. Her brother James died, after a brief but very
distressing illness, leaving a widow and one child. In
a few days after the funeral, Mary went with her only
surviving brother, Benjamin, to Friends' Boarding School
at Fair Hill, near Sandy Spring, Maryland ; Benjamin
resuming his duties as teacher in that Institution, and
Mary entering it as a pupil.

In the early part of the year 1823 we find her teaching a family school in Cheltenham, near the place of
her birth. While thus occupied, she was visited by
members of the Westtown Committee, and invited to
take the position made vacant by the absence of Sybella
Embree, who had gone to Europe in consequence of her
failing health. Ann Mifflin, who was temporarily taking
the place of Sybella, was desirous of being relieved of
her duties at the earliest date practicable ; and as she
was one of the Yearly Meeting's Committee having
charge of the School, she and another member of the
Committee went to Cheltenham, and made the proposi-
tion to Mary. It was favorably received. The appointment was accepted, and in less than a week from that
time Mary was regularly installed, and was performing
the duties of her new position. She began on the 8th of
Second Month, 1823.

It was during her sojourn at Westtown that she
became acquainted with John Mott, who subsequently
established a boarding school for girls, at Rensselaerville,

New York, and secured the services of Mary S. Hallowell as teacher.

In less than a year from the date of her entering upon her duties as teacher at Westtown, we find the first record in her Diary, from which it will appear that she was laboring under deep religious exercise. The baptisms through which she passed to prepare her for the work of the ministry, were mortifying to the flesh, as well as purifying to the spirit; and during all this trying period she was obliged to respond to the daily call of routine duties in the school, and to associate with the members of that large family during the intervals intended for social mingling. Then, as now, there were those who failed to comprehend why a young person should be so serious as to appear gloomy ; so they urged her to be cheerful. No doubt their motive was good, but the advice alone was evidence that they were strangers to the experience through which she was passing. But with all the care that she found necessary to exercise in the social circle (for she was naturally of a lively disposition, and prone to freedom of speech), her surroundings, taking all the conditions into account, were probably about the most favorable that she could have had for her advancement in spiritual things, and as a preparation for her life-work in the training of young women.

The meetings for worship were often favored seasons, being attended by solid Friends who were members of the Committee, and also by Gospel messengers from different parts of this country and from Great Britain, who were traveling on religious visits. In the general arrangement of the school and of the household, there was maintained a conservative strictness that taught the young people by example, as well as by precept, the importance of a steadfast adherence to the practices of Friends. This teaching was not lost on the pupils, but was conducive to the formation of such habits in thought and discipline as to regulate their conduct while in the institution, and to clothe them with a protective armor after leaving its fostering care.

In the case of Mary S. Hallowell, this training proved to be of lasting benefit, and its effects were manifest wherever she had an opportunity and felt it right to exercise an influence over young people.

The exact time of her first appearance in the ministry cannot be given, but it was probably during the latter part of her sojourn at Westtown, or soon after leaving that Institution.

She went to Rensselaerville in 1826 or 1827, and remained there until about the time of her marriage.

In the year 1829 she was married to Isaac Lippincott, of Chesterville, Burlington County, New Jersey. The marriage was accomplished in Friends' Meeting House at Abington, and Mary, herself, wrote the certificate. The company was entertained at the residence of her uncle, Comly Shoemaker, this being her home when not at boarding-schools.

Soon after their marriage, her husband took her to

3

his home, where she entered upon the new duties of
house-keeping and supplying the place of mother to his
two children—a daughter of sixteen and a son of twelve
years.

Although all three of the positions—wife, mother
and housekeeper—were new to her, yet she discharged
the duties of each and all of them with so much fidelity
as to secure the confidence and win the affection of all
the members of the household. The union between
her husband and herself was a true marriage, and her
affection for his children, being fully reciprocated, proved
to be lasting as life.

Notwithstanding the formation of these new bonds
of faith and affection, she did not neglect or withhold
the service called for in the assemblies of the people,
but continued to exercise her *gift*, to the edification of
her hearers, and as we may infer, to the peace of her
own mind. When in her twenty-ninth year her gift
was acknowledged, and her name was recorded as an
approved minister of Chester Monthly, and Haddonfield
Quarterly Meetings. The expressed unity with this
procedure was an evidence that her ministry was not
only approved by the elders, but that it was also acceptable to the other members of the meeting.

She frequently performed visits in Gospel love,
within the limits of her own, and sometimes of other
Yearly Meetings, and the openness on the part of Friends
in the different localities, to receive her, was an evidence

that she was in the line of her duty when on these missions.

To Isaac and Mary S. Lippincott were born four sons and two daughters. The sons all died young (the eldest of them being about eight years old), but the daughters survived their father; and one of them, Margaret W. Lippincott, still lives.

Of Isaac's two older children, the daughter, Phebe W., lived to an advanced age, and looked upon several of her great-grandchildren. Her husband was Granville S. Woolman, M. D., whom she survived nearly twenty years. The son, Daniel P. Lippincott, died soon after his marriage. His only child, Daniel P. Lippincott (born after the father's death), resided in St. Louis, Missouri, and was much esteemed for his ability, energy and many good qualities. He died on the 7th of Eleventh Month, 1892, in the forty-eighth year of his age, leaving a widow and two sons. The elder of these sons, now a young man, is named Isaac Lippincott. The interest that Mary S. Lippincott felt in Daniel and his family, and the fondness for the great-grandson who bears the name of her husband, is abundantly manifest in her letters. There is not to be found in all her writings, more convincing proof of her tenderness and her strong affection, than we find in some of the letters (not made public) relative to "little Isaac."

Daniel and his sons were the only descendants of her husband, bearing the name of Lippincott; and she alludes to this fact in one of her letters to Daniel. She expressed at different times a desire to visit them in their own home; but the distance between St. Louis and Camden, and her feebleness of body, prevented her from accomplishing what would have afforded her so much gratification.

Daniel's marriage was very satisfactory to her, and his wife and boys had, like himself, a firm hold on her affections; and her solicitude for their welfare was un-mistakable; as may be found from her numerous mes-sages of loving interest to those whom she had not seen.

About two years before her death, Daniel brought all of his family with him, and made her a visit in her own home. This event was among the joys of her old age; and the remembrance of it was a source of much comfort to her.

When Isaac Lippincott passed away, he had three daughters living, but no son. His daughter Jane sur-vived her father, but not her mother. She died on the 21st of Second Month, 1885. These family bereavements are feelingly alluded to in the Diary, and in some of the letters of Mary S. Lippincott.

In the Spring of 1843, our Friend, accompanied by her husband, attended New York Yearly Meeting, and soon after their return to their home, she passed through an-other season of bereavement, occasioned by the death of her beloved uncle (who had been like a father to her), Comly Shoemaker. He died of a short illness, and left, as a lasting memorial, the savor of a good name. He was one who liked to help others, and who was noted for his

kindness to all that came within the range of his opportunity, and most especially to orphans. His estimate
of himself, and of his own merits, was very low, so that
he might well have been called one of the " poor in
spirit." His funeral was an occasion of solemn interest,
many, no doubt, feeling that they had lost a friend.
The remains were interred in the Cheltenham graveyard, where those of his parents and a large family of
their children lay. His widow, Sarah Shoemaker, survived him about two years. They had no children.

In 1842, Isaac Lippincott and family moved into
Moorestown — a few miles distant from their former
home—and established a boarding school for girls and
young women. Mary's great energy and untiring industry were brought to bear upon this enterprise, so
that it soon grew into favor among Friends; being regarded—as it deserved to be—as a valuable auxiliary to
the educational work going on in the Society. With
a thorough scholastic training in the useful branches
of a good, plain education, it combined the influences
of a concerned Friends' home. Example went directly
along with precept, and the young women soon discovered that "Aunt Mary" was not only the executive
manager of a large institution, but that she was also
a wise counselor, and a spiritual adviser who could
warn them of approaching danger, and could direct
their attention to the inward monitor that would prove
to them a source of comfort or of distress, according as
they obeyed or disobeyed its teachings. Then, too, she

was so loving and tender; so motherly in her intercourse with them, that they could not feel other than
love for her, and a desire to comply with her wishes.

> " Where kindness on her part who ruled the whole
> Begat a tranquil confidence in all,
> And all were swift to follow whom all loved."

Being ready of discernment in natural things, and
(after the baptism that she passed through in early life)
having an eye that had been spiritually anointed, she
was qualified to administer the Word in season which, in
many cases, probably proved to be as "bread cast upon
the waters." The number of women who are now faithful
supporters of their home meetings, and who are useful
in the transaction of the business in Philadelphia Yearly
Meeting—who were at one time members of her family
—furnishes us with a living testimony to the good re-
sults of her example and her precepts in the training
of young Friends.

When nearly four-score years of age, she accompanied one of her ex-pupils, an approved minister, on
a visit of religious concern to the men's branch of Philadelphia Yearly Meeting. The Friend was evidently
laboring under a great weight of exercise, which she
was favored to spread before the meeting in plain terms,
and in a solemn and impressive manner. Soon after
this young minister had taken her seat, Mary arose
and expressed her full unity with the "dear sister,"
and the sense of duty which *she* had felt to accompany
her on this visit.

It seemed to be just what was needed to supplement and to confirm the former searching testimony.

When the women Friends withdrew there was a solemn covering over the men's meeting.

In the year 1845, Mary S. Lippincott was appointed Clerk of the women's branch of Philadelphia Yearly Meeting, and for twenty-two consecutive years she filled [by reappointments] this responsible position, with so much propriety as to give satisfaction to her friends, and dignity to the large assembly.

She was so modest in regard to this appointment, and the very efficient service which she rendered to the meeting, that in her writings we find but little mention made of it; but the memories of the older and middle-aged Friends retain some deep impressions of the effects produced upon that large body, by her individuality, her quick perceptions, and her close attention to inward exercises.

Upon one occasion, when a stirring appeal had been made to the *young* women, urging them to participate in the transaction of the business—for the reason that their perceptions were keener, and their judgment was better, than was the case with the mothers and the grandmothers, who had been faithful in their day, but who now would better lay down the burden—the Clerk arose, and after a few words of encouragement to the young, expressing her appreciation of their interest in the proceedings of the meeting, she briefly related the Scriptural account of Israel when about to confer the blessing upon his grandsons. Notwithstanding his great age, and the dimness of his outward sight, " he was not to be swerved from the true judgment, but, guiding his hands wittingly," he placed the right one upon the head of Ephraim. The allusion was so apt ; the intro- duction of it so concise ; and the spirit in which it was made, so kind, as to produce a good effect at the time of its utterance, and to leave, on the minds of some in the assembly, an impression which memory has preserved through all the intervening years, and which is still fresh and vivid.

In the year 1847 our Friend had to part with her beloved parent, over whom she had watched so tenderly, and who had been so appreciative of her ministrations of love.

Jane Hallowell was one who had drunk deeply of the cup of affliction, but her last days were made as com- fortable for her, as the infirmities of age would permit. In Isaac Lippincott she found a devoted friend and kind son ; and the hearty co-operation of him and his wife in their endeavors to make " mother" comfortable, no doubt had its influence on the younger members of the family, who early learned that " grandmother" was an object susceptible of their affection, and worthy of their respect.

In the early part of the year 1858, after a period of protracted and intense suffering, Isaac Lippincott was removed by death ; and the blank which Mary felt, as to things of this life—the aching void in her heart—is most pathetically alluded to in her Diary. After this sad loss, the affairs of life seemed to weigh more heavily upon her than they had ever done before, and she began to look toward some way of living that would be attended with less care, and that would leave her more at liberty for the performance of her visits of Gospel love.

Still she continued at the head of her school during more than twenty years of her widowhood. Her two faithful daughters remained with her, and did what they could to relieve her from the heavy burden which rested upon her.

In her intercourse with her pupils, she practised candor as well as kindness; being opposed to indirect or *detective* methods in the treatment or the discovery of cases requiring discipline. Whatever the pupils might do, the teacher, or caretaker, should always be sincere.

This theory, which was based upon positive conviction, was consistently carried out in her practice, and confirmed by long experience.

Her views on this subject were so clear and so decided, as to be well worthy of a place in some standard work on School Discipline.

In Ninth Month, 1877, her brother Benjamin passed away; his wife having preceded him about two years. Mary attended his funeral, and appeared in testimony upon the occasion. She seemed now to be about the last of her generation. Her other brothers had died when she was young, but Benjamin and she had gone hand in hand in their childhood, and so far as distant residences and other circumstances would permit, they had been in close

intimacy through life. On some doctrinal points their
views were dissimilar; but these differences of opinion were
not suffered to weaken the bond of affection which had
united them in childhood, and which remained firm and
bright until severed by death.

His marriage had brought to her a sister whom
she greatly esteemed and loved; and between whom
and herself, there were strong ties of congeniality, as
well as of kinship and affection.

Now, Benjamin and Margaret had both gone; and
another much beloved sister-in-law, Amelia Shoemaker,
had passed away some time before. Her brother-in-law,
David Walton and his wife, lived so far away from her
that she rarely got to see them; a privation that she
much regretted. David had made his home with her
husband and herself during their early married life, and
she liked to speak of those pleasant days.

Nearly all of her first cousins were numbered with
the dead, so that she could look only upon kindred of
one, two, and three generations younger than herself.

While she must have felt—as most old persons do
feel—the strippedness of her situation, yet she kept up
her intercourse with the young, and manifested her
gratitude for their kind attentions. The interest extended, not only to her daughters, and to the daughter
and the grandchildren of her husband, but also to the
nieces and nephews, on both sides. In one of her letters
she speaks of the satisfaction that it gave her to visit
the business establishment of some nephews in Phila-

delphia, and to see the three brothers, and several of their sons with them, all upright, industrious, and prosperous.

But her interest and affection were not limited to her kindred; for they extended throughout the entire circle of her acquaintance; and in a broader sense, we might well say, throughout the whole human family. She desired that all might do right, and thus be happy; also that they might be outwardly comfortable, and might *prosper*, in the best sense of the word.

When attending the Yearly Meeting in Philadelphia, she made her home with her nephew and niece, Joshua and Elizabeth Lippincott, until the latter was removed by death; and during the remaining years of her ability to attend the meeting, she was kindly cared for, while in the city, by her niece, Isabella Lippincott, who lived near the meeting-house.

At these annual gatherings she met with many kindred spirits, who were not bound to her by family ties. It was a touching sight to behold, in the upper gallery, five approved ministers, all past four-score years of age, but bright in intellect, and truly alive in spirit. These five were Sarah Hunt, Deborah F. Wharton, Sarah Hoopes, Mary S. Lippincott and Catharine P. Foulke. Now they have all gone to their reward; Mary having been the first to pass away, and Catharine the last.

Notwithstanding the pressure of home cares, she was a worthy example of faithfulness in the regular attendance of the meeting to which she belonged, and when duty called her to other parts of the vineyard, she had the sympathy and the approval of her Friends at home, before engaging in the weighty undertaking of paying a religious visit.

With certificates thus obtained, she visited, at different periods of her life, all the six Yearly Meetings which then belonged to our branch of the Society of Friends, and many—perhaps most—of the meetings composing them. In the year 1869 she obtained a minute to visit the Quarterly and other meetings within the limits of her own Yearly Meeting.

Soon after returning this minute she obtained one to visit the Southern Quarter; also some neighboring Quarters; and to attend and appoint meetings within their limits. In the performance of these two visits she was occupied more than four years; and this labor, together with the attendance of Baltimore Yearly Meeting, in 1875, and New York in 1879, may be regarded as the evening offering of a devoted and faithful Gospel messenger.

In the year 1880, after an existence of thirty-eight years, the school at Moorestown was discontinued, and in the early part of the year following, Mary and her two daughters removed to Camden, New Jersey. She speaks favorably of their new home, with its many comforts and conveniences, and so long as she was able, she was a faithful attender of Camden Meeting, but her right of membership in the Society of Friends, remained in Chester Monthly Meeting, to which—and particularly to the Chester [Moorestown] branch of it, she was strongly attached by ties of association, of interest, and of affection. The impress left there by the seal of her ministry is still fresh on the minds of the elderly and middle-aged Friends.

The last time, previous to her death, that the name of Mary S. Lippincott appears on the Monthly Meeting book, bears date of Fifth Month 8th, 1879, when she obtained a minute to attend New York Yearly Meeting.

The last Yearly Meeting that she attended in Philadelphia was in 1883. A year later she went to the one in New York, and during the intervals of the meeting she enjoyed social mingling at the house of her friend Jane Russell, whose kindness and tender care enabled her to pass the week comfortably, notwithstanding her feebleness of body. This was her last visit at any considerable distance from home.

We now come to the closing period of a long and dedicated life. The last four years of her earthly journey were years of pain to the weary body, but of tranquillity to the mind; for she was reaping the reward for obedience in having done the will of her Master, while she had the strength and ability to labor in his cause. She could now realize, in her own experience, the happiness of one,

"Whose yesterdays look backward with a smile,
Nor, like the Parthian, wound him as they fly."

Nor did bodily imfirmities prevent her from enjoying the company of her friends, many of whom availed themselves of the opportunity to visit her at her home, when she was no longer able to go out on her wonted missions of religious or social duty.

In some of her letters she speaks of the great kindness of her Camden neighbors, as well as of those friends and relatives from other places, who came to visit her. It was, no doubt, felt to be a privilege to be with her, as it was instructive to witness her enduring patience, her unclouded intellect, and her assurance of the inheritance that awaited her, when done with time.

The parting with her daughter Jane, was one of the close trials of her life, but she accepted it, as she had the loss of her other children, in a spirit of quiet resignation.

Her letters now became fewer and more brief than had heretofore been the case, and the penmanship was greatly changed; but the same loving spirit is still there, and is as distinctly discernible as if we could behold her benevolent countenance, and hear the familiar sound of her voice.

Now, as in her earlier days, her generosity flowed in many directions; and her beneficence was limited only by her want of opportunity; the *will* was still present, and these late letters evince the same desires that had attended her through life, to do or to say something that would contribute to the happiness of a fellow-being.

As the months passed on, she grew weaker in body, but the mental faculties remained unimpaired. Her fail-

ing eyesight not permitting her to do as much reading
as she had been accustomed to, she had much time for
reflection, which enabled her to review her past life, and
to think of the many valued friends whose society she
had once enjoyed. Her love flowed freely toward those
who were still in the body ; and of the others she cherished memories that were so precious as to afford her
much comfort.

During the last two years of her life she was a great
sufferer ; and for about one year preceding her death she
was unable to attend meeting. But even when under
the pressure of physical pain, her mind was bright, and
she was keenly alive to the interest of the Society of
which she was a birthright member, and for the welfare
of which she had labored so faithfully, while health and
ability were afforded her.

Being hopefully inclined, she could rejoice at all evidences of life ; while her quickened spiritual perceptions
enabled her to discover weaknesses, and latent sources of
danger that were invisible to the ordinary observer.

Again and again did she refer to this subject—the
prosperity of the Society of Friends — desiring the removal of all the hindering things, and the advancement
of the cause of Truth.

During her illness, and within a few weeks of her
close, her fervent desires for the maintenance of our
testimonies, were so impressively expressed, that the
concern seemed like a legacy left to her survivors, for
them to accept and to appropriate.

In early life she had entered into covenant with One in whom she fully trusted, and for the sake of whose guidance she was, after a hard struggle, made willing to part with all that stood in her way. This One had carried her over many difficulties, had sustained her under close trials, and He was now her firm support in days and hours of great extremity.

Having done her work as she went along through life, and having left the messages of concern which she had felt during her illness; there was nothing remaining for her to do, but trustingly to lean upon the arm of her Supporter, and patiently abide the time for her release.

On the morning of her departure, she said to her attendant : "I want to see the light ; the light of day. I want to see the dawning of the day."

This desire seemed to be typical of that other dawn, which—as we reverently trust—her spiritual vision was soon to behold.

She passed away in the early morning of Fourth Month 18th, 1888, lacking but sixty-six days of being eighty-seven years old.

Her funeral, which was large, was an occasion of solemn interest to those who attended it; while many who were not present could share in the feeling that a mother in our Israel had passed away.

Her remains were interred near those of her husband, and their children, in Friends' Burial Ground, at Moorestown, New Jersey.

This being " the end of earth," we must take leave

of our subject; which we do with an affectionate regard
for her memory, and a firm belief that she is now reaping the reward of the righteous, in the realms of beatific
felicity.

> " When the good man yields his breath,
> (For the good man never dies,)
> Bright beyond the gulf of death,
> Lo! the Land of Promise lies."

But where the account of her outward life ends,
that of *herself* really begins : for " Being dead she yet
speaketh."

CHAPTER II.

HER DIARY—1823 TO 1875.

PART I.

Twelfth Month 8th, 1823.—This evening W. Flanner
had an appointed meeting here. I felt poor and stripped
before and after it; but during the time we were assembled, I felt that the love of the Divine Shepherd was
towards us. W. handed forth some seasonable and instructive advice—may it never be forgotten! How often
is my soul bowed down with grief, and not able to find
relief—Oh, that it might be stayed upon its God !

10th.—My mind was deeply exercised, under an apprehension of having withheld counsel to one, which
might have kept her from the folly she engaged in. Oh !
how I mourned, and cried unto the Lord in my agony,

4

"Have mercy upon us!" My tenderest feelings were pierced as with a sharp arrow—may I humbly seek forgiveness. How often do I feel condemnation and woe; when shall I become willing to submit entirely to the Cross, and know a dying daily, yea, and hourly? I shall never find peace till my will is slain ; but the carnal part in me is continually striving to wage war with the spiritual—with the Lamb. Oh! that strength may be given me to overcome the wicked one. Oh! most adorable Father! strengthen me to resist temptations; chastise me, but not as I deserve, lest I be consumed; try me, prove me, and make me willing to bow and say: "Thy will be done," in me, "as in Heaven."

11th.—By reason of my inactivity and wandering thoughts, I became burdened, and found the seed was suffering. I sat meeting in distress, and thought I had gotten to a place where two ways met, and that I had not strength nor confidence in myself, sufficient to pursue the right way ; and I felt if I should take the other, as though the angel of God was waiting with his sword, to cut me asunder. I wept, and knew not what to do ; I looked for my Beloved, but I found Him not. Where is my Beloved gone; I seek Him, but He cannot be found. I am as one destitute and forsaken—bowed down with grief, and none to unbosom it unto ; my flesh waxeth old, as a garment, and my bones ache; my sighs come in the morning and continue until the evening; sleep flees from my eyelids, so that I know not my former rest. Oh! that I were old, for then should I have hope that I should return to the dust from whence I came—there should I hope to rest from all my troubles. Were I worthy to live, or had I hope of better days, then I could look forward with a ray of comfort; but my heart is too hard to yield to the will of my Heavenly Father, so that I am afraid that I shall fall a victim to the second death. Oh! that I had faith, for then would I pray, but I almost despond, knowing my poverty and weakness; poor indeed am I, hardly worthy to raise my eyes towards Heaven, yet am ready to put up my feeble petitions to the Most High. I abhor myself, "why hast Thou set me as a mark against Thee, so that I am become a burden to myself." I can feel with David, when in his agony he cried out, "My God, my God, why hast thou forsaken me?" When wilt thou return, O Lord, and enlighten my countenance; when wilt thou break me to pieces, and form me into a vessel for usefulness in thy house. Make me willing, I beseech Thee, O Father! to give up everything, and with obedience, give glory to Thee in the highest, then shall I know "peace on earth and good-will to men!"

27th.—This day, for a little time, my spirits were animated, and caused me to say that which has been a source of grief unto me, and has made me work for repentance. Oh! that I might be more watchful, that I may not at any time give way to levity for a moment. When shall I be able to trust myself in company, without fearing to enter into conversation lest I say too much, or something that will cause grief?

28th.—My soul was deeply bowed in awful reverence before Him whose frown is terrible as the roaring and boisterous ocean. I passed an almost sleepless night, on account of what took place yesterday. I went to meeting, but sat as in a dry and sandy desert, mourning, but could not weep, till our Friend, William Flanner arose, and in the true life spoke at considerable length; part of his testimony touching the place in my heart which was under suffering, melting me into tears, so that I felt a confidence there was a possibility of returning and finding forgiveness. After meeting, I took my book, but felt restrained from reading, could not suppress my tears; when W. Flanner took me by the hand, and affectionately pressing it, said—"What art thou learning? Learning to preach?" This was too close a question for me to answer, and therefore I wept as he pressed my hand, and gently added, "Thou canst not learn it from the Good Book, but only from the Master. It will be made easy to thee. I love the flock wherever I meet with them," &c. I felt tendered all day, and found tears relieving. Oh! that I may lay my foundation *sure*, so that it cannot be shaken; that I may be found faithful! But Oh! this heart, when will it become obedient; when shall I be able to bow and say with sincere heart, "Lord, not my will, but thine be done in all things." I commit myself to thy care, and in Thee is centered all my hope. Enable me, I beseech Thee, to give thanks to Thee always, and let the praise be thine forever. Amen!

29th, 30th, and 31st.—My spirit mourned during

those three days almost continually ; and it seemed as
though all the life in me was under suffering. I be-
sought the Lord to be with me, and direct my steps, and
praised be his name, He heard my cry, and permitted
me to feel, at times, that I was not forgotten. I earnestly
craved that the next day I might be favored to begin
anew my journey and my life, and find Him to be my
Alpha and Omega ; also, that He would enable me to sit
Monthly Meeting in a gathered state, and to feel with
Friends while there. I lay down to rest, with my mind
turned inward, and endeavored to keep it directed to the
Light ; and after some meditation and reflection, sank
into the arms of sleep. So ended the year.

First Month 1st, 1824.—Endeavored to have my eye
single and directed to the Fountain of Life, that I might
renew my covenants and my diligence. Found a little
trial at meeting, the enemy striving to ensnare me by
tempting me to sleep for a few minutes, and when it
became almost irresistible, I burst into tears, thinking—
" Have all my prayers and solicitude been ineffectual,
have my cries not been heard, and has my concern for
the last two or three days not been fervent enough, so
that the Lord would enable me to resist any such temptation that might be presented to me !" But, blessed forever
be the name of the Most High, He caused these words to
be spoken to my spiritual ear, " My grace is sufficient
for thee !" I believed it to be his own voice, and I had
faith—so Satan left me, and I had an unusually comfortable meeting, which I hope will never be forgotten ;

my heart almost overflowed with gratitude and love. May my soul dwell deep in the Valley of Humility, and never forget to look to its God for help.

2nd.—Still bowed down and mourning, laden with heavy burdens, but still I have hope in God.

3rd.—My soul still travailing and humble. The death of my dear brother was brought afresh to my remembrance by a letter from a near friend; also a fresh load of heart-rending trouble and grief, added to that which I already bore. I have long been wounded by the arrows of affliction, but all these things are doubtless ordered for my further refinement and purification; and, Oh! that they may have the desired effect, saith my soul!

4th.—Bowed in spirit and sorely oppressed, got no relief in either meeting—sighs and groans my almost constant companions; I see fields of labor, at times, opening before me, but feel almost like a dried stick, and cannot do anything. The little life seems almost gone, and I cannot find Him whom I long for. Tell me, O ye that know, where has my Beloved hidden himself, for how can I live without his presence? And yet I can hardly find strength to seek Him. Oh! that I may keep my place, and not go astray, that I may dwell deep, and repose full confidence in Him who never leaves nor forsakes those who put their trust in Him.

Permit me, Most Holy Father, to supplicate Thee on behalf of my afflicted soul; permit me to raise my voice, unworthy as I am, and call thy attention from on high. Look down I beseech Thee, with pity, on a poor, frail mortal, whose heart is ready to sink, and who is almost overwhelmed. Leave me not to perish, but keep me, I entreat Thee. Suffer me to abide under the shadow of thy wing. Cleanse me, purify me, try me, prove me, baptize me again and again, if consistent with thy holy will, "create in me a clean heart, and renew a right spirit within me;" teach me humility; yea, keep me down deep in the valley, that I may not think much of myself. O, gracious Father! lead me wheresoever Thou desirest me to go; and make me willing to bow in full submission; fill my heart with thy holy presence, then shall I be thy devoted servant, having a song of triumph in my mouth, even praises, glory, honor, and thanksgiving to "Thee, the only true God and Jesus Christ, whom Thou hast sent!" Amen!

Sixth Month 20th, 1824.—My occupations, and the weak state of my body, have not allowed me to take up the pen for a long time, but now I am at liberty to add more to my Diary, and may it be in humble simplicity. Though I am favored at times to feel the inshinings of Divine Light, and the sweetness of his countenance, yet it seems transient. Oh! may I abide in the patience, through all my afflictions, seeking to profit thereby, favored still, as I often have been of late, to feel the overshadowing of Heavenly Love. I have long thought, at seasons, that I was fast hastening from time into eternity, and increasingly so of late; but at other times have looked forward to what has appeared as work for me to do, but now all seems veiled from my sight; and alas! my best feelings seem cold and dead. And yet, I have faith that the Lord will, one day, "arise with healing in his wings;" his former favors having been abundantly sufficient to fix my trust. And finding my bodily strength failing, I desire to be doubly watchful, that I may be prepared for whatever may befall. I would rather die, seeking to enter in at the "strait gate," than live a careless, unconcerned life, left to my own devices.

21st.—On looking over the past, I do not feel that I have done wrong to grieve, though I am striving to be quiet and composed; yet truly I feel stripped of every good thing, and deeply humbled, earnestly craving that I may patiently abide under the hand of the Former, that I may be rightly formed to his own liking. I am very often reminded by my friends, that "Christians should be cheerful." I am brought to query what "cheerfulness" is; and whether it is possible for persons, in every state of spiritual exercise, to be the same, and to evince, by the expression of the countenance, that they are free from care, joyous and light-hearted, carrying no burdens. I have felt what I consider *true cheerfulness*, when perhaps the tears have flowed down my cheeks, and my countenance has been very grave; cheerfulness arising from the overflowings of Divine love in my heart, the sense of gratitude for the mercies shown me, all unworthy as I am. I do believe it is best for me to be sober in all my movements, quiet and retired, that I may be more watchful over myself; feeling that often "by the sadness of the countenance the heart is

made better." Oh! that I may be ever waiting, ever
watching, ever ready; that at whatsoever hour the
Bridegroom may come, I may trim my lamp, and joy-
fully go with Him into the marriage chamber.

Eighth Month 5th, 1824.—Much favored this morning in meeting, a precious season to me and to others;
much good counsel being also given to the children by
J. Cook. I was afraid to go to meeting, as I sometimes
am, lest more should be required of me than I am willing to yield unto: and though I so often covenant that
I will do anything asked for, if peace may be mine, yet
when the time comes for the public avowal of my allegiance to the Lord, I shrink. I struggled awhile after
I had taken my seat, and felt the tender touches of
Divine love.

May I be content to be brought low, and humiliated,
after such favored seasons as I have lately had, at times,
such heartfelt relief from the sorrow that, for a time, was
a daily companion.

PART II.

[*Found in a book containing miscellaneous items. The only dates in this
collection—where the year is given—are those of 1823 and 1824. To some of
the entries the day of the month is prefixed, but not the year.*]

Blessed be the name of the Lord, "for his mercy
endureth forever."

Oh! how I do desire that I may be kept from entering into trivial conversation, or from going into unprof-

itable company, lest I be cast off forever from having any part in the Kingdom of Glory.

On hearing of a person whose expression was that he was "as a brand plucked from the burning," I was ready to say within myself, if *I* am saved, I also shall be; for I was told by a Gospel minister [William Foster, from England], when I had escaped from the prospect of a sudden death—and I have since wondered how I escaped—that through mercy I was spared; for had I died then, I should have been a brand for the fire.

"Those that seek me early shall find me," saith the Lord. "Behold I stand at the door, and knock; if any man hear my voice, and open the door, I will come in to him, and will sup with him, and he with me." If thou wilt be my disciple, I will lead thee into green pastures, and beside still waters, by which the Shepherd of Israel feeds his flock. Then thou mayst quench thy thirst, and satisfy thy hunger with that bread and that water which the world knows not of; only be thou faithful, and thou shalt be saved. How hard it is to yield my stubborn heart. Why am I not willing to have my mind always occupied aright? I love to go to meetings, and often feel my meetings refreshing seasons; but at other times, O, how the enemy comes and tempts me with drowsiness! How long shall I be thus tempted? There is a possibility of overcoming, but not by my own strength; for I have found that of myself I can do nothing. "Return, repent and live;" for it is high time.

How often does the encouraging language which my beloved friend, J. M., gave me, come to my mind, and strengthen me so that I endeavor to persevere. O, how encouraging was the language which he handed forth, at a time when I was laboring under discouragement, feeling that all my striving and grieving would prove vain ; for I was ready to think I was not in the path which I had been placed in when I first gave up to take up the cross! The second time that he visited us here, he called me to him, after he had bid me farewell, and said that his coming here again was uncertain, and that he wished to speak with me. He then addressed me about as follows : " Mary, I want thee to be encouraged, for thou art in the right path ; and be particular to take good care to preserve thy health. The formation of discipline is not a sudden thing, but requires time, and thou wilt find times of rest from all thy cares." I suppose he meant for me to improve those times, which I hope I have been favored to do often, but I fear not always.

The next time he came here, he called me to him in the evening, and said, " Mary, it has long rested on my mind to establish such a school as I have been speaking of, and if I should succeed, thou wilt hear from me, as it seems to me thou art the person ; but perhaps thou wilt not like to live out in the back woods." I replied that it would make but little difference where I lived, if I was only doing my duty. He said, for some years of my life, he supposed it would not make much ; and that he had felt me nearly and tenderly united with him, and had been much refreshed in my company; that when he first saw me, he saw that there was an extensive service for me to perform in some department. I answered that, if I was only obedient, *that* was all that was necessary. "Yes," said he, "and if my feelings do not deceive me, thou art obedient." I then said, I felt weak at times; he replied, that after feeling weak, we could acknowledge that we received strength. We had some more conversation which I hope was profitable; may I never forget it.

Oh! how can I ever be disobedient after having advanced so far as I have? Did my friends know what baptisms I have passed through; could they feel the weight, the burden, that bows down my soul frequently, and did they know the agonies of my spirit—when my body is reclining upon the bed which is intended for a couch of rest—they would feel pity, they would feel sympathy with me, and then, I think, they would place no temptations in my way. How often do I lie, sighing, groaning and weeping, being, as it were, shut up in darkness; my Heavenly Father seeing proper to withdraw himself from me that I may feel my own weakness and poverty, and hence the greater need of his strength. But, blessed be his name, in his own time, He is pleased to visit me again with his presence, and give me to taste of his gracious goodness; others also have been baptized, before me, with the same baptism, and by adhering to it have become pillars in the church of their

Heavenly Father. Such examples afford me much encouragement, and teach me not to despair, but to seek
after strength to have self brought low, and to become
obedient in all things, that I may neither dread to live,
nor fear to die.

This day have my thoughts been turned towards my
dear, deceased brother. I consider that for more than
two years he has been released from a world of trouble,
that his body has moldered into dust, but that his spirit
is at rest, singing praises day and night, to the King of
kings. Oh! that I also may be prepared to go; that
when I am called upon I may go, rejoicing, to the mansion of rest. No one knows—save by experience—what
it is to lose a near relative. But I will not dare to complain, but will try to be thankful that my tender mother
and one dear brother are left. Should these be taken,
be pleased, O Glorious Father, to enable me to bear the
stroke without murmuring! All thy ways are just and
righteous.

Our dear Friend, J. H., spoke in meeting some
time to me, or to the exercised mind which was present.
It applied to me, so that I knew it was for me to profit
by; for truly I was under deep exercise, and could
hardly suppress my feelings; the tears streamed from
my eyes, and my sighs almost choked me. He said,
during his discourse, that he believed it was with the
person now, as with Saul formerly, who, though he knew
he was anointed of the Lord, yet wished to abide in the

stuff. This was true concerning me. I have been, at times, made sensible, in a degree, of my calling; but my natural wish was for another thing; for not much longer remaining in a single state, but uniting with the object of my affections; which course I find is not right yet, though it may be at some future time.

Oh, may I remember what J. H. also said, for it has been shown me for some years past that I have been spared and nourished up to do a *work*, which if I do not give up to do, woe will be unto me. Oh! that I may only be obedient in all things ; that my soul may not be lost.

Oh, how was my soul bowed down to-day, after leaving meeting, having been there tempted, at the beginning of the meeting, with drowsiness! I feel almost ready to despair, and have been made to cry—" My God, [Oh,] why hast thou forsaken me !" Even since then have I been tempted to do wrong, but not so strongly as to yield. I sat down alone and queried with my God, why am I thus shut up ? What must I do ? But I cannot find his presence as heretofore. When wilt thou return, O Lord, to fill me with thy presence, that I may again rejoice ? My only hope is in Thee. I am very poor and needy ; I hunger and thirst ; I long to be fed by thy own hand, and to drink of thy cup, for I feel almost ready to faint by the way. Oh, that I may be strengthened to press forward with hope. If I could relieve my mind by revealing my situation to some friend, it might afford me a little comfort ; but I find no liberty to do so, though I am frequently asked what ails me—whether I have the headache, &c. Can it be that none of this family have any idea what ails me? Are they not capable of judging by the spirit? I fear I am not competent to do my duty here, when my mind is so burdened; but I do not often feel the burden while in school, as my mind is otherwise occupied while there.

It is hard to be found fault with, by those around us, but I desire to bear it patiently, and not to retaliate, believing that with all my might I strive to do the best I know, to do my duty to those placed under my care, though I sometimes feel ready to give up my own judgment in school matters.

Oh, that I may wait in patience, and not run before I am sent, nor yet hang back when I ought to go. That I may not give to others what is meant for myself, nor keep what is intended for others. The pain in my head is often violent, so as to make me think of former times. It is good for me to be afflicted, that I may not be unmindful of the sufferings of others, or of myself at other times. This day hath been one of sorrow and heaviness of heart.

On Seventh-day afternoon I felt much distressed, but found little opportunity to be alone, till evening. Then I did not feel well in health, and the distress of my mind is beyond the power of language to describe. The anguish, the rendings, the heart-felt sorrow that pierced me, seemed to admit of no relief. I walked the floor of my room, and poured forth streams of tears, while my

sighs almost stifled me. At a late hour I retired, not yet
finding any relief, neither knowing the cause of my distress. I thought I should have some deeper baptism to
pass through. I lay on my bed groaning and weeping, till
I found liberty to close my eyes. I then recommended
myself to God, desiring that He would be pleased not to
withhold his hand from chastening me. In the morning
I felt no better, but went to meeting and sat down in
the quiet, desiring to be still and wait. I found no
relief: could not discover that I had sinned, save in
being over anxious to see one thing the day before. The
time between the meetings was passed in sorrow, believing that death was to be my lot, and that soon. Went
to meeting in the afternoon, and was favored with a ray
of light and hope. I wondered that I could think of
nothing, not even of passages of Scripture; but could
only sit breathing for help; when it presented to my
mind that new wine must not be put into old bottles, lest
the bottles become marred, and the wine spilled, but new
wine must be put into new bottles, that both may be
preserved. Then I saw that the old in me was not entirely done away, and I craved that I might be created
anew. I felt not much better till Second-day evening,
when I was taken more unwell, and could see nothing
but death before me. I sat down alone, in the kitchen,
by the fire; and in my meditation and distress, some
things opened to my view, and so on, till the cloud passed
away, and a brightness as of the Sun of Righteousness
shone forth. I now felt entirely weaned from earthly

things, and perfectly resigned to die, thinking that I soon should, I prayed that I might bear my sickness throughout patiently; then I began to feel that death was not so near, and that this conflict was to wean me more from the world, and make me more willing to do the Lord's service, which He was about to require of me. I feel yet bowed, for fear I shall not willingly give up to open my mouth in public, if He still requires me to, as I have had many reasons, for this long time, to expect He will. I feel bowed down to the very dust, willing to creep on the earth with my face covered with the dust thereof, for Christ's sake; and yet it seems almost worse than death to think of the service before me, even opening my mouth in public. Oh! that I may be obedient and faithful, for if I am not, woe will be unto me. There will be no greater service imposed upon me than I am able to perform, if I am only obedient. But Oh, what I have yet to pass through! I must be broken again and again, until I am willing to give Him my heart. O glorious God! O righteous Father! be pleased to chasten me still, but not in thine anger, lest I be consumed. Baptize me with deeper baptisms; dip me still deeper in Jordan; choose me in the furnace of affliction, according to thy just will, that I may be made willing to give up my life to thy service, and give Thee the glory, honor, and praise forever. Amen.

If I could dwell alone, then would I pour out my soul aloud to my God; but perhaps it is right that I have employment.

I thank Thee, Oh Father, that Thou hast not suffered me to be tempted with drowsiness in some of my late meetings, and I have long found Thou wouldst not suffer me to be tempted when I asked for help in faith.

Sixth Month 24th.—Oh, the griefs of my heart! The distress! What shall I do? I fear I am sinking into a state of melancholy.   Having my mind partly engaged through the day, makes the distress press more heavily at night; and in my lonely hours, sleep has almost fled from me for some time past, and I feel as if my health would be injured more and more, unless I can find some remedy. I cannot find that I have been guilty of evil that is working upon me; my sins have appeared to me to be blotted out, through my repenting, and trying to do my best.   This trying dispensation must be to wean me entirely from all earthly things.   Already I feel so far weaned, that I can wish to live for nothing but to serve my God.   It is good for me to be afflicted, that I may continue to be weaned, for I know from experience that sin bringeth sorrow.   I feel that I must give up all, and submit to the cross; but I regard myself almost as one unworthy to perform a service.   My night visions, what is their interpretation?   Being, as I think, not asleep, but lost in sorrow a few weeks since—I saw as I lay upon my bed, a large chain lowered down from the ceiling to the floor, and it seemed to move towards me, and to disturb me so, that I shook with fear.   Last night, as I lay in deep sorrow, I saw another chain, with three cords of very fine iron strands, of a bluish color, let down from the ceiling on to my bed, close by my right side (I think there were not more than three cords), and I saw them shake, which alarmed me so greatly that I trembled for fear, and was almost choked with grief. What can be the meaning of so extraordinary a sight? Persons sometimes have to be chained, but I hope that this is not to be my lot. It has occurred to me that the interpretation, in part—or perhaps all—is that I must be fastened with that iron chain which is an emblem of the golden chain which was let down from Heaven, whose three cords were " Faith, Hope and Charity." I do not know that such a thing has ever been spoken of, but I think it must have been, or it would not have been presented to my mind. Oh! that I may be helped to have faith and hope, believing that my gracious Master will in his own time return, and that I may also have charity for those who trespass against me.

Tenth Month 3rd.—Oh, wretched one that I am, where shall I flee for safety? I fear that for these two weeks past I have not been advancing toward Zion as fast as heretofore. What is it that has turned me aside, or impeded my progress? Who can tell? Oh, that I may not be at ease, lest He " spew me out of his mouth," with the lukewarm. I have not known, I believe, for several months, what it is to smile with an easy heart. Indeed, for several years I have felt something within, restraining me from indulging in levity; though I have sometimes bordered on it. I feel deeply concerned lest

I shall be cut off in the bloom of life, for not being willing to give up freely to putting my talents to usefulness in the church. That I ought to do so, or I shall be found wanting, has been shown to me by the inspeaking Word, as well as by the Lord's servants. I often think I could willingly close my eyes forever—feeling no strong ties to bind me to this world—and often feel as if my end were near; and a few evenings since, when dwelling under this feeling, these lines flowed spontaneously from my mind :—

I feel my days as almost past,
And look to Him with hope at last,
From whom all blessings come :

May He be pleased to condescend
To be my Father and my Friend,
And guide my spirit home.

Help me, O Thou most righteous and adorable Father! Be pleased to help me, thy poor afflicted, humble, dependent child, who goes sorrowing on her way. Keep me humble, suffer me, unworthy as I am, to raise mine eyes to Heaven, and admit me to partake a little of the bread of life. With thy rod correct me, and chastise me according to thy righteous will, until I be purified from the dross, and cleansed ; then shall I be able to worship Thee in spirit and in truth. Thou who alone art worthy of all praise, honor, and glory, forever—I feel a little of thy strengthening presence ; I taste a little of thy goodness, so as to acknowledge that Thou hast not left me in the vale of woe, but that Thou still hast mercy upon me ; still lookest down with an eye of compassion, as a tender Father on a repenting child. Bow me down, I humbly beseech Thee, into the dust ; cause my bread to be mingled with sighs, and my drink with tears, that I may, through these dispensations, be made willing to turn my back wholly upon the world, and my face to Zion. Then shall I become obedient to Thee, who alone can save me in the hour of temptation, and keep me from falling into the pit. Blessed be thy name forever. May thy kingdom be established above all in me. May I serve Thee with all my might, power and strength, even unto the end.

Oh ! that I may find Him (the Alpha and Omega), to be present with me when I awake in the morning, that I may renew my covenants, and double my diligence, to press forward toward the glorious prize.

PART III.

First Month, 1844. — It has been steadily my intention to look over and adjust my writings, as some of my early experiences and exercises of spirit, may be profitable to my children, at least, and perhaps unto others ; but as yet opportunity has not served. I also feel it right to leave on record my views on some subjects.

I am now in my forty-third year, and on looking back to what occurred in my youth, it seems so long ago as to be almost like a dream. Oh ! the deep provings and exercises that were mine, no mortal knows; but, thanks be unto God, He showed me the beauty of the " New Jerusalem," and steadily instructed me that the righteous should inherit it, and find joy and peace in dwelling therein. The Lord has not forgotten his handmaiden, even in her low estate, keeping me in " perfect peace," as my mind has been " stayed on Him, and I have " trusted " Him fully, to " supply my every need."

Second Month, 1845.—How swiftly the years roll around! To think that so many years of my life should have passed away, and so little of the great work shown me, (at the time that I was a school-girl, when the language saluted my spiritual ear, " Simon, son of Jonas, lovest thou me? Feed my sheep;") so little of the work seen in the opening of visions has been accomplished.

Oh, that I could extricate myself from my worldly concerns, so as to attend more fully to requisitions of duty; or that, by my own industry, I might procure pecuniary means, so as to feel warranted in paying visits in Gospel love, in accordance with the clear manifestations of duty—a work to which more faithfully to attend, I believe would be a blessing to me, in every sense of the word. Thou only knowest, Most Holy One, what the exercises of my spirit, the deep baptisms, have been and are; Thou only knowest what I have passed through for months past, because my way seemed hedged in on every side, so that the shrinking from known duty has brought weakness and darkness, till I have felt ready to adopt the language, " My foot had well-nigh slipped."

Yet, Thou art matchless mercy, and in Thee have I
hope, that, as my soul boweth in awful reverence and
prostration, desiring nothing but to serve Thee, that
Thou wilt cast up a way before me into the South;
whither, for many years, thou hast shown me that my
feet must be turned; that the glad tidings of the Gospel
of peace and salvation may be proclaimed, tending to
the opening of the prison doors and setting the captives
free. O ye Southern States! the "voice of thy brother's
blood crieth unto me from the ground," saith the Lord.
Hear ye the voice of the quickening Spirit of the great
"I am," that ye may escape the judgments of the Almighty, by turning aside from the iniquity of oppressing
your fellow-men! Men, made by the same good Being,
for the same great end, and whose salvation is equally
precious in his sight; for, "All souls are mine," saith
the Lord. As that of the master, so of the slave. Poor,
bowed down, and oppressed, with a load of ignorance
heaped upon him by his more depraved superior, the
white man—more depraved because he sins with his
eyes open; sounding abroad his belief in the New Testament, while living in open violation of its precepts.
Oh, the weight of the concern that I have felt, increasingly so, for years, for the United States of America, that
it might become a truly Christian nation, having no
other banner than the "banner of the Prince of Peace;"
that as our written "Institutions" are, so we may be—a
light to surrounding nations, in peace, in uprightness,
in temperance, in meekness, in brotherly kindness and

in charity. That the sound of implements of war·be not heard, nor the glistening of weapons be seen in our Western Land ; that the groan of oppression be no more heard throughout our borders, with nothing to hurt or destroy, because righteousness covers the earth, as the " waters cover the sea," and justice reigns, from the " rivers to the ends of the earth."

Tenth Month 4th, 1853.—Thou knowest, O Lord! that my request, on the bended knee of the soul, has been in regard to the arduous undertaking of re-opening school. If thou, Lord, wilt be with me, and keep me in this way, that I go, and give me " bread to eat, and raiment to put on," then Thou shalt be my God, and of all that Thou givest me, a part of my *outward substance*, as Thou directest, shall be devoted to the use designed ; so that I may be found following the footsteps of thy dear Son, when He appeared in the outward life, doing good to the bodies as well as the souls of men. In what way can this be used to more profit, than in aiding the dear youth in receiving a *guarded education*, that they may grow up prepared to be helpful, as social beings, in the community, and useful members of the militant church ? But, Thou beholdest my frailties, and seest my weaknesses. Of myself I can do nothing in this concern. Help me, O Father! for on thy name do I call, having none to look to but Thee, nor to pour out my feelings unto! To Thee do I make known my cause, while the mountains, as it were, are upon my shoulders, weighing me down. I ask not for an easier path, but that in patience and resignation I may bow under the burden, and walk in the way appointed, till the mountain of difficulty be removed, the outward debts be paid, and the inward accounts be squared. The former I have longed for more than anything else in the world, the latter, more than life! O Father! Thou knowest my besetments, and that Thou hast made a way for me from my youth up, when both inwardly and outwardly, no way appeared. Thou hast done much, and forgiven much; therefore, may I love much, and serve Thee all the days of my life. What is the world to me, only as thy gift? What are all its riches compared with heavenly treasure? When the light of thy countenance is beheld, all is beaming with joy; when clouds and darkness are around about the habitation of thy throne, then sadness reigns! But, when sadness covers my spirit, owing to the weight of responsibility resting upon me, I have to put on a cheerful countenance for the sake of those entrusted to my charge, lest I make my own words of no account; viz: "This is a world in which little is given us to complain of, but much to enjoy;" and again, Having in all things "a conscience void of offence toward God, and toward men." This constitutes that peace which the world can neither give nor destroy! I have had a diversified path through life, many trials and sore conflicts; but in all, my God has never forsaken me!

I have known of his goodness and his mercy, and that they fail not. He is surely on my side, and will uphold me during the few, fleeting days yet allotted me in this lower world; and when my time here closes, will take me to himself in eternity. Oh! what a bright and glorious prospect! Often, very often, dearest Father, hast Thou given me, in the visions of light, a view of the existence beyond the grave, and a foretaste of the joys to come, to buoy me up while journeying in the deeps, alone in the midst of company, and as an orphan in the wilderness of this world. Keep my precious children, O Holy One! that they may dwell in thy courts, and walk in the way of obedience; loving Thee more than the world, and thy law and thy testimonies, more than the glory and the glitter presented to their youthful view.

I feel that I am rapidly approaching "that bourn from whence no traveler returns," and Oh, how I long for retirement and indwelling of spirit, that I may be prepared from day to day, so to order my footsteps aright, as to encourage others to walk in the fear of the Lord, and to love righteousness.

My love for my fellow-beings increases with the increase of years; but I love the Truth and its testimonies too dearly to sacrifice them in order to gain the friendships of this world. The love of God enlarges my feelings in love to Him, and to his servants; unites my heart to them in the fellowship of the Gospel of his dear Son, and overflows in desire for the gathering of the scattered tribes, for the return of the poor wanderer and the salvation of all. Peace to him that is afar off, and

to him that is nigh, if his face is only turned toward Zion
—if he is journeying thitherward—but "there is no peace
to the wicked!" These must turn from their evil ways
before his servants can have fellowship with them. And
from whom must the servant withdraw sooner than from
thieves and robbers; those who are striving to climb up
some other way into the kingdom, than by "Christ the
door?" Such are they who are erecting creeds, substi-
tuting rites and ceremonies; calling upon men to bow
before images and put up petitions unto them, as though
these could save them, or empower them to overcome
their enemies, or "turn the battle to the gate."

Such are they who are running in their own time
and way, to convert the world, and to reform their fellow-
beings. "By their fruits" shall ye know them. Are
their fruits humility, simplicity, self-denial—a renunciation of the world's customs and policies? Or, are not
too many of these seen gorgeously attired, and conform-
ing to the world in its flattering titles, and in its salaried
ministry, studied sermons, prayers, and such like? Or,
are the times changed since the days that the Holy
Jesus found, among his bitterest enemies, the High
Priests, and professors of a Pharisaical religion—the
Sabbatarians, and those who were sticklers for their
church rites, making them of account in direct violation
of the doctrines of Christ. "It is the spirit that quick-
eneth, the flesh profiteth nothing." Have not Friends
fallen into the current that is rushing onward, and bearing down almost everything before it; a current of unity

with this working with all (whether qualified or not, by the preparing Hand) to bring about by outward means, a reformation? We need not again an outward Saviour, for it is declared, "He died once for all." In that prepared body, He "bore our iniquities," He was bruised for our transgressions, and with his stripes are we healed." A *spiritual* Saviour is now needed to take us within the veil where the life is, and where we are to learn the way to "work the works of righteousness," which are peace, and the effect of which is "quietness and assurance forever!" Oh, my people! come ye unto the light of the Lord, and raise an ensign before the nations; say ye to the inhabitants of the earth, "Christ is risen!" He is not *in* the earth, but *above* it; come up hither, in spirit, and behold his spiritual appearance, the Christ of God, manifested in man—a Saviour to save him from sin; a Redeemer to redeem his spirit; a way by which to approach the Father—the way, the truth, the light and the life! All the angels in Heaven are subject unto Him; his kingdom is an everlasting kingdom, established when all others are overthrown. No man knoweth the Father but the Son, and he to whom the Son revealeth Him; to have the Father revealed, the Son must be born in us—the Son of God, and the Son of Man—the Lord's Christ! "Manifest in the flesh, justified in the spirit, preached to the Gentiles, believed on in the world, [and] received up into glory." May Friends unite in a *saving* belief in Him; which is to "know Thee, the only true God, and Jesus Christ, whom Thou hast sent," for this is "life eternal." O Lord! keep me in a humble, teachable state, ever learning in the school of Christ, when and where only, Christians are taught.

First Month 1st, 1854.—My time is so occupied with the many pressing cares connected with our Boarding School concerns, that my pen is often laid aside unused, even when very much arises to place on paper, or to convey to others. I fear that my thoughts, like the water that lacks an outlet, will become stagnant; a circulation keeps them pure if they flow in a pure channel.

Another year is begun; O, time! how rapid is thy flight; and ah, how little work is done! I look, and behold childhood and youth far in the past; the strength and energy of middle-age gone; and now I am descending the hill that leads down to the silent grave, the dust from which I was taken. How soon the period will arrive, when a veil will obscure terrestrial objects, and the things that have been visible will be seen no more forever. How has the world changed to me, an evidence that I myself, have changed. Many things delighted me once, even when my life was in the midst of bitterness; now I feel that I would gladly retire from everything, for the welfare of the church, and the good of my fellow-men. Everything now is a hardship, save only the *work* to which I have feebly put my hand. And yet, I do but little, and keep back from labor, being beset on every hand. Oh! how faithful were our early Friends, and how devoted to the cause which they so heartily

espoused : neither their outward business nor the arm
of power, arrested their progress; thus they were made
" fruitful in the field of offering, and joyful in the house
of prayer." O that way would open for me to cast off
my burdens in those parts of the vineyard to which they
severally belong! For I feel pressed down, as a "cart
[under] sheaves."

Twelfth Month 2nd.—Nearly a year has elapsed
since I opened my book to write, but I have penned
a great many letters, &c. Believing it right to do
so, I correspond with many friends on the subjects
which most nearly interest me,—the spread of the peaceable religion of Jesus ; the advancement of the glorious
cause of Truth ; and the welfare of our highly-favored
Society—that this would return to first principles and its
first love, thereby to be a " burning and a shining light,"
bearing witness unto the Truth ; and pointing to the
" Lamb of God which taketh away the sin of the world."

First Month 1st, 1855.—Another year has unfolded
itself to view, ushered in with a placid serenity befitting
my retired feelings ; and with a brightness analagous to
the glory which breaks upon my mental vision. Last
evening, passed away the purified spirit of my beloved,
my revered friend, Mary Jessup; taken from us in the
midst of her usefulness, and when her path, as the just
man's, was brightening to the " perfect day." The time
spent with her in her sick chamber, was a memorable
season ; it seemed as though the Almighty was beheld
there, sitting upon his throne, his train filling his holy

temple. I said in my heart, as language distilled like
the dew of Heaven from her lips, "while *in*, she is *above*
the world." God maketh her face to shine, and giveth
her strength and language more than human. Oh! if
I had ever doubted a happy immortality, I could have
doubted it no longer. Her happiness amidst extreme
suffering and great bodily weakness, no language can
portray. The brightness of her perceptions; the sweet
composure with which she gave to her dear husband and
children, and many others, her dying admonitions; her
parting counsel and fervent prayers, contriting every
heart. None but a Divine Hand could have sustained
her. The reward of a well-spent life, was, in part, received, ere the vital spark was quenched. She is gone,
and I am sad, though rejoicing in her release from suffering. She asked for me a blessing, and prayed that
some of the youth might be raised up to bear up my
hands in old age. That in near feelings of unity, she
had done it, we having been closely bound together.
Ah! I have indeed lost a friend; may my spirit be humbled and kept at the feet of Jesus, so that I may be cared
for and preserved during my pilgrimage journey.

First Month 24th.—The twenty-fifth year since the
birth of my first child! What changes since then, and
how many trying dispensations. Five sons (the eldest,
mine by adoption, a choice young man, the son of my
dear I.), removed from this to a better world; all innocent
and happy! Close as were the trials, blessed be God,
He always gave me the spirit of resignation, so that I

could bless the hand that afflicted, not asking their stay ; and could adopt the language, "Thy will be done!" And now, in looking back over all the trials of my past life (and these have been many), they sink into insignificance when compared with the "goodness and mercy" that have followed me all my days, even in the time of my greatest rebellion, when met by the "reproofs of instruction," which are the way of life. As judgments then, his mercy was shown bidding me to bow at his presence, while his "mercy covered the judgment seat." Oh! how shall I ever tell, in the fullness of his "loving kindness to the children of men;" or how speak of the many bountiful gifts dispensed, both spiritual and temporal, to poor wayward man, to insure his happiness in this changing state, and in that which is unchangeable —a brilliant scene?

This earth, formed as it is, and surrounded by yon orbs of dazzling beauty, has not been formed in vain, for man to live upon and despise. Ah! no; it is the Almighty's footstool, where the prints are seen of his all-potent tread. Walk where we may, there may we see his Heavenly impress; in the plants that grow, from the greatest to the least; in the beasts that roam the forests; the birds that soar high in the air; and in the varied tribes that inhabit the waters—these are all the works of Deity, who pronounced them "good" when He created them, and gave them their position. At the head of the animal creation He placed man, the "lord of all." As head of these, a harmonious head, should he

keep his position. But, alas! he fell; by disobedience
he fell, and sorrow and suffering came into the world.

27th.—I have learned more in the school of affliction, than in all the joyous seasons I have ever known;
for in times when outward springs of consolation were
closed, then the poor mind resorted, as did the woman
of Samaria, to Jacob's well, and there found the Master,
with living water, waiting to give freely, and to instruct
with his loving counsel;—in this school I have had
many a lesson to learn. To use the words of dear James
Simpson, the elder, "I took my degrees in the back
part of the wilderness, where the spirit of the Lord
moved Samson, in the camp of Dan." I had none to
look to as my teacher, or to depend upon but the Most
High God, who spake to my mind by the language of
impression, and who also, made the Holy Scriptures
instrumental in my instruction, opening passages answering to my state of mind; and showing me the wonder-
working power of the Invisible One within his rational
creatures, to bring them into a state of preparation for
the enjoyment of his presence, and of his glorious Kingdom forever!

Touching visible things, man by his wisdom, even
the "spirit of man" which is given him, may comprehend them in their appearances, in their movements,
and in their changes; knowing at the same time, that
"there lives and works a soul in all things, and that
soul is God." But, touching spiritual things, these
cannot be understood by the natural man, neither can

6

he comprehend them, only as in passive obedience to
that "sure word of prophecy," he gives heed in all
things, "until the day dawn, and the day-star arise in
[his] heart;" giving attention to the first preparing for
an increase of Heavenly light and knowledge, and of
that wisdom which cometh down from above, making
him "wise unto salvation."

First Month 1st, 1856.—This, the first day of the
week, of the month, and of the year, comes clothed in
robes of spotless white, none of the defilements of the
year just departed, nothing to soil the garment that covers the trees and ground! How is it with the hearts of
the sons and daughters of men? Let us view our own,
in that light that dawns upon our understandings, and
see whether the same purity and spotless innocence
abound! Whether passively, through the night-season,
as one year was retreating and another advancing, we
spread out our minds to receive the grace of God in its
descendings, to obliterate all crime; to wash away our
sins, and remove every defilement; so that, with the
ushering in of a new morning, we might arise from our
beds of slumber, as new-born babes, fitted to begin our
labors in the new creation. And to behold more beautiful than heretofore (because of a preparation to admire
and adore Him) the wondrous works of an Almighty
Power. Oh! my soul, search and examine well, ere
thou answers, search and know the truth; hast thou not
slackened thy speed of late, and have not thy senses
became less keen? Hast thou been poured out like

wine, for thy fellow probationers, or, like Ephraim, hast thou "settled upon the lees?" Hast thou not been resting secure and at ease in thy ceiled house, while the House of God is lying desolate and waste; and all this lukewarmness and slothfulness, even after thy many covenants, and the mercy and loving kindness of which thou hast bountifully partaken? Arise now from thy lethargy, renew thy energies, and put on thy armor, and go forth in the name of the Lord, for the time is short, and the labor is pressing! How swiftly the years roll around! A few more and thou shalt pass into Eternity—if thy work is finished, into a happy Eternity, if not, awful the reflection! Oh! that I may put on strength, and be renewed for toil; spreading my tent in the Valley; and there dwelling with Him, whose abiding place is in the hearts of those who have become temples fit for the "Holy Ghost to dwell in." There is the only safe dwelling-place, and there, too, is refreshment known, for the gentle dews and celestial showers, descend upon the green pastures, and enlarge the quiet streams.

Twelfth Month 31st, 1857.—This evening closes another year; bright, calm and serene. There is a solemn silence within doors and without—a fit season for meditation! Since this time one year ago, how many dear to me in life, have passed away—their removal leaving a void not to be again filled—among these, dear N. P. Thou wast most beloved, my more than sister; my bosom friend, to whom my soul was knit by an indissoluble tie, to whom I poured out, fearlessly, all my

heart's joys and sorrows! And now, there is no one
left to whom I can so freely speak, sure of being understood ; my sorrows must be locked up in a casket, undisturbed. Art thou far away, dear friend ? No, our affection cannot be dissolved; death surely could not have
power over unchanging and unchangeable love. May I
not follow thee to the Spirit world, and behold thee ar-
rayed in glorious robes, one of the beauteous throng
surrounding the Throne of Omnipotence ? Oh ! that I
may join thee there, when I shall have filled up the
measure of my days ; there may we be reunited, to know
parting and sorrow no more. As we have worshipped,
prayed and praised together *here*, so let us there, in the
presence of the King, join in songs of praise forever.

Father, prepare me to bear the portion of trial yet
to be meted out to me, with patience and resignation.
" Hitherto hath the Lord helped " me, in great straits
and close conflicts. Oh ! bring me more and more into
the true quietness ; for, in the world there are strife,
noise and confusion, but in thy presence, peace. Oh,
Father ! keep my dear children so in the innocency,
that they may receive thy holy anointing oil, so that
their eyes may be anointed to see the glories of thy
Kingdom, and the loveliness of the Truth ; for the Truth
needs advocates. Many are running into theory and
speculation ; climbing up into the tree of knowledge to
become wise above that which is written ; when the
heart is not established in God's love, the creature is
exalted instead of the Creator. Oh, my soul ! thou art

settled with regard to *doctrine*, and satisfied that enough has been given thee for thy day's work ; thou knowest that Infinite Wisdom unfolds his truths to dedicated minds, that to these He gives the key to open, when none can shut.

First Month 1st, 1853.—A new day, a new year, has unfolded itself in the brightness and beauty of a mild winter morning. It is an auspicious morning ; and I feel that I have blessings to enumerate, many and bountiful ; temporal blessings not a few, as well as spiritual, when my heart is spread out before the Lord to receive them. He withholds " no good thing " from those that love Him. Many have been the trials and tossings that have beset my pilgrimage path ; into many straits have I been brought, but the Lord never forsook me, but delivered me out of them all. He has borne with all my weaknesses through life, has thrown his mantle of love over me to cover them ; and still sheds abroad his glorious light, to enlighten my pathway to the haven of rest. I have abundant cause to bless and magnify his great name forever. In adversity, in loneliness, in youth, in temptations on every side, thou, Lord, wast by my side, though I knew it not ; Thou wast on my right hand, to sustain from falling into perdition. In childhood, when sorrow melted my heart because my dear mother was sorely afflicted, and my mind shared in her grief, then did thy love and tenderness contrite me, even to tears, I knew not why ; not only for my fellow-mortals, but for the poor, dumb beasts, did I pour forth my sympathy, if

any were suffering or in want. Mysterious to the mind
are thy workings in the deeps, to form the soul to thy
liking, and to mould it for future use ; but, if the material
is there, and passive, as " clay in the hands of the potter,"
however rough and unpliable at first, Thou canst fashion
it in thy way and time, and prepare it to endure the
furnace, without receiving crack or flaw. Not only me,
O Father! but Oh, remember my children, and let thy
hand press upon them to break them to pieces, and then
form them anew, and anoint them for service in thy
church. It is not too soon for them to begin to be engaged in their social and religious duties, for we have,
at best, little time in which to finish these. How it
pains my heart to see the young, and those just passing
from youth, trifling away their precious time in light
reading and light conversation, so much as to encroach
upon hours that should be given to devotion, and to making the inquiry, " Lord, what wilt Thou have me do,"
that I may serve Thee in time, and enjoy Thee through
the endless ages of eternity ? In childhood I will seek
Thee ; in manhood (womanhood) I will serve Thee, working in the garden of my own heart, and in the vineyard,
as Thou appointest me, that I insure the reception of the
blessed " penny " at the close. Oh ! that this resolution
might obtain with the rational family of man ; then how
much more would this earth resemble a paradise, and the
inhabitants thereof, the saints in Heaven. If the children
of Friends, favored as they are, do trample under foot
our testimonies, as things of naught, the time will assur-

edly come, when "strangers shall feed [our] flocks, and
the sons of the alien shall be [our] vine-dressers." My
soul mourns to see our testimony to plainness of address
so violated ! Offending in one part of our law (Discipline)
we are offenders, and shall never prosper in supporting
the work of the testimony of Truth. "Be ye clean that
bear the vessels of the Lord." We may slip, through
unwatchfulness, and find repentance and forgiveness ; but
if we knowingly violate our Discipline, we are inconsistent members, professing more than we possess ; and
thus we become a by-word to honest-hearted Christians,
who are not of our fold.

No people have been more highly favored and blessed
than Friends ; no religious teaching is better fitted than
theirs to advance the Redeemer's kingdom, which brings
peace on earth and "good will toward men."

How great, therefore, is the pity that we should be
trammelled by inconsistency—lame and halt, instead of
firmly supporting the banner of Truth, and marching
foremost in the ranks.

Second Month 9th, 1858.—At half-past five o'olock,
P. M., my beloved husband, my trusted companion, quietly
passed away, after much suffering, to a blessed and happy
eternity. He was aged seventy-two years and nearly six
months.

Oh, how it sustained us in the hour of bereavement
to know that his work was done ; that his mind had been
gathered and centered, trusting in the hand of the Al-

mighty to conduct him, through sickness and death, to his home in Heaven.

He lived and died a Christian—much devoted to his Master's cause. I asked that his mantle of deliberation and quiet might descend upon me, a lonely widow, that I might be guarded on every hand, to journey on my way alone.

Fifth Month 16th, 1858.—Sad and solitary, in my lonely chamber, do I sit down to read over the last lines written in this book. Sad and solitary, for I feel, what is all the world to me now, without my dear partner? In every place there is a void; but *he* is at rest. If spirits can watch over the inhabitants of this earth, surely his spirit will watch over me and mine.

How swiftly time passes by; one week ago I was preparing for Yearly Meeting. Now it is over, and Friends dispersed. I look back with satisfaction to the freedom and harmonious feeling that prevailed. But Oh, for more heartfelt concern! Silence and self-denial are greatly wanting. Were there not those present who would "sell doves?" The dove-like nature cannot be sold for honor, nor for any other price, by man or woman. The Father gives it; and its descending must be as it was upon the Holy Jesus—the "Spirit of God descended as a dove, and rested upon Him." I fear ministers forget sometimes, that the first duty is to *love God*, that by this redeeming love, we be constrained to love one another, and in love to reprove the evil-doer.

Sixth Month 23rd, 1858.—This day I am fifty-seven

years old. My thoughts yesterday and last night, were
turned back to years gone by; to my dear mother and
her trials and privations, during my infancy and childhood; the good Shepherd who careth for his flocks, prepared for her, better days and happier times; she was
able to bring up and educate her children, and for many
years was spared to see them comfortably settled in life,
and engaged in useful and honorable callings. She
spent her time pleasantly among them and her grandchildren; and as she advanced in years, was so situated
as to be able to retire from labor, resting, and waiting
her appointed time to depart. She calmly passed away
in a good old age; but she passed not away from my
affectionate remembrance; her countenance is vividly
before me, and I need not any semblance to tell me how
she looked. Dear to me was she to the close; and I
feel not yet severed from her, though she is unseen by
my outward eye.

Eighth Month 6th.—Again has the Angel of Death
broken the tie that most closely bound me to life; yes,
more closely than all else! Six months to-day, did my
beloved partner close his earthly pilgrimage; and I am
left to plod on my weary, lonely way.

Who can participate in my sorrow, for the young
have their delights? Oh! the widow only knows the
widow's grief. A companion in every way is nearly
one's own self; and when such a one is taken, the bereaved
one is surely stricken. Thou, Lord, carest for, and canst
sustain me; to Thee only can I look! There is none

else in Heaven nor on earth to call upon; for I feel as one alone, and desire none but Thee to be my stay and staff. Keep me in the littleness; and, Oh! enable me to get through the world honorably, that the Truth may not suffer, and that my peace may be secure.

Remember my dear children, and stain the glory of this world in their view, that they may come to love the Truth, and the simplicity into which it leads. Thou knowest, O Father! my heartfelt pain, because the testimonies dear to me as my own life, are so lightly esteemed, and so lightly spoken of.

First Month 1st, 1859.—Last night closed the saddest year of my life. This morning has found me still dwelling on the departed, and following to the Spirit world the host of dear ones, who were once lovely in the body, and who are now saints in Heaven. How the cords that bind to earth are severed, as our friends and kindred depart. Though lovely the succeeding generation, as they come upon the stage of action; though we can pleasantly mingle with them in social intercourse, yet we have passed from the season when their pleasures were ours; from the friends who were our contemporaries —who felt as we felt, whose tastes and inclinations were in accordance with our own. It is wisely ordered to be so, that we may prepare for the evening of life, to retire in quietude to await our approaching change. The hurry and bustle of life over, the children reared, and prepared to act on their own behalf, it is our rightful privilege to become more and more lookers on and advisers, than energetic laborers in business. And fast approaching the end of time, to dwell more upon eternity and the things connected with the Eternal world, and the joys to be entered upon, when this life is swallowed up in death, and the captive soul is liberated from the shackles of mortality. My dear, beloved partner, to me a husband and a father, thou art no more my spiritual adviser, and my temporal help-meet; thou hast left me to bear the conflicts of life alone, and unsheltered by thy presence! By my side I find thee not, when tossed and tried, and I look around for a consoler and a friend. I retire alone and weep, and pour forth my plaints to Him who seeth in secret, and counteth the widow's tears, having compassion on her. Sometimes it seems as though the "brass" of "Heaven" and the "iron bars" of "earth," prevented the penetration of sighs; then again the outstretched arms of Omnipotence, invite my approach to Him for sustenance and shelter. O Father! keep me in this hour of affliction deep and proving, when thus severed in my affections from a being so near and dear; near and dear because of human ties, and doubly so from the precious spirit that dwelt in him and kept him in the Christian's path! He is at rest; the grave holds the body, lonely and beloved, but the spirit is not there. Shall my thoughts continue to hover around the narrow house, and penetrate into the darkness of the tomb, to see the lifeless body in its repose? For a time may not this be permitted? Gradually the thoughts must ascend with the part that lives forever, and must dwell upon the joys that are partaken of in Heaven, and that have no end. There must they center, for there is the Christian's hope, and expectation, and perfection. Father, strengthen me, that there may terminate my highest wish! In the outward, clouds, and storm, and rain, cover the earth with dullness and shade—a likeness of my inward state. Before the approach of evening, the sun may stretch himself forth, and shine brightly, dispelling the clouds and darkness that surround him, and shedding a radiance on all below; then may the spirits arise and gratitude ascend, with thanksgiving and praise, from the altar of many a heart, not even *mine* excepted.

Third Month 27th, 1859.—Lonely and alone, this lovely spring day, I sit and think on the past pleasures of life.

What is life? A little while and it ends. The grave takes that that was animated and busy, because endowed with life ; but it has to be buried out of sight, because there is breath no longer. Alas! what are we?

> " An angel's arm can't snatch me from the grave,
> Legions of angels can't confine me there."

Tenth Month 3rd, 1859.—Entering again the sphere of duty, as the head of an Educational Institution, O may the arm of an Almighty Being sustain me!

Sixth Month 23rd, 1860.—This day consummates fifty-nine years of my earthly pilgrimage; during this period many have been the vicissitudes, the bereavements, the trials; yet in all and through all, so far, have I been sustained; and can bless my God that He has been with me through "ups and downs," and has made my way each succeeding year more pleasant and happy, because increasingly confirmed in the feeling that life is a blessing—that man, to be truly happy in this world and in that to come, must comply with the terms offered, even obedience to the Spirit of Truth in his own soul. A spirit sufficient to teach, to guide, and to open the understanding to receive all truth, both immediately and instrumentally, and to reveal the Father and the Son, whom to know is Life Eternal. And this Spirit is the Light, the Life, and the Power (it is called by various names); it is the dawning of the day of the Lord; and whoever dwells in the light, keeping a single eye to it, will receive the "child born," the "son given," who is the Saviour and the Redeemer of the world. I am as fully comfirmed in this view, as I am that the sun shines in the fullness of his glory, shedding his beams upon the earth to sustain life, and to cause vegetation to come forth in its season for the sustenance of the animal kingdom. Clouds may obscure the outward sun at seasons, but they do not diminish his luster; so sin may obscure the Divine Presence from our finite view, but it cannot change the nature of Him who is "light," and in whom is "no darkness at all." Oh! my soul, cling thou more and more to Him, and henceforward let "obedience keep pace with knowledge,"—then will all thy seasons of "darkness be turned into noonday;" and thy God will be to thee, in the decline of life, as a "morning without clouds," and will cause thy "sun to go down in brightness." For thou, Lord, hast been very good to me; Thou hast always been my Friend and Father. I have had none to look to but Thee; Oh! be Thou with me, and keep me unto my life's end.

Tenth Month 7th, 1860.—Returned, last evening, from a neighboring Quarterly Meeting, pained at heart from the position of Friends. Oh! how these are lifted up in an imagination that *our own* works will be "working the works of God." Where is the clearness of vision to see that there is but one place for Israel, and that is to dwell alone, with their minds spread in the valley before God, and *not spread* in their imaginations, on the heights around about. Oh! they cannot see or understand, methinks; they will not see that there must be *spiritual* harmony, and *spiritual* unity; nothing else will do. Ah! it is surely now as in the days of Ahab, the many are believed, and Micajah rejected, proscribed and denounced; yea, imprisoned to be fed on the bread and water of affliction; but undoubtedly his prophecy will be fulfilled; for God has not changed, neither has He changed his law in regard to this people, called Quakers.

Sixth Month 23rd, 1861.—This day I am sixty years old. Yesterday I began to reflect upon passing time and events, calling up before my mental vision, a host of dear departed friends and relatives; and especially a dear and honored mother who gave me birth, and nurtured me in my infancy and youth. My spirit is closely bound to hers, and my love knows no abatement, though fourteen lonely years (lacking a few days) have rolled over my head, since she passed out of this life. But thou art at rest, dear mother; and many dear to thee and dear to me, have followed thee across the River of Death—amongst them, thy ever-kind son, my beloved husband, who has left me to tread alone a rugged path! Well! the Lord willed it so, and I have tried to submit, and say, "Thy will be done." O mother! art thou conscious of my sighs and tears, as I view the world in its faded aspect—faded in my view; for, in reality, it is in its pristine beauty; but I, having become a lone pilgrim, living in the midst of a new, a young and buoyant generation, have had my view extended beyond this transitory scene. And, Oh! hadst thou lived to have beheld the desolation by war threatening our land, causing the hard earnings of thy dear son and thy grandsons, to be wrested from them, how low thou would have been bowed under the weight of sorrow! Happy was it that thou was spared all this painful experience, taken away, as it were, from the evil to come!

Yet there is wisdom in all God's purposes; and may we learn wisdom through strippings, whether these be of kindred ties, of loving friends, or of property—and be the better prepared to enjoy that felicity which is not derived from earth, but from Heaven alone!

Long has been my pilgrimage journey, though " few and evil" may have " been the days of my life ;" having had a large portion of happiness, as well as my full share of deep sorrow. But, the Lord Almighty has never forsaken me, and in Him do I trust, looking unto Him to lead me onward and upward, till the life of the body is swallowed up in death, and the soul ushered into a new existence. In these troublous times, the future, as to the outward, is veiled from view ; none can reveal it but God alone by his " Light" within.

Third Month 1st, 1863.—My mind, through the night, and renewedly to-day, has been afresh convinced that whoever abides in God, knows his protecting and preserving power to encircle him on every side, keeping him secure from his enemies ; and I was engaged in prayer for my poor soul, that those Heavenly surroundings may be mine, whereby nothing shall ever overcome me, or draw me away from the light, life, and power of God. Oh ! that everything of an earthly nature in me, may give way before the arisings of the " Sun of Right-eousness ;" that my affections may be placed on things above, and a greater willingness be wrought in me to obey the will of my Heavenly Father, in all things, even in promoting " peace " on earth and " good will " to men.

As now surrounded, I am like a pent-up prisoner. O the weight of care and responsibility that rests upon me ; sources of sore trial, known only to myself and my God ! But in the midst of all the turnings and the over-turnings, the predominant feeling of my heart has been, " Thy will be done !"

Third Month 2nd.—My feelings have been solemn

and retired for a few days and nights past, and renewed
desires have been awakened that I might become wholly
weaned from the world, and from looking to the things
thereof, as affording any certain enjoyment. There is
little to attract a mind pressed with care, and strug-
gling with adversity. The buoyancy of spirits that
used to be mine, return no more. The heart is pressed
with a burden of responsibility without any earthly
hand to remove it. Therefore, trusting in God, I must
pursue my journey, hoping that the Truth may never
be dishonored by me; but that I may make an honest
livelihood for myself and mine, and honorably discharge
the trust reposed in me by my departed husband.

Twelfth Month 31st, 1864.—With the close of this
day terminates the year 1864. The outer world, as far
as the eye can take cognizance of objects, is mantled in
spotless white—an emblem of purity and innocence.
May our spirits be so robed, as the year passes out of
existence, and so welcome in the succeeding one, that
its beginnings, to us, may be favorable to lives of piety
and devotion. The day is calm and quiet, as though it
were the closing scene of some auspicious event. And
is it so? To many it is, no doubt, as they are about to
bid adieu to all transitory things, and enter into another
state of existence. To those who have their loins girt
about, and their rod and staff in readiness, such is a
glorious and happy period; for, putting off mortality,
they lay aside the pains and conflicts attendant thereon ;
while putting on a happy immortality, they enter into

7

"joy unspeakable and full of glory." How great and
varied have been the changes, since the beginning of
the year just expiring! In the family circle, in Society,
in neighborhoods, in the world at large! Could a history be furnished us, written by the pens of thousands,
each giving in the line of his own experience, it seems
to me, a Fountain of tears, seeking vent, would burst
forth from eyes unwont to weep, and sighs would heave
from hearts unapt to feel. How many have passed
through the chambers of death to the cold and silent
grave! Stalwart men, the bone and sinew of our country—the hub and spoke of the wheel of commerce, of
the loom, of agriculture, and of the various arts and
sciences. Young men, the pride and promise of their
parents' expectations, either mowed down in the field of
battle, or wasted by some enfeebling pestilence; or, too
horrible to relate, starved in noisome prisons, before the
eyes of cruel and hard-hearted beings in human form.
And not a few of the aged patriarchs, who seemed to
have belonged to a generation gone before; the loving
and gentle wife; the mother and the infant in arms;
the little prattler; yes, a great host, pursuing their
journey through time, have been arrested in their course,
and taken from this state of being. Many are the
mourners, up and down in the land! And is not the
feeling with these, "Attempt not to comfort me; I will
go mourning all my days, until my gray hairs are
brought down, with sorrow, to the grave?" Yet this
sore mourning need not be, save on behalf of those who

have come to a premature end. They who have pursued
a steady, straightforward course, who have followed their
Holy Leader in the way of uprightness; they whom He
has lifted into life, and let them fall "just in the niche
they were ordained to fill," all these having finished
their day's work here, are taken hence in fulfillment of
the decree, "Dust thou art, and unto dust shalt thou
return," only to be transplanted into a happier clime.

———— 1868.—Alone as to the outward, and stripped
of all that can possibly cheer the animal spirits, for
there is a void that nothing can fill, no earthly object
can supply. More than ten and a half years have rolled
around since my beloved partner was called hence, and
released from the shackles of mortality, and all the pains
and conflicts of life, to be reinstated in his presence
who spake the never-dying soul into existence by the
word of his power! Truly there is no other separation that can compare with that of husband and wife,
who are joined in the Lord—one in the body (in affliction) and one in spirit. Happy might we conclude
it to be, according to our human calculation, could these
beginning at the time of their marriage, continue and
end their journey together. Yes, go hand in hand
through life, and hand and hand in their passage over
that river that lands them on the side where stands the
Celestial City, in which dwell the redeemed of the Lord.
But that great God, in whose hands are man's destinies,
has willed it otherwise. One is taken and another
left, and sorrow and suffering, and many a bitter cup

are apportioned to the survivor. If these bereavements are received without murmuring, and esteemed as good gifts, they will be refining in their operation; and will fit and prepare the soul to cast off all its cares and sorrows, as filthy garments, in order to receive a robe that is pure and spotless, and owned as the "wedding garment," when presented at the marriage chamber of the Lamb, as an invited guest. My partner, thou art not, and yet, thou art forever an angel in Heaven, a glorified spirit, forming one of that innumerable company, who surround the Throne of the Lord God and of the Lamb! Oh! how many loved ones are there, my equals in age, my companions, the guardians of my childhood and youth, the comforters of after years; and my tender offspring; and here am I, bereft indeed, weary, and careworn, hastening on my way to the close! Bound to time and the cares of this world, for my dear children's sake, and perhaps, also, for the sake of the church. For, feeble as are my efforts, the prosperity of the church, and the spread of the ever-blessed Truth, are dearer to me than aught else in this world. Oh! how I long to see the loving visitations of God extended to my own, and other dear children, that they may be seen coming up "adorned [as a bride] for her husband;" not in gay apparel, according to the fashions of a vain world, but in the simplicity produced when everything is formed according to the pattern shown in the Mount.

Through life, ever since very young, the care of making a living has always devolved upon me, and now,

probably, always will; though I have ever looked forward with hope and faith that rest and a quiet evening
would be allotted me, preceding my departure from this
changing scene. I look around and see many women
who are exempt from such care; who are provided for,
and can use, at their pleasure, what they wish. They
have time to devote to duties at or from home, without
seeming to be sacrifices. Why it is thus, has to be left;
yes, I must believe it is wisely ordered for some good.
I seem forced into business, that Truth may not suffer
on account of any failing to receive their due, from
losses which we had to endure. And my God knows
that I have tried to labor honestly and diligently, that
everything should be just and right. And yet, truly,
amidst adversity, disappointment, in many a strait, a
way has been made to move on, beyond any human calculation; but it has been the "strait and narrow way,"
that I should not be elated by prosperity, nor too much
cast down by adversity. It must be that the Most High
has interposed when prospects were flattering, lest I
should take my flight on the Sabbath-day; and removed obstacles, when these were too great, lest in the
winter season I might be off. May all the praise be
unto the Lord, if I hold out unto the end, and may his
name be exalted in the earth! Oh! my soul, trust thou
still in God, who is the light of my countenance and
my help!

If thou, Lord, wilt give me bread to eat and raiment
to put on, and wilt be with me in the way I should go,

and finally, bring me home in peace, I will serve Thee
with all the might and strength that Thou givest, for I
have none of my own! Thou knowest, gracious Father,
that this is my petition from day to day, and from year
to year, and has been since early youth; and yet, how
feebly have I walked and worked, and how little good
have I done in the world! Oh! that thou mayst be near
to me supporting me amidst my trials and sore conflicts,
which are deep and many; and enable me to keep my
head above the troubled waters, though the billows roll
and threaten—for all forever is thine, in Heaven above
and in the earth beneath. Ah! how much of the time
I have to wear my sackcloth underneath, that my countenance may not be the index to a heart oppressed with
care. May all these things refine my poor soul more
and more, and prepare it to dwell forever in that Holy
City that hath a sure foundation, whose " Builder and
Maker is God."

> " In thy pavilion there is peace and rest,
> Thy saints are there, and are forever blest."

First Month 3rd, 1875.—A beautiful day in the
outer world, the trees and shrubs being covered with
sleet. It was too slippery for our horse to take me to
meeting, and dangerous for me to walk. My daughters
went on foot.

I have felt sensible that the Divine Presence is
everywhere, and his love offered to every son and daughter of Adam, the world over.

This has been an unusually open winter; so that is seems as if a gracious Providence has favored the many poor and destitute in various parts of our country.

Last Fifth-day we had a most excellent silent meeting. It seemed as if the Most High spread his wings of love and mercy over us all, and made us rejoice, and give adoration and praise to his adorable name. O such seasons! how they renew our faith and trust in Him in whom we "live, move and have our being." I often feel to exclaim in spirit, "The earth is full of the glory of God." He is not afar off, but nigh. He tabernacles in man and fills all space.

Sixth Month 23rd, 1875.—I am seventy-four years old to-day. Keep me, O Father, in thy love, forever. Amen!

MARY S. LIPPINCOTT.

CHAPTER III.

PART I.

A letter from a niece, this morning, says George and Catharine Truman are both ill—the former very ill; she also speaks of the illness of other dear friends, and of the death of some. But, so does the race of men pass on and off the stage of life. When one is ready and waiting, happy and glorious must be the exit from a world of change, to a state of unchanging felicity. Then, the sadness to us who mourn the loss, rises into joy and thanksgiving; and I hope that we may be able to rejoice in the end, by our sun's going down in brightness, and our souls arising into eternity.

I tenderly sympathize with thee, dear A., in thy varied feelings. A diversified path is the poor pilgrim's portion on his way to the Celestial City. If he has not "Evangelist" to direct him and give him a "roll," he has a greater in his own soul—"Christ in you, the hope of glory!" The Life, Light, Wisdom, and Power! Everything to be as armor and as counsel, while a lone

traveler, ofttimes in a weary land. No, not alone! A
Friend is near to urge him on!

When my " tent door I open wide,"
I hear his footsteps at my side,
And hear his voice, to sweetly say
Fear not ;—thy drooping mind I'll stay.
Thy God is *near* -*not* far away '

Abraham was proved, not in displeasure, but for the
trial of his allegiance. See how he was blest in withholding nothing! All given up! This is what we
must know. Saying, "Here am I, O Lord, do with me
as Thou wilt! Then, as we become the clay, the Potter
can do his work, with none to hinder! He forms the
vessels, refines them, fills them, then there is a pouring
out for use! How wonderful are his ways and his works,
all in wisdom, for our greatest good.   And when we are
ready to conclude that He has hidden his face and with-
drawn himself, He is not far off, his eye is open, watching us as a loving parent watches a darling child!

Children must learn to work, without depending
too much upon the parent to sustain them in inactivity ;
so they have to be stripped at seasons, deeply tried and
proved, that they may look around and see whether or
not they have occupied their strength rightly. "My
Beloved is mine and I am his;" as much when sought
and *not* found, as when He is seen, and his face is comely
with smiles. Be of good cheer, my dear, tried one, the
Light will shine, the clouds break away!

"In quietness and confidence shall be your strength," is addressed sweetly to all the Lord's children in every condition of life.

For, in this state, even the doubting and troubled, as was Elijah, hear and understand that the threatening Tempest, Earthquake and Fire, cannot destroy, overwhelm, or overturn, for God is not in them! They are elementary, changeable; but, in the still, small voice that follows, is this holy calm, this quietness and confidence. Oh! how strong then, to wrap the "face in the mantle," and receive the counsel of God; to go at his bidding, to instruct and edify his people, those who have "not bowed the knee to Baal, or kissed his image." "Rejoice evermore, and in all things, give thanks;" because of the true declaration, fulfilled in the Christian's experience, in this waiting state,—

> "God is coming, God is nigh,
> Hear ye, God is passing by!"

And with his presence comes light, peace, and a "certain evidence of Divine Truth." The soul bows, the will is subdued, and the heart-language is, "Not my will, but thine, O Father, be done!" In this passive, waiting state, He reaches forth his arm of love, in his own time, and his voice is heard, saying, "Arise and journey on!"

In the Beginning, it was many days (or epochs), ere the elements were brought together, and the right arrangement made, and the growth for the support of life. Lo, in the new creation, out of chaos comes forth order, life, food, raiment, and ability to labor, under Divine guidance, and in the light. The night for repose, the day for labor! The analogy between the outward and the inward is very striking. All the commotions, doubts, fears, and whatever else has been thy experience, dear child, has been the experience of those who have trodden the way of the cross before thee. All these have been allured into the wilderness, to be drawn away from all the glitter and vanity shining so enticingly in the open day; there hath He "spoken comfortably" unto them; and, staining the beauty of the first, they have become enamored of the second, the invisible glory and beauty not to be seen by the outward eye.

For the elect's sake, these days of suffering and anguish of spirit, are shortened, when the work of preparation is effected, then it is enough. Wash me, make me clean; "purge me with hyssop," and " I shall be whiter than snow;" pure within, holy; in accordance with the injunction, " Be ye clean that bear the vessels of the Lord." I had, in my exercises of spirit, to tread the loneliness of my way, though I had counselors, by letter, who had entered into my condition, and their words were as the gently distilling dew, and refreshing rain.

Our Father raises up servants to lead and instruct, as He did Moses to Israel. " Bear ye one another's burdens," and " be ye one another's helpers in the Lord." Help to cleanse, prepare and strengthen those whom the

Lord has chosen for his disciples. But the *Master must send them*, and show, them where, when, and what to speak; must give them their "Urim and Thummim," and be to them "mouth and wisdom, tongue and utterance."

Many things pass through the mind; all these must give place to the Master, who brings a solemn quiet, out of which springs up a language for the people. "It is not I that speak" but the "Father who is in me." His voice through his instrument, who is as a mouth for the Lord! Trust Him who opens the way, enlightens the path; is present to anoint, to bless, and to prosper his own work; and to roll together the clouds and scatter them, that the "Sun of righteousness" may illumine heaven and earth.

Although my health is nearly restored, yet it is so cold and icy to-day, that my children were unwilling for me to venture out to meeting. Not mingling as much as usual with Friends generally, as I am much at home because of the "imfirmities of the flesh," I often feel poor, and the streams very low! I question myself whether there is a withering, yea or nay. There are many poor in the world, in "basket and in store" outwardly; there are many poor in "oil and wine," spiritually, for their own refreshment, and to hand to the needy. But, if they know who has in store a supply, they can "ask in faith," and, in his own time, they will surely receive. There was something for the disciples to do at

the time of the miracle, and there is for us now. "Fill
the water-pot up to the brim." What a placid surface—
not a ripple, or there would be an overflow. All the
thoughts (so unstable) gathered, still, the eye of faith
directed to the Master—waiting. O the change! The
water agitated, threatening, overflowing; changed into
the "wine of consolation." Draw out now; give to
others, and "drink thy wine with a merry heart; for
God now accepteth thy works."

It is no new thing to be tried; to be tossed as with
the tempest, and "not comforted." But the "Comforter"
is nigh, saying to those who love Him, "Lo, I am with
you alway, even to the end of the world." I could recur
to the days of my espousals, when at seasons, I can say,
from experience, "I remembered God, and was troubled,
I complained, and my spirit was overwhelmed;" seasons
when I sought my Beloved, and found Him not, for a
long time. Ah! many such seasons have been known;
but when my allegiance was *proved*, then He arose in
his beauty, and his face beamed with love. Such is the
experience of his children, that our dependence may be
on an Almighty Arm, and that we may be led in a "new
way," in the everlasting Light; then we see for ourselves, without any doubt or uncertainty, what that good
and acceptable sacrifice is, which the Lord requires of
us; not what man requires, but what man in Christ,
assents unto. I often think how little heed is given, by
the fashionable, church-going people, to the voice of the
Spirit, impressions, silent prayer, heart-praises and melo-

dies. Therefore, book-religion, vocal prayer, and owning creeds, are substituted for practical religion. Oh! what a privilege to be educated in a belief that we have Immanuel, God with us, ever, unless we wilfully go from Him, into disobedience; and then He follows us to the very ends of the earth, whether we be rich or poor, saying, "Come unto me, all ye ends of the earth, and be saved." The more children are taught to look to this inward principle, the better it will be for the community at large. I believe First-day schools among Friends will be a blessing, *if kept in their right* place. Good seed, sown in innocent minds, must take root!

What will my dear A. think of my long silence, after such a letter as hers? Well, dear, it has not been for want of loving interest and sympathy; but because of my close travail of spirit and sympathy with the sick; in view of the approaching end of some, very near and dear to me. And that which was looked for, has come, and is past; and I feel more links broken in the chain of affection; not only one, but more! Thus it is; the circle brightened by loved ones, lessens rapidly, and ere long, my turn to be gathered will arrive, and, Oh! then to meet the glorified spirits of the dear departed, where separations will be no more known, is, in prospect, some joy in the midst of grief.   *   *   *   O how many valued members of our Society we have lost since our last Yearly Meeting! Pillars in the church! I feel sad when I think how we shall miss them, though I know it is all in wisdom. The mantle is left, if only caught up. But, thou may say this does not meet my case. My dear A., the Master tells thee his will, and gives thee wisdom. Be faithful in all humility, and He will clearly show thee thy stepping-stones in the true path. He will be thy bow and battle-axe, and will cover thy head in every day of conflict.

As obedience is kept in, an enlargement will be known. For the little streams lead to " broad rivers and streams," in which the bark can move on in safety. Have faith ; it is the gift of God ! It will remove mountains, yes, and make an easy way through the deeps. I feel assured that thy mind is spread out to receive the dews and the showers of his love ; they will descend not only for thy refreshment, but 'for thy growth. No good thing does He withhold from them that love Him ; but He chooses his servants in the furnace of affliction. We are human and must know refinement, purification, sanctification, justification. The "just shall live by faith." Press on in the way cast up for thee ! Trust in the Everlasting Arms to support thee ! Pour out thy soul to Him, who is a friend close at hand, with an ear always open to hear, an eye to pity. I can read in thine, my own experience in the day of my espousals, when my Maker was my husband, and from the world I was divorced. Yes, dear, I often " ate my bread" in the bitterness of my soul, and trod a lonely way. Yet God was nigh and watched over me, and how marvellously did He make a way where I could see no way.

Words would fail to speak his praise! May the "ark" be kept in Israel in safety!

I recur with heartfelt satisfaction to my attendance of Baltimore Yearly Meeting, from which we returned in safety, and with the sense of unspeakable peace, as the reward of obedience. Can we not all say, "it *was good* to be there." Our spirits were refreshed, our strength renewed; and we can live on the food received (if abiding in humility) many days, or go forward through the wilderness, in the strength thereof. We had, indeed, an excellent meeting, interesting social minglings; and under all, a current of love and good-will flowing, almost universally, an evidence of the "peace on earth, and good-will to men."

I find a peculiar, heartfelt satisfaction as I ponder on these evidences of life; so many seem under the preparing Hand, ready to step into the ranks, at the word of Divine command, and carry on the good work in which others were engaged when called home. Oh! these dear ones, how they are encircled by the Father's love; and how wise, how tender, should the fathers and mothers in the Church be, so that they may shield these inexperienced ones, steady their faltering steps, and aid them to walk safely in the rugged ways that they may have to tread. Some have entered early, others later, into the harvest-field, but each one is entitled to the "penny;" enough to procure the Bread and Water of Life—sufficient to satisfy the hungry soul.

Some of the dedicated have always had suffering, in greater or less degree, for their portion—not for themselves alone, but for others. So it remains to be, if we are poured out for others, so to fill up our measure for the "body's sake." I have partaken of the cup of suffering also; but the good Father has not forsaken us, else where would have been our hope? So hope on, trust on, dear one; the Lord's presence can make amends for all other privations. He has rich blessings in store.

I know, dear friend, thy conflicts have been many, and will be. Trials are added by the disposition to remove landmarks, and to do away with all mystery, as they say! And to divide what God has joined together, "Jesus and Christ!" Such efforts scatter and divide. I have no sympathy with such views; neither do I believe that Friends will be instrumental in gathering to the true sheepfold if they depart from original ground. There is *no Scripture* for Jesus being the son of Joseph. Besides, my own instruction by revelation, as I sat in a meeting about fifty-two years ago, was in entire conformity with the Scripture account that the "prepared body" had no father but God—a "body hast thou prepared me," sent for a special purpose; Divinity in humanity! A Saviour to the Jews, and his mission was to lead into a higher dispensation. The Law and the Prophets having been fulfilled in Him, then the visible Jesus was removed, that a spiritual head of a more spiritual religion might be known. Can not an

8

Almighty Being perform any work? Is not his power unlimited? Is it wise in man to try to remove the connecting link in the great economy of God, in restoring a fallen race? There is no flaw in God's works! How gradual are his mercy and long-suffering! And what encouragement to a fallen race that He sent into the world, one tempted in all things, yet never yielding— inviting us to trust in the same Power to keep us.

I cannot write much, for I am not well enough; but I must say that I am very sorry that there is such a desire for reform as to try to *reform Faith*, which is God's gift. "By grace ye are saved, through faith, and that not of yourselves, it is the gift of God." If we doubt the emphatic testimony of the Scriptures, in what shall we have faith? In the Spirit only? That is true, but we must have speech also—some channel of communication. If Jesus *is* Joseph's son, why look to his sayings more than to other men's? Or, how hold Him up without being idolaters? Oh! that we would get into the Gospel stream, and keep in it! No distrust, no doubt, no contending doctrines there! Christ would guide our little barks safely, and still the threatening storms.

The more I read and hear of philosophical investigations, designed to remove a belief in miracles, and in the account of the outward advent, the death and the resurrection of Jesus Christ, the firmer is my faith in the truth and the reality of the record, as in the Holy

Scriptures. How can any one who believes in God (who has all power in Heaven and in earth) doubt any miracle, at any time or age of the world. Who would dare to limit his power; the finite to limit the Infinite. There is no difficulty, it seems to me, in reconciling occurrences, if we are steadfast in our faith that God's ways are higher than man's ways, and his thoughts than man's thoughts. "God is Light," and as we remain, as men, in our true position, upright, our reason unclouded—not perverting God's ways, nor disobeying his laws—our minds clear and thoughts pure, his light will shine upon us to give us to know the Truth. To see things not before revealed to us, to behold the angels (ministering spirits) ascending and descending to feed us with food convenient for us; and the Son and sent of the Father coming in love inwardly, as truly as He came outwardly, to redeem us from all evil; to lift us up with Him; and to give us an inheritance among all them that are sanctified; and herein we see the end of the outward, the work accomplished. How great the danger of doubting! Those who doubt, and cavil, searching for errors, faults, inconsistencies, can always find them, in everything; real in some things, imaginary in many, and wholly imaginary in Christianity. Inconsistencies appear in too many professed Christians; but the religion of Jesus Christ is not blemished thereby. It remains pure.

John Woolman saw and heard "certain evidence of Divine Truth;" and I have long believed this. Atheists and skeptics have long tried to dig and undermine the Rock on which Truth rears its edifice, but they have failed; I hope and trust they ever will fail.

— - —

PART II.

LETTERS TO HER NEPHEW, ROBERT SHOEMAKER.

MOORESTOWN, Ninth Month 18th, 1847.

My Dear Nephew :—I was in the city yesterday, on a Committee, but having to sit there from ten o'clock until three, I had no time to call, or to attend to some other things that I wished to.

We are all well, and have been for the most part through the summer, which is cause for thankfulness. The country looks beautiful; the corn and buckwheat crops are promising, the pasture is excellent, and the conditions are cheering to the heart of the farmer. How much we have to be thankful for, and yet how little evidence of an humble acknowledgment of the good gifts of the Great Giver, do we discover in the busy world where men are wasting and destroying these good gifts, and furiously slaying their fellow-beings merely to get a little more! How long will these things be? When will men learn wisdom by the things that they suffer? Oh, that Christian professors everywhere would unite in promoting the peaceable religion of Jesus. Then how sweetly should we dwell together, where joy and gladness would be heard, and the voice of melody. The true Christians in every denomination know no feeling other than that of love: toward the vilest sinner they feel that love which induces pity. Oh, what an example did our dear Redeemer set us, in eating with publicans and sinners, that by this condescension he might gain their love and convert them, by calling them to repentance. Oh, that we might pray unto the Lord of the harvest, that He would send forth faithful laborers into his harvest-field, that there might be more of a gathering to the flock and family of Christ — for these are to be found in every nation, kindred, tongue and people; and however different their profession, they are all *one* in Christ. They are one with the Father and with the Son, and in this oneness they have fellowship one with another. Ah! how soon will that period arrive when it will matter not to us concerning anything but this— that our names are found written in the " Lamb's book of Life;" for these, and these only, are entitled to an entrance into the joy of our Lord.

I remain with much love to thyself and family, and with desires for your welfare, affectionately thy aunt,

MARY S. LIPPINCOTT.

Sixth Month 1st, 1879.

My Dear Nephew :—The weather is very warm these last two days. I had pleasant weather while in New York, also a very satisfactory Yearly Meeting, and much affectionate kindness from Friends. I parted from them feeling that it would probably be my last visit, and I feel peaceful and thankful for the many favors received, and for none more than for the loving care of my Heavenly Father, who, I hope will sustain me till He takes me home.   I also hope that He will care for mine and for all others, when I am gone, for I feel a desire that all souls should flee to God for refuge, and be saved.

We miss our horse much ; but I am thankful to be able to walk to meeting.   To-day I had a ride part way, and walked the remainder ; a good meeting rewarded me.

We are all three of us troubled with aches and pains, but I often count my favors and blessings, and try to hope ahead.   There are many trials and adversities, but there is also an assurance that there is a joy to cover all these, if only we are redeemed and made partakers of God's salvation offered to all.

I hope you are all well, also thy brothers and their families, to whom love abounds in my heart.

" I love my own dear kin and kith
With love that is no sham nor myth."

Thy affectionate aunt,

M. S. L.

MOORESTOWN, Eleventh Month 25th, 1879.

My Dear Nephew :—Thanks for the nice pictures, received yesterday.   They are excellent likenesses of a dear nephew and niece, as I hope ever to be privileged to call you, while I am tottering on to the goal which lies at the end of my pilgrimage.

We are much tied at home with business that claims our time and our thoughts—yes, more so than I would wish in old age ; but perhaps it is better to keep in the harness till the end, and so "to wear out, rather than to rust out." I hope never to grudge what I have freely done for others, but we have met with some losses which are hard to bear ; for had they not occurred I might have been relieved from care and anxiety long ere this.

I am like Jacob; I like the Shoemakers and always did ; and it does me good to step into the store and look upon you as you are engaged in business; you all look as if you are trying to do right, in every sense of the word, and that is what constitutes true happiness and usefulness—to help yourselves and to serve others. This is so in lawful business, and in higher duties as well. A Friend once said, "We are all servants, from the highest in authority down ;" and so it seems to be. To serve well in our temporal things, and to accommodate others, evinces that we are faithful stewards over temporal goods, and to such are given "durable riches." How happy would it be for mankind if it were always so, for then there would be no over-reaching, no defaulting ; but the observance of the Golden Rule would enable us all, as "brethren to dwell together in unity." Oh, how often and increasingly I rejoice because the good Father loves the human family, and reaches out his hand to gather all ; to raise even out of the pit of pollution, and to place the feet upon a rock, which rock is Christ. "How often would I have gathered" you, but "ye would not." This is the pathetic language to all poor unconverted ; and to all backsliders for whom Christians must be poured forth in spiritual prayers. I believe throughout Christendom, prayers ascend and reach the ears of the Lord of Sabaoth, that the way of salvation may be known, and the wanderers return and live.

The recent visit that we had from thy brothers and their wives, with the dear little ones, was truly pleasant to us. I recurred to your father in his youth, when he was in business at grandfather's, and we all there. Then and always, he was as a brother to me. He was very conscientious, kept out of harm's way, and was a good example to young people. Yes ! I loved your parents, and I hope to meet them in eternity. May we be gathered there when done with time—gathered in one company ; none missing from the family circle surrounding the throne of the Lord God and the Lamb forever.

Thy loving aunt,

M. S. L.

MOORESTOWN, First Month 13th, 1880.

My Dear Nephew :—I have desired that I might have strength, mentally and physically, some time soon to call to mind and write down many names of the former members of our families, and some others who used to be prominent, active inhabitants and useful citizens of Shoemakertown. They were many, and were well known as an intelligent people ; and many of them were well educated, and were not inferior in business

ability, in practical piety, and in religious observances
to their worthy successors. Such is my belief, and if
any of my age remain, they will, I think, sanction my
view and confirm my testimony. And the harmony and
good feeling! Why, I often recur to my childhood, when
from all that I heard and saw, I thought of no faults in
any, except occasionally a rare case of intemperance was
seen. Visiting was frequent, and evenings together
were passed pleasantly and instructively; for the conversation would be upon the better times since the
Revolution, the improvements in schools, in farming,
fruit-raising and other branches of business; also the
prosperity of A., B., and C., who were doing so well, &c.
There were comfortable homes with well polished furniture, and nice "rag carpets;" parlors with a nicer
kind, and pretty furniture; and then the welcome —
yes, the welcome! And the easy, cosy mingling! How
sweet is the remembrance. There was thy double great-
aunt, Nancy Leech, descended from the royal Stuarts.
Seated in her ebony chair she looked like a queen, to
whom her husband, children and domestics delighted
to do honor; and she was worthy of it. Her family
were trained in ways of true politeness. Thy great-
grandmother Martin was another lady. Uncle John
Shoemaker's family, and his sons John and Charles
and their families, and many, many others, including
what are left of their descendants. Thy great-grand-
father (my grandfather), Benjamin Shoemaker, was a
gentleman, and was regarded as such, and highly es-

teemed by Friends and others who visited at his house, and were friends to him as he was to them. It is now a long time since these worthy predecessors and their not less worthy neighbors, passed away, but their characters, their worth, their gentleness, and their Christian deportment remain with me; and I often consider it a privilege to have been reared with such, and to have had the opportunity of hearing the instructive conversation of so many of them, as I sat beside my venerable and much respected grandsire.

Oh! how it animates me to recur to the past, and to thy dear father in his youth, and a little later to thy own dear mother; so kind, and affectionate and bright. How many pleasant hours I spent with her.

How I am bound to my kin, and to those whom they have chosen as helpmeets. Farewell.

Thy attached aunt,

M. S. L.

MOORESTOWN, Fifth Month 31st, 1880.

My Dear Nephew :—I feel lonely to think that B. S. and the others have gone to stem the great water, and to pass the summer in a foreign land; and I have an idea it is a stripping time with thee and all the rest, nearly allied and cheered by their presence, as well as with the sons left at home. I hope that it is right, that it may prove a benefit, and that they may safely return, and not encounter floating ice-bergs on their way. The day [of their sailing] was auspicious, so far as weather was concerned, and to us who must remain at home, the showers have been refreshing.

While the weather is beautiful, there are cares and trials that sometimes weigh heavily, and there is a longing for some one to confer with. The financial pressure affects more or less all who are engaged in business, and I have to assume my share. I do not want to complain, for though I have had a long and checkered journey, I have never been forsaken. I often turn to my dear kin, with longings to be more with them during the little time allotted me here.

Love to thy dear self, to A., and to your children.

Thy affectionate aunt,

M. S. L.

MOORESTOWN, Sixth Month 29th, 1880.

My Dear Nephew:—I intended to write thee on my seventy-ninth birth-day, 23rd instant, but I first wrote to Benjamin, and then my head ached so that I deemed it not prudent to write more that day, and the extreme heat and indisposition have prevented since.

I have not been out since First-day week, though I hope I am better this morning, having slept more last night than for some time previously.

Such a drought and heated term in Sixth Month, none can remember ever to have known before. We try to keep as bright as we can, and J. is remarkable for bracing up.

I had an interesting letter from Benjamin, written

on the second and third insts. I presume that he and
many others partook some of sea-sickness, and probably
more after he wrote. How many accidents we hear of,
but most of them nearer home. How thankful I feel
when I hear that the dear ones are safe and comfortable,
and I trust, thankful, too—with all the withholding and
the blighted prospects—for food and raiment. These
will be needed a little while longer to sustain and clothe
the poor body, and then it must return to the earth.
But if the soul is only safe, and fitted for immortality,
Oh! what a favor from that great, good Father who holds
all—except those that fall away—in his everlasting
arms of love. May He enclose thee and thine, me and
mine, and all those who love Him, and who delight to
think upon his goodness and mercy. And, Oh! that
all the wanderers and prodigals would " return, repent,
and live." Happy would it be for such in life, and
happy would it be for them in death; because the captive spirits would return, in peace, to God who gave
them. Love to A. and to your children.

Thy loving aunt,

M. S. L.

PART III.

LETTERS TO HER GRANDSON.

[The boy, the youth, the young man, the husband,
and the father, to whom the following letters were ad-

dressed, was the only child of her husband's deceased son. His name was the same as that of his father—Daniel P. Lippincott. Most of his married life was passed in St. Louis, Missouri.]

Third Month 21st, 1859.

My Dear Grandson :—I received thy very acceptable letter duly, but have been prevented by company, from replying. We are all pleased with the prospect of seeing thee soon. We should like thee to come to our house to stay until some other arrangement is made.

All thy friends manifest a great deal of interest in thee, and want thee to do well, and to be comfortable and happy.

I do not want thee to go into a store, as I would not choose that business for thee; it is so confining for those who have been used to the open air. Thy present need is to go to school, and get a thorough education. I am pleased to see thy good penmanship, and well composed letters. I hope thee will keep well.

I shall be glad to have thy likeness when thee comes.

Take good care of thyself, and try to keep well. I shall be glad to hear from thee if thee has time to write again before coming.

Farewell. Jane and Margaret unite in love to thee.

I remain thy affectionate and well-wishing grandmother.

MARY S. LIPPINCOTT.

Fifth Month 16th, 1859.

My Dear Grandson : — I received thy acceptable letter while in Philadelphia, attending our Yearly Meeting, and as I am Clerk of the Meeting I could not get time to write and tell thee how glad we always are to hear of thy welfare.

We are all pleased to learn that thee has employment, and hope thee will keep well and be able to fulfill thy part pleasantly.

Our Yearly Meeting was large (more than three thousand in attendance), and was a good, comfortable meeting throughout. It held nearly a week. To-day we are again on duty in school. The weather is lovely, clear and cool, and the country looks flourishing.

17th.—The birds are singing very sweetly, they and myself being about all that appear to be up, in our immediate neighborhood. Our family mostly allow me the privilege of being alone a good while, mornings. They love morning naps.

We often think of the pleasant time thee spent with us, and hope the like will occur again.

I hope thee will continue to make a selection of reading that is profitable and elevating to the mind and morals ; for there are many publications emanating from the press that are no better for the mind than poison is for the body. Their contents sicken the moral sense, and then destroy it. Refined, substantial books, accompanied by virtuous and good society, shed a happy and beneficial influence on the character of the young, which often proves a blessing through life. Correct principles early imbibed, and habits according therewith, seldom leave us; neither is it in the power of the vicious to overthrow them. Very rarely, at least, does it occur that such are swerved from their purpose of doing well. I hope that thine may be a useful and happy career. Thy business campaign was early attempted; but an over-ruling Providence is the care-taker of his children, and I trust and hope that He will have thee in his keeping, and guide thy footsteps aright through life; then it will matter not on what part of the globe thy career is finished, thy end will be peace.

With love from all the family, including myself, I remain thy affectionate grandmother,

M. S. L.

Eleventh Month 20th, 1859.

I hope this will find thee as cheerful and happy as I left thee, and as well in health, for I am interested in thy welfare and improvement, as much, I believe, as if thou wert my own son. Dear child! I feel easy about thee, believing thou art placed in a very favorable situation, and I hope thy progress in study will be satisfactory to thyself and to thy teacher. I was much pleased while in the school, with the appearance of so nice a company of youths, and I do hope you will be an advantage to one another. Self-government is better than observance of rules (though this is right) for few rules are needed where each one controls himself.

I had a pleasant journey home, and found all well and getting along nicely.

We had an interesting lecture on Fifth-day; expect to have them once in two weeks.

I had a severe turn with my head one day, but it passed off; for which I feel thankful. We are having lovely weather, after much rain.

A. R. was here yesterday, and seemed glad to hear of thy safe arrival there [at Gwynedd Boarding School]. I think thee will love all the family. I hope thee will not feel discouraged if thee is not able to answer all the questions, for thee is young, and I have no doubt will get along well, time being afforded thee. I want thee to tell me about thy studies, and whatever else there is of interest. I feel a deep interest in the family and the school. How do you spend your time between schools? What do you play? Exercise is very essential.

I have had a good deal of company, and do not feel as if I had much to say, for I have interruptions while writing. With love and desires for thy welfare, I am thy affectionate grandmother,

M. S. L.

Eleventh Month 30th, 1859.

I received thy acceptable letter and was pleased to notice the improvement in thy penmanship and spelling. We have delightful weather, and anticipate a mild winter's morning, when we arise to hail another day. We have been favored for the most part with the privilege of lovely walks over the green fields, and through the woods to gather mosses, and other relics of the season, that remain uncovered by snow, and unbitten by the frosts that blight so much.

Twelfth Month 1st.

A fine morning, but hardly light enough to see to write. I suppose another day will decide the fate of poor John Brown. We can form some idea of the seeming security of the South, by the array of military men on such an occasion. To my mind it conveys the idea that our favored government rests on a slender basis. How Friends feel at the South we may conjecture. Those with whom I correspond have not yet made the first allusion to the subject in any of their letters. A Friend, just returned from Virginia, says that in Louden County, some think they will be ordered to leave the State. The measures of the Governor of Virginia seem like a challenge for a civil war. The result we must await. I mourn over our country, that we have, with our eyes open, traveled the direct road to such a crisis.

The institution and perpetuation of slavery on the one hand, and the zeal on the other (always manifested more or less to meet wrong) have provoked this ebullition, and where is it to stop? Well would it be for the United States if our rulers, peaceably, should remove cause and effect: then would this be the most favored nation of the earth, and an asylum for the oppressed

9

from other lands.   But at this time great prudence becomes the people of the North.

I reverently trust that more can be affected by " fervent, effectual prayer," than by freedom of speech, to
change the hearts of those who are agents in the iniqui-
tous system of slavery.   Much was effected in days of
old in that way, and the Supreme Ruler of the universe
makes use of men now for a wise and glorious purpose—
even to stay the flood of iniquity by wielding the sword
of the spirit, to slay spiritual foes, enemies to the Truth,
to the people, and to God.   Poor John Brown ! who can
pronounce judgment upon him ?   He may have thought
as Saul did, that he was doing God service.   Surely
he has been prompted by very many, and I trust his
rash act may be pardoned, and he go to rest.

Please give my love to the family, take good care
of thyself, and be a good boy ; these two injunctions
embrace all that is needed.   I am always glad to hear
from thee.

Thy affectionate grandmother,

M. S. L.

Twelfth Month 20th, 1859.

I am pleased to see thy improvement in penmanship and spelling, and infer that thy progress in other
branches corresponds.   I feel very sure that thy situation
is eligible to receive a good education, and that every
attention will be paid to polish thee, as thee is growing
to the age of a young man.   In America now, juveniles

soon reach a responsible time of life, when the appellation of young man falls pleasingly upon their ears.

I was favorably impressed with the appearance of thy schoolmates, and I trust that you form an agreeable "social circle," and that by your gentlemanly deportment, and accommodating manners, you may be an ornament to the school, and a comfort to those who preside as guardians over you, while there. It yields much more real satisfaction in after years, to look back to school-days with the consciousness that they were well-spent—industriously and profitably—than it would to have to remember idle freaks, and antic performances that made the teacher's care doubly onerous, and caused the students many unpleasant deprivations. Innocent recreation and amusement I always encourage in the young; it is good for their bodies and strengthening to their minds.

I am obliged for the paper; those exercises are useful in calling out your energies, and promoting care and precision. Do thy best, but be not too anxious to perform too much. Time will be afforded thee to accompany application "up the hill of science." At thy age it is not wise to tax thy brain too much.

I am glad you all keep well, and that thee is happy. Accept my love and believe me to be thy well-wishing grandmother.

M. S. L.

First Month 30th, 1860.

I find that it will not do to depend upon others to write to thee, so if I do not tire thee with my letters I shall continue to tell thee how we are and how we fare. D. W. has been extremely ill, so that at one time we despaired of his recovery; but he is now convalescent, and likely to be well again.   It was a severe case of pneumonia.   Other relatives and friends in usual health.

We have very cold weather and some sleighing. Thy letters evince improvement in both penmanship and composition.   I hope thee may feel encouraged to persevere, but to proceed carefully, and not be anxious to acquire more than is best in a limited time.   In ascending a steep mountain, it is best not to go too fast at the beginning, and thus spend the strength which will be needed for the latter and more arduous portion of the journey. Health of mind and body must be attended to — neither should be over-taxed.   Does thee need any additional clothing for this very cold weather ?

I am pleased to learn that thee is so happy there amongst kind friends.   I am very easy about thee, knowing thee is so well cared for and protected.   A. R. was here yesterday.   I gave him thy letter to read.   He seemed much pleased, for he feels a deep interest in thee and in thy improvement.

A man has been tried for murder at Mount Holly Court, and has been convicted and sentenced to be hanged.   I am sorry that an execution is to take place so near us. It would be dreadful even if far off, and yet it is distressing to think of the murders committed.

I do not go to the Town Hall to hear lectures, as I do not feel like going with the crowd; but if I were near enough to you I should like to hear some of your performances. I presume thee does not now fail to answer questions in grammar, unless thee is embarrassed.

I fear my letter may seem dry to thee, but thee will have to excuse it, remembering that I am old, and that I do not see so many things to animate as when I was young. Especially is this the case since I have been deprived of the company of thy dear grandfather, who was everything to me to make life comfortable.

With much love to thee, and with desires for thy best welfare in every way, I am thy affectionate grandmother,

M. S. L.

Second Month 7th, 1860.

My Dear Grandson :—I have been gratified with seeing thy different letters to notice the improvement, as well as to be informed of thy health and happiness. The inclemency of the weather prevented J—— from getting to see thee when she went to Philadelphia.

We are progressing pleasantly and harmoniously, and I think we never enjoyed school more than we do this term.

I expect to go to Virginia; leaving home on Sixth-day next, to be absent perhaps nearly two weeks.

Has thee been able to keep warm out of doors these cold days? I hope so, for it is needful to use plenty of exercise in the fresh air, and to be clad so as not to take cold.

I want thee not to be too anxious to acquire a great deal of knowledge in a short time. Remember thy age, and that there must be a physical constitution forming while an education is being acquired. These should be balanced, that a sound mind may inhabit a sound body. An eminent scholar would not like to embark on a voyage of discovery in a rickety old vessel; the vessel should be properly cared for, as well as the passenger, in order that both may be preserved.

I send thee a little " pin money," though not to buy pins. With kindest love to thee I am thy affectionate grandmother,

M. S. L.

Third Month 6th, 1860.

My Dear Grandson : — I returned on Second-day from the South. Left my brother and sister indisposed, though better. My neice, C. H. M., buried her little son while I was there. The other quite ill with same disease, a catarrhal affection. I enjoyed mingling with my friends and relatives ; everybody seemed glad to see me. I was not afraid even to go near to Harper's Ferry. The Quarterly Meeting was unusually large ; perhaps the excited people wanted to hear whether or not Friends would have anything to say about John Brown. They heard no allusion to him or to politics. We desire nothing but to persuade men to be Christians.

I do not feel able to write much to-day as I am weary from traveling. My journey was performed in cars, stages (over bad roads), carriages, sleighs, and once on horse-back. I do not enjoy the *traveling part* of a visit.

I hope thee keeps well, and gets along comfortably to thy own and thy teacher's satisfaction ; then the days passed there will be recurred to with pleasure. Please give my love to the two families and to such of the students as remember me. I desire the welfare of all.

With love I am thy affectionate grandmother,

M. S. L.

Third Month 26th, 1860.

My Dear Grandson :—We have been much engaged and have had a good deal of company. I have not, however, been unmindful of thee, for I think of thee often, and desire thy health, happiness and progress in study. I was interested to hear that your examination was coming off soon. Interested, because I hoped it would prove satisfactory to all.

My dear child, I do very much want to see thee, and I expect thee wants a little recreation at home. It speaks well for thee to allude so favorably to thy teacher, to the school, and to every accommodation there. I think thee will always be able to recur with pleasure to the time passed there, and I feel grateful to the caretakers of that Institution for their attention to thee.

To-day it seems as if winter were returning. We have had the cheering music of birds from the woods, and frogs from the waters, adding to the interest of a ride or a walk. These now must hush, and await the termination of the snow-storm and the howling wind. What a change from yesterday! So it is often in the spring of the year.

I close with love to thee and to the two families, and remain thy affectionate grandmother,

M. S. L.

[In the spring of 1860, Gwynedd Boarding School was discontinued, and D. P. L. went to Freeland, Montgomery County, Pennsylvania, to school.]

Eighth Month 17th, 1860.

I hope, my dear D., that thee will keep well, and be able to progress to thy own satisfaction, and to do well every way. I know that such is thy desire and intention, and I have confidence to believe thee will make every effort in thy power. [In a former letter she had expressed her regret at his having to leave Gwynedd, and go among strangers.]

Now, do not get disheartened if any tasks are hard, or if thee does not come up to what thee could wish. I have no doubt of thy success; and—health permitting—I have confidence in the prospect that thee will be able to engage, at the proper time, in some useful and profitable business. I. and J. join me in love to thee, and in our interest for thee. I hope that thee may ever find in us friends who desire to do the little we can to pave thy way to manhood. I'trust my prayers will ever unite with thine, that blessings may rest upon thee, and the meek and quiet spirit of thy father be thine. Farewell,

Thy affectionate grandmother,

M. S. L.

First Month 2nd, 1861.

My Dear Grandson :—Did thee ever see more beautiful days than were the last of last year, and the first of this? The snow, mantling earth and trees, and the sun by day, and the moon and stars by night, making everything glisten with gem-like grandeur.

To-day is the time appointed by President Buchanan for fasting and prayer. I believe that the Most High requires of us, not for a day, to "fast for strife, and debate, and to smite with the fist of wickedness," but to pray without ceasing, day by day. If the people were righteous, and engaged in prayer, it would avail; for "the fervent, effectual prayer of a righteous man availeth much." But how different when people lay down their war-like weapons, their war-like speeches, their strife and debate, *for a day*, to bow down the head as a bullrush, and to-morrow arm themselves as fiercely as ever. This is not the way to call down a blessing upon our country. If men (in power) will not learn wisdom, the people must suffer. If those who are citizens will not adhere to the precepts of Jesus, the Gospel spirit will not rule in our land. Surely there is trouble in the camp. If might were right, our country would prosper still, and rise above all other nations of the earth, because of our liberal institutions. But, then the rattling of the chains of the bondman would no more grate upon our ears, neither would the man at the *bar* hand forth the poisonous cup to the weaklings of the flock.

I do not know of any news of importance. The condition of our country seems to be the all-absorbing topic. I hope our young men will not look toward war with an expectation of lending their aid. Will not the people, in whose power—humanly speaking—it is, settle the difficulties amicably. Slavery has ever been a blight, and if war should grow out of it, it will be a ten-fold calamity.

Write when thee has time. With love I am thy affectionate grandmother,

M. S. L.

Third Month 8th, 1861.

My Dear Grandson :—How is thee in health, and how is thee getting along? We want to know, and we want to see thee. I have had many cares and many anxieties, as our school has not been so large as usual, though we have brighter prospects for another year, and hope all is right. Thee knows in such a concern as this there must be calculations ahead, and anxiety to be lay-ing up something from year to year. I hope I am grate-ful for my favors. I also hope that good may come from

the turnings and overturnings in our country. I hope
there will not be war, but trust to Him who controls the
destinies of nations, that his power may stay the cruel
oppressor's hand. A country like ours ought not to have
the stain of slavery upon its robe. All men are born
free and equal. Let all have their rights. It may be
a work of time, but right must prevail.

A. R. often comes in to talk about thee, and mani-
fests much interest in thy comfort. Other friends often
inquire about thee—so thee is not "out of sight, out of
mind."

I remain thy affectionate and well-wishing grandmother,

M. S. L.

Fifth Month 21st, 1861.

My Dear Grandson :—I received thy very acceptable letter duly, and ought to have written to thee long
ere this, but the state of the country, the trials of my
near relatives in the South, the Yearly Meeting, and my
increased school duties seemed to disarrange my plans
for attending to correspondence. While I still feel a
great deal, I have become more easy under it; trusting
in the arm of Divine Power to carry on his own work,
and in the way to produce the greatest good to the
people. It is an awful day, but who could expect any
other than that it must come, if cruelty and oppression
were suffered to prevail to such an extent? We wait the
result with great anxiety.

I hope thee is progressing with thy studies, unmoved by the sound of war, or of the trampling of horses rushing to the field of battle. It is a fine spring to be in school, the weather continues to be so cool and pleasant.

Farmers have plenty to keep them busy, and I am thankful that enough remain at home to till the ground, and to attend to various branches of peaceful industry, so that our future wants may be supplied. · But I lament over our people, that, blest as we are above all the nations of the earth, we cannot be grateful for our prosperity, and live as brethren on an equality, in harmony and peace, guaranteeing to one another rights and privileges that are due to all, irrespective of nation, race or color. Had this feeling and these conditions existed throughout our land, instead of the roar of cannon and the glitter of bayonets, there would have been the anthem of " peace on earth and good will toward men." Our common Father, I am sure, willed it to be so, and nothing is lacking, but a want, on our part, of obedience to his will. Disobedience bringeth death, and all manner of cruelties and oppression, with their concomitants, sorrow and misery. What a waste war makes of life and property !

We shall be glad to hear from thee soon. With love, I remain thy interested grandmother,

M. S. L.

Eighth Month 14th, 1861.

My Dear Grandson :—Several of my relatives have come from Alexandria, some to New Jersey and some to

Pennsylvania. They look forward to returning soon, and now are hoping to be able to remain at their homes. I have lately been more comfortable concerning them, still feeling confidence in the Divine Arm that is able to protect them, even from their excited opposers. The beginning of this struggle has indeed been terrible, and what the end may be, who can tell? .

If men would only learn wisdom by the things they suffer—but the *natural* man is always the same; it is only the Christian that changes; and if mankind ever embrace, in its purity, the religion of Jesus Christ, wars and fightings will cease, and harmony everywhere prevail. This would be the restoration of all things; and what a pity that such is not now the condition of intelligent beings, made but a little lower than the angels, and intended for eternal life and happiness. Happiness in time, and happiness throughout the boundless ages of eternity.

Thy loving grandmother,

M. S. L.

Eleventh Month 5th, 1861.

My Dear Grandson : — Thy acceptable letter just received, reminds me that none of us have written to thee since thy return to school.

Last week I passed in Baltimore, attending the Yearly Meeting. My brother and sister, and many of my friends from Maryland and Pennsylvania, were in attendance. Very few came from Virginia, none being permitted except those who are within the Government lines, and many of these deemed it prudent, in these unsettled times, to stay at home. From Louden County four men came without asking passes, and hoped to return, though the banished and refugees are not permitted to go home to their families.

The deprivations of those within the Confederate lines are very great. Groceries are very scarce, and salt is nearly all used up. Coffee is fifty cents per pound, and the commonest sugar, twenty cents.

We had pleasant weather and an excellent Yearly Meeting. Nothing occurred on my visit to annoy me, except that, while I was passing through Philadelphia, a woman got her hand into my pocket, and succeeded in stealing my watch. I could not account for her behavior, but did not think of my watch till a few minutes too late. My money being in my satchel she did not get that.

I am sorry that your pupils are so unsettled by the sound of war. Oh! how glad I should be to have the war ended, and the Government peaceably sustained. We are all well and getting along very pleasantly. We have forty pupils, twenty-one of them boarders, and are expecting more. We have never had a happier company of girls, or a more agreeable time. The autumn is delightful, and favors late pasture, &c.

I remain, with love, thy same

M. S. L.

P. S.—I think thy mind is settled to stay in the quiet.

First Month 12th, 1862.

My Dear Grandson : — Everything would seem pretty cheerful, if it were not for the times, which cast a damp over all ; for we don't know what is to be done in the future, nor how to calculate for our business. It is needful to deliberate before we take a step ; the movements seem fraught with so much uncertainty. In the South the suffering is great, and the deprivations are many. Even the innocent have to suffer for the necessaries of life, on account of scarcity and high prices. In Louden our friends feel their wants, yet try to keep in the patience. As they can send only open letters they do not write the worst. Cotton is eighteen and three-quarter cents per spool ; candles, fifteen cents apiece. No more candle-wick, and some have cut up their cotton clothes-lines to make wick. No more kerosene in the stores, and no calico, &c.

I believe our friends and neighbors are generally well. W. C. met with a serious accident recently. His horse ran away, threw him out of the vehicle, and injured him very much. It is now thought he will recover. All were well at thy Uncle W's when we last heard.

With love, and with desires for thy health and best welfare, I am thy affectionate grandmother,

M. S. L.

Second Month 14th, 1862.

My Dear Grandson : — Thy acceptable letter was duly received, and it claimed our interest, more than usual, by expressions of sympathy with thee, though late, as it appeared thee had well nigh recovered from the measles. Thee must, indeed, have felt lonely and desolate with such disease upon thee, and among strangers. .I should have felt very anxious if I had known it at the time. I do hope that thee has not taken any cold, and that thee will be careful of thy eyes, for they may be weak for some time, as such is often the case after that disease.

I approve of thy plan of going to college, and leaving the other arrangement at present. We are getting thy things ready for thee. All join in love.

Thy affectionate grandmother,

M. S. L.

Fourth Month 6th, 1862.

My Dear Grandson :—Last evening I received thy acceptable letter, announcing thy safe arrival [at Exeter, N. H.] It was gratifying to hear from thee, for we had thought and talked much about thee, thinking of thy lonely journey, and then arriving at the end of it, amongst friends, unknown and untried. Yet, we had faith to believe that thee would get on without difficulty, and that—health permitting—all would be well. I am glad to learn that appearances are favorable, and that thy boarding place promises fair. If the family should prove to be pleasant, it will be more home-like to be there than it would to be where there are many ; especially if any in the large establishment should be given to misdemeanor. I am not partial to rigorous ruling, though I love discipline and order. A few rules, and these well obeyed, are far better than too many; and I believe kind and social intercourse between preceptor and pupils, with private admonition when needed, establishes confidence, and a disposition to govern with love on one part, and to obey with cheerfulness and simplicity on the other; thus making school a pleasant place, and every duty in connection with it, interesting to perform. I think, too, that the more we love our Heavenly Father, and the more we desire to serve and please Him, the more we shall love his creatures, and the greater will be the kindness and tenderness which we manifest towards each other. Especially will this be the case with those having charge of young people. It is better to lead than to drive. If teachers are led by the unerring spirit of Truth, they will dwell in the light, and walk in the light, thus becoming leaders that do not cause the people to err, and agents in the Divine Hand in raising the young into life, and letting them fall just in the niche they were ordained to fill. Hardened, indeed, must be the youth that will not follow in such a pleasant and promising path. In that peaceful path, God's love and grace abound to sustain the wayfarer, and settle the mind with composure, let come what will. I, indeed, have great cause to acknowledge that the Lord has been my support when I could look nowhere else for any; and I have no doubt that, at thy early age, thine can be the same acknowledgment.

10

I have no fears of thy being expelled from the school, and if thy health should not suffer from too close application, I shall feel easy. The climate there being so much colder than ours at this season, I hope thee will be careful to dress warm enough.

I have often heard that the New England villages are picturesque, having an abundance of shade, &c. The people, too, are persevering, and know how to earn a livelihood. They are to be esteemed for this, as it makes them valuable as a class of citizens.

I hope that thee will be well satisfied with having chosen to go there, also that thee may be able to pass the time profitably during the vacation of the school.

We shall always be glad to hear from thee. With unabated interest, I remain thy affectionate grandmother.

M. S. L.

Fifth Month 6th, 1862.

My Dear Grandson :—I have not written as soon as I should have done. The distressing state of affairs in our country, and the pressure in business matters resulting therefrom; the slain on the battle fields, of the sons of our people, the desolate homes of the widow and the orphan, the suffering of the sick and wounded who are pining away in the hospitals—these things combine to almost disqualify me for the regular routine of business, and for the use of my pen as in times gone by.

The cause of all this great trouble, and slaughter and devastation; indeed of the evils and wretchedness that are in the world, has been man's revolt from his Maker. He has disobeyed that inward language of impression, " If thou doest well, shalt thou not be accepted? and if thou doest not well, sin lieth at the door." What happiness all might enjoy in this life, and in anticipation of the joys to come in the eternal world, if only all would hear and obey, that their souls might live. This earth might be as a paradise ; for those trials and deprivations, incident to a state of probation, would be received as good things in the wisdom of Providence, and hence they would not render us unhappy.

I desire for myself, and for the human family, that we may increasingly set a right value on human life, its uses and intentions ; and therefore prize our privileges and number our blessings.

We often talk about thee, and we all feel deeply interested in thy welfare. I never doubt thy *doing* well.

Farewell, with love and desires for thy continued improvement.

I am thy affectionate grandmother,

M. S. L.

Seventh Month 7th, 1862.

My Dear Grandson :—Take good care of thyself; follow that *inward guide* which leads in the way of righteousness and peace—the way of justice, humility and truth ; and all will be well with thee, let what may attend thee.

I hope thee will have a pleasant trip, and see the

natural beauties of New England, not failing to observe the industrious habits of her sturdy sons and frugal daughters.

We often think of thee with deep interest, desiring thy prosperity and happiness, and thy advancement in the way that leads to usefulness.

In haste, and with love from all, I am thy affectionate grandmother,

M. S. L.

Twelfth Month 13th, 1862.

My Dear Grandson :—I *did* see Asa's letter from thee, also one to him from G. L. S., mentioning thy programme and speaking in kindly terms of thy deportment and progress in study while at his school. Thy letter to me was also received.

The business arrangements will be properly attended to, and provision made in case of thy not returning, though I hope that we may see thee again.

That thee will experience pretty fully the privations and hardships of a life in the navy, I have no doubt; but to be fortified for these, and to bear them patiently, will make them supportable and lessons of self-reliance. By looking to the great and good Spirit as the alone true guide and director in all that is right, lessons of this kind may be abundantly spread before thee while tossing to and fro upon the boisterous ocean, with the port far distant, and probably unknown. We are all on the ocean of life during our earthly sojourn—some on the briny deep and others on *terra firma*. All are in danger of shipwreck if not vigilant on the lookout; or if we have not efficient strength and a trusty Helmsman to man our little barks. In time of storm and danger we should have a present Saviour to call upon, who can arise and rebuke the winds, and command an immediate calm. Many are the storms of life, but the Great Pilot who rules the tempest as He does the calm, often, when the elements are in fierce strife, and the raging seas threaten to overwhelm our little bark, teaches us lessons which in the quiet we should never have learned. But a seaman's life is one of peril — one of instability and change, and a *fighting* sailor knows not when a formidable foe may attack, sending his body to a watery grave and his soul to the invisible future. To live so as to be ready to depart in peace is the great business of life, and I know of no other way to attain this state than to keep a conscience void of offense toward God and toward man. In the New Testament the life and character of the Christian is set forth, as well as the design of man's existence, &c. He is to glorify his Heavenly Father in this life, that he may enjoy Him evermore in unmixed felicity.

I do not know that in my day this once favored country will again be blest with peace and prosperity; but I trust we shall find a portion of happiness, and be the partakers of many of the good gifts of a bountiful Giver. Gratitude should, therefore, prevail in our hearts, and a desire that He will teach us wisdom and give us understanding, that we may know his mind and will concerning us.

I suppose thee saw the eclipse of the moon. Our large family were up some time observing it. It was a beautiful, clear night, the snow adding splendor to all around. When thee writes again we shall be glad to know what position thee has, thy engagements, &c., that we may think how it fares with thee, and know the destination of the vessel. It is an awful thing to think of the war that is desolating our land. I desire not in *any way* to encourage its continuance, believing, as I do, that it is not the design of the great and good Being that men should destroy one another.

I hope thee will have books to read, and that thee may keep thy conversation chaste and coupled with fear, so as not to be influenced by any surrounding circumstances, and especially by the hard language so often used by the sailors.

With love, and desires for thy preservation, I am thy affectionate grandmother,

M. S. L.

Third Month 9th, 1863.

My Dear Grandson :—On the 7th instant I received thy acceptable letter dated Second Month 15th, and was very glad, once again, to hear from thee. I should have written again, but was not sure of the right direction, therefore waited anxiously, desiring to receive intelligence from thee. Your situation seems perilous, both on account of your isolation and the leakiness of the vessel. There are so many vessels afloat in Government service, that we supposed you were with a fleet.

Deliverance from the present thraldom *may* come, and *will*, I trust, if people humble themselves, and call upon a Power higher than man's to control events, to deliver the captive from cruel bondage, and to bring about a peace not to be again disturbed. Maybe good will grow out of the evil; for in the North the slave system has been so sanctioned and sustained that we have partaken of her sins, and must therefore receive of her plagues.

I am glad thee keeps well, and am pleased that a situation more favorable for improvement offers. I hope thy great care will be to improve thy mind and protect thy morals. No doubt thee is exposed to profane and coarse language, but let it not influence thee to depart from that which is chaste and becoming in the most refined society.

Should you get to Philadelphia next month, as I hope you may, we shall be very glad to see thee. Thy mother is very anxious to hear from thee, and no doubt more so to see thee. Since thee left Moorestown there have been many changes by removals, marriages and deaths. I believe thy relatives are as well as usual.

The birds are beginning to sing. I suppose that you, in that southern climate, have warm weather nearly all the time. I should think the constant motion of a vessel would be unpleasant to the head; but there is a great deal in use. I wish thee could have some of our apples and other edibles; do you have pretty comfortable provisions? I know thee is not particular, and is easily satisfied with regard to food; but a wholesome variety never comes amiss. I hope thee may not have to go to battle. Oh! how it would comfort the feelings, on returning from the navy, to have hands unstained with blood.

We often talk about thee, and wonder where thee is, and how thee fares.

With desires for thy preservation, I am thy affectionate grandmother,

M. S. L.

Fifth Month 4th, 1863.

My Dear Grandson :—I received thy truly acceptable and very interesting letter, in less than two weeks after it was written. I should have replied immediately, but I have had so much headache this spring that my daily round of duties seemed to be about as much as I was able to perform. But I have remembered thee none the less; for very, very often, by day and by night, do I think of thee tossing on the unstable element, isolated from female society, and deprived of the luxuries, and of many of the conveniences of life. How I long for the termination of this war. How unwise has been the course pursued by the South, that might have been made prosperous and happy, had they been content with the best government in the world; and been willing to liberate themselves from the evil of slavery. I pity them for their ignorance, or whatever else it was, that caused them to rush onward to destruction and desolation. I sympathize with the destitute among them—women and children suffering great deprivations, while husbands and fathers are on the battle-field. Well, they and we are in it—in war and in slavery ; and I still believe that the two must end together, or else we shall have only an uncertain peace.

Many friends inquire for thee with much interest, and I believe desire thy health and happiness, and will be glad to see thee again, if thee can be favored to get home.

I hope that you will not have to join the battles on sea ; I dread them so much.

I do not know of any interesting news, and I can-not send thee anything good that I know of, or indeed thee would often get some of the comforts of the table.

With much love, and with desires for thy preservation in innocency, and for thy health and happiness, I conclude, and remain thy affectionate grandmother,

M. S. L.

Sixth Month 3rd, 1869.

My Dear Grandson :—I did not intend to let so much time pass by without again writing to thee, but my many close engagements must be my apology. I often think of thee, this busy season, when, to make a living, so many have to earn their bread by the sweat of

their face. But honest bread is sweet, and it matters not
much how closely occupied we are, mentally or physically,
so that we " pitch upon that course of life which is most
useful, and habit will in time render it most agreeable."
I have faith that in the most part this is true, even
though at times we may sigh for deliverance from a burden that presses heavily; yet, as we look around us,
and see a plodding multitude more unfavorably circum-
stanced, and engaged in occupations less pleasing to us
than our own, and seemingly having greater cause for
unhappiness than ourselves, we learn to be, at least
measurably, contented with our present lot.

I hope that circumstances may favor thy getting
permanently fixed, without having to anticipate changes.
If thee can be engaged in fruit growing, without undue
encroachment upon thy studies, it may be well; and
when ready to enter upon the practice of law, perhaps
thee may establish thyself where thee is, and find the
environment as agreeable as the home of thy childhood.
I often think it is not a matter of great moment whether
we are amongst our relatives or strangers; for if we conduct ourselves as we ought, we find friends—whether
our kindred or not—who cheer and gladden our lives
by kindness and affection. Though we have had a very
cold spring, yet the abundance of rain has favored the
growth of vegetation, and everything with the farmer
seems to promise fair. Strawberries are plentiful in the
market, and our own are beginning to ripen. Our school

is to continue four weeks after this, and then we are to
have a vacation of twelve weeks.

We have a First-day school at our meeting-house,
on First-day afternoons, and a Reading Association on
Third-day evenings, in both of which I am interested.
I have often looked at the lads, since I have been a resi-
dent of Moorestown, and my heart has warmed at the
thought that these are to be our future men; and my
desire has been that they may be trained up in the way
they should go, that in manhood the Good Being should
have possession of their hearts, in order that their course
may be directed aright. Then would there be wanting
wise men to save a city or a country? Surely not. So
at least I think, for I have great confidence in a guarded
education, and in the social mingling of old and young,
that a close intimacy between these two classes may be
established; that experience and activity may go hand
in hand, age being enlivened by youth, and youth stead-
ied by age; and that, as their interests are identical,
their sentiments should harmonize on all matters of
vital importance. The farther I advance on the journey
of life, the more anxious I am to see a host of men and
women doing all the good they can in the world, in their
every-day life.

Our country has passed through a sore ordeal, but
everything now favors prosperity and happiness, if only
there is a sincere intention on the part of those in
power, and of business men as well, to pursue a right
course, and to regard the common weal as paramount to

all selfish intrigues and over-reaching avarice. I am aware that there is much corruption, and that vice and immorality are making fearful strides; but we may take comfort in the assurance that where sin abounded, grace did much more abound. I believe in abounding grace to redeem from pollutions, and to save; and this belief, together with the hope that there are enough good men to bear up above the flood of corruption, leads me to anticipate brighter, better and happier days for these United States.

The time may come when thee can visit us, and see for thyself the many changes that have occurred. Thee will find some improvements, some strippings, and many of us traveling the down-hill of life. Can thee see thy grandmother sitting in the library, writing to thee; thy grandfather's picture hanging there so smiling; and the books, &c. Wouldn't thee like to be here a little while? I should be so glad to see thee, the only male representative bearing the name of Lippincott in my family. Well, dear child, continue to bear it honorably, and then thee will meet those in Heaven who were bound to thee by kindred ties on earth. Yes, and thee will also be happy in time, during the days and years that may be allotted to thee in this state of existence. While I live thee may rest assured that there is one whose interest in thy prosperity and happiness cannot be lessened. Accept my love and sympathy with thy every privation and hardship, and think of me as

Thy affectionate grandmother,

M. S. L.

Ninth Month 16th, 1869.

My Dear Grandson :—Thy letter is just received. We were very anxious to hear from thee, for we feel sympathy with thee in thy illness, but hope that the hot season will soon be succeeded by weather favoring thy recovery. I often think that sickness is a service for our profit; and the purpose that it should serve is to raise our thoughts from *this* life to *that* which is to come —this, so short and uncertain, the other, ever-enduring.

I am much improved in health, but my head is still weak, and the continued heat affects me — particularly in the middle of the day, and my hand continues unsteady from that cause. I hope I am thankful that I am so much better, for I desire to be restored and spared longer to my precious children. But we must all of us, in all things, endeavor after resignation to the Divine will. In this there is patience to endure all things, and to await every event.

Jane seems much better, but whether or not the improvement is permanent, we must wait to see. Margaret is well. We are to open school on the 27th instant. Schools have so multiplied, that few are filled as they were formerly, and the few are those in which the accomplishments are taught.

I cannot write much this time, as my head is painful. My fervent desires are for thy welfare, and my hope is that thy health may soon be restored. I hope, too, that I shall be better able to write.

Farewell, my dear grandson. May the Lord keep

thee and bless thee. My love to the good, kind family
with whom is thy sojourn.

I am thy affectionate grandmother,

M. S. L.

Eighth Month 28th, 1879.

My Dear Grandson :—I have been thinking a great
deal about thee and thine—more than usual for some
weeks past, though I trust I do not lose sight of you, nor
suffer my love for you to wane, however long my silence
may have been. The heat has been great, and it has
been accompanied by misty days, which were very de-
bilitating. This condition of the weather, together with
a rheumatic lameness in my right arm, disinclines me to
write, even though my desires to do so are very strong.
I have been much at home for the past year, being less
able to bear carriage-riding than I was formerly. Remember, I have passed the seventy-eighth mile-stone on
my pilgrimage through this world of lights and shadows.
My pathway has been diversified with joys and sorrows,
and many companions with whom I have traveled in
close intimacy have gone over the river before me, leaving
a blank that nothing below can ever fill. Yes, but the
loveliness of God's earth remains, and many lovely and
beloved younger people. A few in the gray white of
winter's frost, more in the sear of autumn, and many,
very many, in the loveliness of youth and buoyant
childhood. Toward all of these—but most especially to
the youth—my heart bounds with a feeling of love and

good will which bids them pursue the path of uprightness, and labor that the world may be better because they have lived in it.

It may seem late to tell thee of the number of our friends and neighbors who were and are not, but who, I trust, live forever in the Celestial City. Thy uncle, David Walton and wife and myself, are the only ones of that generation remaining. They are living in Virginia, and, as they do not incline to travel, we seldom meet. It would be a pleasure to me to meet him once more and talk over the happy days of the past. For about two years he was an inmate of our family, and as he was then a childless widower, thy dear, good father and he roomed together. Thy *attractive, amiable, good* father was then a boy from twelve to fourteen years old. The good qualities of his boyhood ever remained with him, and his lovelineess and lovableness continued with him to the end of his earthly career. Just before passing away, when taking leave of his father, he said : " Thee has been a dear, good father to me. There has never been an unkind word or a hard thought between us." To which we could both reply, " Thee has been a dear, good son."

Well, he passed on to a higher life early ; in his twenty-eighth year, happy and resigned ; a great loss to survivors, but as he said, "I shall miss much trouble." His sensitive mind was grieved to see suffering and to know of wrong-doing ; and such sights and such knowledge are the experience of the observant. He had

led an innocent and useful life, and being assured of a
clear record, he was not afraid to face the just Judge.
Oh, what a blessing to him, and what a comfort to survivors, that he should have this assurance when the
awful period arrived. I had buried four sons before him,
and he was as dear to me as they were; yea, more dear
as a companion, for he was older (the oldest of the
others was in his ninth year when he died), and a
kinder brother to little boys and girls, and one more
loved by them could not be. His kindness I can never
forget, nor his fondness for children. If ever so busy
he must take up the little ones in his arms to caress
them; and when they were sick he was a most affectionate and efficient nurse. Tell thy dear, little Isaac,
that he had another nice grandfather, younger than thee
now is, when the Heavenly Father took him to heaven.
We have no visible likeness of him; but on my memory
I have the impress, fresh, ever fresh. Thee shall have
thy grandfather's likeness and mine, also those of thy
aunt's, if we can arrange to get them taken while we all
live, which I hope we can.

We are very glad you all keep well. We have
watched the papers, hoping that the fever would not
spread and reach Cairo. I am much gratified to learn
that circumstances direct thy course to teaching and to
study; believing it increases thy usefulness to be engaged in that way. For years past, thee must have
had a busy life, including thy clerkship; but when
business is profitable, it makes the labor seem less

wearisome. I suppose thy farming is carried on by proxy; this answers quite well, if a watchful eye takes cognizance from day to day. I have never thought that work on a farm would be adapted to thy constitution.

If I were ten years younger and had ample means, I should not long delay a visit to you in your own home. Aunties, too, would love to go as much as I should. If we had seen you there, just once, we should then be able to look in upon you with the mind's eye, and see you just as you are. Tell little Isaac that we intend to send our pictures before long; we also hope to see him and his mother face to face, sometime ere we pass away. Farewell! With our united love to you all,

Thy affectionate grandmother,

M. S. L.

Tenth Month 1st, 1883.

My Dear Grandson :—I am aware that it is a long time since I have written to thee, as I do not write much of late years, and less each year. But, could thought reach thee in words, there would be no lack of intelligence or communication, for I keep in remembrance those loved and cherished in childhood, in youth, and in old age — those who still live, and many, very many, gone from this world to a future home. Yes, I seek their presence, and they pass before my mental vision in their loveliness as seen when present, and often a momentary joy flashes over me as though a sweet commingling were realized. I hope this may ever continue

11

while memory, the mirror of the mind, remains untarnished, for it makes voids less felt, and removes, partially at least, a loneliness, a sadness, that intrudes at seasons, as the separations are realized. Many are in far distant places, and many more have passed to the spirit-land.

At my age I cannot visit much—not even a few miles off — without headache and fatigue. So, loving home, and enjoying this beautiful world, as I have in consecutive years from my infancy onward; I remember the many blessings and favors dispensed, and that my life has been brightened by the company of those around me. Yes, life has its pleasures renewed day by day, and for these, gratitude fills my heart to the Supreme Giver of all Good, and the stream of his universal love flows out toward all who live, accompanied by a fervency of desire that every soul may be separated from sin, may be redeemed, fitted and prepared for the true enjoyment of life here (the intention, no doubt, of the Creator) upon the terms of obedience to the Spirit of Truth, and the full fruition of bliss in the spirit-world—peace and joy forever.

The neuralgia, from which I have long suffered, has now become my chief complaint. It has lamed me some, and it causes stiffness in my right arm. In other respects my health has improved.

Jane's throat is better, though her cough continues, and the doctor says one lung is nearly gone. M—— is pretty well, though not very strong, and we are all bright and cheerful. We greatly enjoy our home life, in a private way, after so many years with a large household. We can now enjoy the visits of our friends, with nothing to call us away during an hour of social converse, or longer time, as occasion offers. How we should love to see you here, and to become acquainted with Lizzie and the children. Perhaps the time may come when a visit can be accomplished. We shall, at least, have it in anticipation, for there is enjoyment in planning for time to come.

Many changes have taken place, but many remain of thy relatives and friends. The improvements almost everywhere are marked ; and I hope they may continue, as prosperity, if rightly received, is adding to the elevation and usefulness of the inhabitants in every place.

Thy aunt P's children and grandchildren are doing well, I believe, and are mostly well. There are several great-grandchildren—interesting, of course. All live in love and harmony.

A good many of my nephews, nieces and others in whom I am especially interested, are at Swarthmore College. The number of students there this term is larger than ever before. Our new school-house at Moorestown has been enlarged. The school numbers nearly one hundred pupils this term. The meeting and First-day school are large, though many have died. We go there often to Monthly and Preparative Meeting. We have a meeting and a First-day school here in Camden, but we cannot yet sever ourselves from Moorestown.

I hope you are all well. Does Isaac learn well at school? Does he speak German? How I should love to talk with him, and to hear him talk; and Richard, too, the little prattler; and dear Lizzie, and thy dear self. All of you, including Lizzie's father, accept our united love, and desires for your health, happiness and prosperity in every way.

Thy affectionate grandmother,

M. S. L.

Eleventh Month 1st, 1883.

My Dear Grandson :—This is a lovely, bright day, with a cool, bracing air. It is very acceptable after the damp, foggy, oppressive weather that has prevailed for several weeks past. It was quite unusual for the autumn, which we anticipate as the loveliest of seasons. Still, the occasional days of pleasant weather have kept a little balance in favor of strength, so that Jane has improved a good deal, though she still has a hard cough. The season has not been a sickly one, though we now hear of colds and some fevers.

My head and eyes are still weak, owing to my suffering from neuralgia. I am improving now. Thy aunt P., her children and grandchildren, get here pretty often.

Nathan Conrow died lately, also William Borton. The meeting, though still large, has been much stripped. If thee were to visit Moorestown now thee would miss many from meeting, and as for the place, it is so enlarged and improved thee would hardly know it. Many Philadelphians live there, and attend to business in the city.

One of our Camden neighbors has a son in St. Louis. I send thee his address, and with it the information that it would be a comfort to his mother if he and thee would become acquainted. He is a stranger in your city, is young, has been well brought up, and probably would be glad of a kind word, or even a little counsel from one who came from his old neighborhood, and who is much more familiar than himself with the West and its ways.

I hope you are well, and that Isaac can " talk Dutch;" also that Richard grows, and entertains his mother. How we'd like to see the children and their parents. I wanted to write, as I have more leisure than thee has, but the two great drawbacks to my correspondence are dim sight and lameness in my right arm. I hope thee can read this writing.

Our united love to thee, Lizzie and the children; also to your father.

Thy attached grandmother,

M. S. L.

Third Month 3rd, 1884.

My Dear Grandson :—We recur with much comfort to your visit, and hope that you did not take cold, or feel worse for your journey; also that you continue well. We have thought much about thy accumulated business, and hoped that the increased pressure would not weary thee too much.

Have you had any share in ·the loss and suffering occasioned by the terrible floods? As we have not seen any mention to that effect, we hope that you have escaped. The loss of life and property seemed heart-rending; and the idea of rebuilding on such low lands seems almost appalling.

In Philadelphia there has been a very destructive fire recently. Perhaps you have seen an account of it; the chemical works of Powers & Weightman. The loss is very heavy, many laborers are thrown out of employment, and so much quinine has been destroyed, as greatly to advance the already high price of that drug.

In other places, too, there have been accounts of destructive fires. It is wonderful how so much waste in that way occurs, when so much professed vigilance is exercised to prevent fires. It is to be hoped that some check can be given to prevent so much destruction by this devouring element.

Jane longs to get out, as being confined to the house always increases her lung trouble. I do not get either to Philadelphia or to Moorestown at this season of the year; but I greatly enjoy the visits of my friends. This mingling with loved ones keeps the mind bright; so that there are enjoyments even in sickness.

With love and best wishes from us all, to you all,

I am thy affectionate grandmother,

M. S. L.

Eighth Month 19th, 1884.

My Dear Grandson :—It is a good while since I
wrote thee, and since we have heard from thee. We
have had a cooler summer than a year ago, and sometimes very heavy rain (almost a flood once), which has
been favorable for vegetation, but the heavy mists have
been unusual, causing oppression when lungs are weak.

I recruited so much during a few days passed at the
shore, that I continue pretty well, and have a good appetite. We have not been much from home, as Jane gets
sick from fatigue when she goes out riding.

A great many go away from the city for the summer, having two homes. This makes it more lonely for
us that remain ; still, we cannot complain, for our neighbors have been very kind in visiting us.

I suppose thee has seen accounts of the earthquake.
Did you feel the shock ? It did not damage us, but was
so severe as to occasion noise, swaying of walls, and in
some places a rising of the ground, swinging and rattling
of chandeliers, ringing of bells, &c. The walls of one
house on Market Street cracked, and glasses were broken
in some places.

If thee is busy, perhaps Lizzie will tell us how you
and your dear boys are. Love to you all.

Your attached grandmother,

M. S. L.

First Month 27th, 1885.

My Dear Grandson :—What troublesome times, at
home and abroad, occasioned by party strife ; but—to

those who can hear it—there is whispered in secret, "In me ye have peace." Oh! that love and peace might reign; "peace on earth, and good-will toward men."

Your dear little boys, I trust, grow, and are lights in the house. Has Isaac been able to go to school, in the cold. Has not the cold been more severe than is usual at St. Louis?

Our united love and best wishes to you all.

Thy attached grandmother,

M. S. L.

Seventh Month 13th, 1885.

My Dear Grandson :—During the two weeks since we came here to Rancocas I have had so much neuralgia that I put off writing. I am now better, but it occasions so much weakness in my head that I go out but little; only to meeting, and to mingle with our family circle living in the village. We are very comfortable in our boarding place, which we find airy and pleasant, and all are kind and affectionate, and we are mostly cheerful.

We are better than when we came here, but we feel lonely without dear Jane. Go where we may, we miss her so much, with her loving and faithful kindness. M. feels as though life is a struggle without her. But we are sure she is happy; she was so willing and anxious to go to rest, so centered in love to everybody, and so trusting in her heavenly Father to receive her. We must look forward to the time of a reunion.

P. and her children and grandchildren do seem to

be so loving and happy with one another, and so interested and helpful where they can bestow aid upon anybody, that it is a delightful neighborhood to be in. The poorest are sought after and cared for, and P. is as a doctor to them when they are sick.

We often talk about you. Has R. recovered from his hurt? Is I. better, and has he returned home? We should all love to see you, and to welcome you. Do not tax thyself too hard. We send love to Lizzie. her father, and to the dear children. A blessing to all, from

Thy affectionate grandmother,

M. S. L.

— — —

PART IV.

GENERAL CORRESPONDENCE.

TO GEORGE HATTON.

First Month 19th, 1850.

My Dear Friend: — I must acknowledge my remissness in allowing a very interesting letter, received months ago from thy dear son and daughter, to remain so long unnoticed; also the Extracts from your Yearly Meeting, and a tribute to the memory of their dear, departed mother. For all three of these we are much obliged; and though my pen has lain idle, my thoughts have not remained so, neither are our affections lessened toward thee and thine. Often do I feel as if it would afford me much pleasure could I sit down and converse with thee, and see the little group assembled at the fireplace of thy son's home. As I am not privileged to do this, may I not hope, some time, to greet you at our own habitation.

Dear George, there are many *instructors* in Israel, but few are the fathers and the mothers. Ah! for want of these, where are the children ? Will not the language yet be applicable (if not so already) that was spoken to the prophet Eli, who restrained not his sons. Alas, for the Society of Friends? Where shall we be landed? After all that our predecessors suffered that they might come out from the Nations and dwell alone ; are we now to declare that this was all a *delusion;* and that we are to *mix* with them, partaking of their merchandise, and joining in their traffic ? Ah! I believe the true Quaker is called out of the professing world now, as much and as truly as the Israelites were called out of Egypt. "Out of Egypt have I called my son." And if so, and if the disciples are with him, they must come out too. And what greater bondage than Egyptian bondage ? What darkness equal to Egyptian darkness ? Why it is to be *felt !* Quakers never can be popular with the religionists of the day. When they aspire to popularity, they run out. When Ephraim offended in Baal he died. Had the watchmen been faithful to chase the enemy out of their borders the city might have been saved. Are not their eyes now opening to see the effects of their remissness ?

There are those among us who seem to think that *doctrine* is of little account. With these I differ, believing as I do in the promulgation of sound doctrine where truth sustains truth; and feeling it right to discountenance the opposite, where error sustains error. If the doctrines of the Society of Friends are true, and if the embracing of them tended to make men better and more peaceful; if they have been proved to be no cunningly devised fable, but the basis of a religion sufficient to live by and to die by, then they are worth standing up to support, even before a host of opposers. Shall we forsake the Master (within) when He is about to be taken and crucified?

We are told by some that every one is to attend to the dictates of his own conscience. This advice, to a certain extent, is good, but conscience is *educated*, and one by its dictates, goes counter to another; so come confusion, strife, division. No, this will not do. George Fox says " mind the Light." He also says that Christ is the Light, and that minding it brings all to Christ, where there is no division; brings all into one fold, where they will support the same testimonies, walk by the same rule and mind the same thing. Here we can hear every man in our own tongue (with new tongues) wherein we were born (of the Spirit); and without this spiritual union how can we have fellowship as members of the same religious Society.

I have been thankful that John Comly has been

strengthened to get out to meetings, and that he is so alive to the interests of the Society.

. Elisha and Sarah Hunt have gone to the Western Quarter to attend some meetings there. Benjamin Warrington and wife are in delicate health. I have a Minute from the Monthly Meeting to appoint some meetings, and have attended but partially thereto; for finding my health inadequate to the prosecution of the concern, I think it best to return the Minute and wait till another time. I have been absent from our own meeting very often of latter time, though my indisposition has been such as to lay me by only for a few days at each turn.

In these parts we are very much exempt from the dividing spirit, the Truth being, I trust, strong enough to withstand it. For this we ought to be thankful, and to keep humble, trying to be prepared for the trials that may await us at our next Yearly Meeting.

Has thou been out much since thou left us, or has thou been permitted to rest awhile since thy heavy dispensation of trial and stripping. Surely it has been such, and thou must feel thyself lonely, and the weight of exercise must press more heavily without a sympathizing partner to share it with thee. We have felt for thee much, but we had no doubt that thou would find a support to thy tried mind. Then, too, thou has consolation in thy children, who will, no doubt, endeavor to smooth thy path and to hold up thy hands. Also thou has dear friends around thee whose spirits are in unison with thine. These are consolations, and though they cannot fill the void, yet they can soothe the sorrowing heart. None, as I apprehend, can know the feeling of the widowed state, until it is realized by experience; and yet, blessed be the Father of all, the back is fitted for the burden. He can give resignation, and then hard things are made easy.

I remain, with much love from Isaac and myself, thy truly attached friend,

MARY S. LIPPINCOTT.

TO THE SAME.

Eleventh Month 13th, 1851.

Beloved Friend: — Thy truly acceptable letter brought a confirmation that my dear husband and myself retain a place in thy memory and thy feelings, amidst all the fluctuations of time, and the conflicting of the elements in the civil and in the religious (?) world. To be thus remembered by one of the Lord's servants is an evidence that we (however unworthy) are still numbered with the household of faith.

We rejoice to hear that thou and thy wife are joined together as yoke-fellows to labor in the Church of Christ, for the support of the Ark of the Testimony, and to keep it from passing over into the camp of the Philistines. We, as a Society, are besieged by a formidable foe, grown to the stature of Goliah of Gath; as formidable in appearance and in array. No power can reach it, but the power of the Highest; none can smite it but those who are armed with the whole armor of Light—

the name of the Lord. When we have a sense of our own frailties what blushing and confusion of face do we feel in the presence of the Most High. Ah! my friend, I know what I say; for verily do I feel that I have no might of my own, even to keep my own spirit in subjection; to keep *self* under. Where, then, are the boasting and vaunting of poor, erring mortals? Truly, as thou says, belligerent parties may form armies, and pitch in battle array. Israel, like the sons of Jesse, may engage in the Lord's battle, because they see the desolation and wasting they make. These may speak great, swelling words, and may extend an arm to pierce, but they cannot conquer. Oh! what hard work it makes for the Lord's anointed, when their own men go unskilfully to work. They hurt the cause. As David went, so must go the servant now, that smites the champion, and puts the armies to flight; and that servant must first have slain the lion and the bear. A conquest must be made at home, in our own experience. The world assumes the forms of the lion and the bear, to devour the lamb-like nature in us; and if we have not power to keep our father's sheep, how can we help our brethren or meet our common foe?

I, with others, am led in a close way, and cannot find peace, without being obedient; and if I have to be regarded as *not* being one of the philanthropists, I must bear it patiently; having an evidence within my own breast, that I feel nothing but good-will to men, desiring their everlasting welfare.

We have been engaged in some religious visits in Bucks and Burlington Quarters. There are valuable, exercised Friends in those parts, also *some* who are up in the air, as if they had found a new way, and another key to open the secrets of the Most High. I am favorable to that charity which reproves those that are out of the Truth, and approves Truth's advocates, all in the same spirit—for the *real welfare* of both classes. I think the time of trial will come, when we shall have to show on whose side we are; whether on the Lord's side, or on that of Baal. Who shall stand the day of trial?

Priscilla Cadwalader attended our meetings, I believe to general satisfaction. Her doctrines are sound and scriptural.

We have eighty-nine in family. It is a great responsibility, but I hope that it is right for us to have our school, as a guarded education for the young is needed, and a care to restrain them from hurtful indulgences.

I hope thou may be preserved in that faith in which thou has heretofore stood; for then, shall none be able to pluck thee out of the hand of Him who called thee to espouse his cause.

With love, in which Isaac joins, to thyself, wife and children, I remain

Thy sincere friend and well-wisher,

M. S. L.

Beloved Friends :—Although I am unable to decide whether or not I am indebted to you, I am inclined to write, and say that you are not forgotten amidst the multiplicity of business in which we are immersed; and to hear from you is always pleasant.

For awhile I did not answer my friends' letters, because I felt too poor to write; and thought that nothing interesting could emanate from my pen; and though I have not changed this opinion, yet I did not feel quite satisfied to close my correspondence; and, besides, thoughts repressed may become as stagnant waters.

This has been a genuine, old-fashioned winter, whose character resembles that of which our aged grandsires used to speak, in the days of our childhood, when the family group was collected around the great fireplace in the kitchen, where the fire burned briskly. Oh! for those golden days of the olden time. But those days are gone; times are altered; dress takes the place of simple sports, and reading, of the ingenuous chat.

Education is, no doubt, a blessing; but, like everything else it must be in moderation, or its use ends. I love to see the native sports of children, and I enjoy domestic scenes, such as I loved when young. I am a great admirer of Cowper, and his views of enjoyment are in accord with my feelings.

But, though the winter has been cold, it has not congealed the stream of love that flows towards our friends, and binds us to those who are like-minded with ourselves. As such we regard you and your parents.

Your loving friend,

M. S. L.

TO HER DAUGHTER.

PICKERING, Canada, Eighth Month, 1853.

My Dear Jane :—I do not know whether or not I gave, in my letter to M., an account of our visit to the Falls of Niagara; but I could not give a full description of their magnificence if I were to attempt it. We viewed the Rapids and the Cataract from many different positions, going as near as we deemed it prudent to venture; and we are prepared to acknowledge that nothing which has been written, by way of description, has even half reached the reality, and therefore it has failed to impress the mind of the reader with the sublimity there displayed. One morning the sun shone out so clear that we saw the beautiful rainbow, forming about two-thirds of a circle, and a dim one reflected beyond it. Well may it be considered, as some who have traveled much have termed it, the greatest natural curiosity yet discovered in the world. I hope that both of you, my dear daughters, can have the opportunity of seeing these Falls for yourselves. I took leave of them with the feeling that they would still flow on in awful grandeur, and be gazed upon in wonder for ages yet to come. The motion from the very beginning of the rapids is such that it impresses the spectator with the idea that the *hurry* will subside, but

12

however long he may gaze, he finds no abatement; and in amazement he traces the waters to their starting-place. He considers how great a volume of water is rushing down this river from the lakes, and that the supply is equal to the overflow.

From Niagara, by way of Lewiston, we crossed Lake Ontario, a beautiful sheet of green water, to Toronto. The sun shone brilliantly, and hot as the weather was, I sat awhile on the upper deck, viewing the placid bosom of the lake, and seeing the sky and water meet in every direction. *Terra firma* had been removed from view entirely.

We dined on board the steamer, in company with several Englishmen, who treated us with much politeness and attention.

On reaching Toronto we rode some distance through the flourishing city and through a well-improved country beyond it, to Nicholas Brown's, where we arrived just before midnight. However, even at that late hour, we were made welcome by our kind friends. Indeed, they seemed almost overjoyed to see us. They had not received my letter, and therefore were not looking for us, though Margaret had been talking about me.

We are all pretty well, though the weather is exceedingly warm—as warm perhaps as any that we have felt this summer, and so dry here that the fields are brown and parched.

I am anxiously looking for letters, feeling that I

am far off, and a long time absent from home. If I can
only hear that you are well, I shall feel easy.

Thy loving mother,

M. S. L.

TO GEORGE HATTON.

MOORESTOWN, Tenth Month 27th, 1854.

Beloved Friend—Whom I esteem as an elder brother
in Christ—I often feel it in my heart to salute thee in
the love of the everlasting Gospel, and bid thee God-
speed on thy journey toward Canaan.

How pleasant it was to behold thy face once more,
when in a land of strangers; but still more pleasant to
feel that, with all the perils and buffetings and commotions, our faith in the saving principle and power of
God, manifested within, remains unchanged; that we
have not parted with the stable truth for all the cunningly devised fables, gotten up in the will and wisdom
of man, who by adhering to them is unstable as water.
"See the Quakers, how they love one another." This
remains with those who have passed from death unto
life, for their love is founded on and centered in God,
who is love, and who is unchangeable. They are bound
in one bundle, united in one spirit, and are prepared to
rejoice together in his presence, where they mingle in
prayer, in baptism, in suffering for the body's sake, and
in thanksgiving and in praise. These beholding each
other's countenances are made glad, for they see reflected there the image of that Divine Being whom they

love, whom they adore, and whom they desire to worship in spirit and in truth. If this consolation is afforded kindred spirits here, while shackled with clay tenements, how complete must it be hereafter, when these are cast off as a worn-out garment, and the spirit, the soul immortal, is robed in Light. O the unspeakable joys of the Celestial world! Neither the tongue of man nor of angel can declare it to the full, while we are finite beings, though we may have a glorious foretaste thereof, even in this lower world. When our hearts are raised in fervency of prayer to our God, He lifts us above transitory things, for a little time, that we may believe in Him, and in his promises, so as not to give back in days of trial and sore conflict, neither to despair of his aid.

How beautiful is the world in which we are placed, and how numerous are the blessings that descend upon our habitations. If mankind would only live in obedience to the in-speaking Word, this earth would be like a paradise, and our happiness would be augmented from day to day. No man would harm or hurt his brother, or do any violence to his neighbor; but all would act up to the injunction of our Saviour, " Therefore all things whatsoever ye would that men should do to you, do ye even so to them." Thus would each be promoting the happiness of his fellow, and helping him through *this* to another world, even his everlasting home. Then, the nearer the approach to this home, the happier should we be, from the assurance of "joy unspeakable and full of glory."

Oh, that the children of men were wise unto salvation! Then would they obey the Light within, which is a certain Guide, and a faithful instructor, always ready to show the way to peace and everlasting Life.

Oh, that Friends would come home to this, and be established in Christ: that they would hold up Jesus Christ; that they would "preach Christ crucified, unto the Jews a stumbling-block, and unto the Greeks foolishness:" but "the power of God unto salvation to every one that believeth." This would do more to reform the world, and to make men Christians, than would all the *works* so lauded by a busy and active generation.

The stream cannot rise higher than its fountain, nor can its waters be of any other nature than those of the source whence it issues—if impure they cannot cleanse, if bitter they cannot console. Is it not time for people to gather around the living fountain, and there wait for the *living* water, that they thirst no more, because the well of life is in them bubbling up for them to drink? I feel an encouraging hope that there is an increasing concern on these accounts; and that it is not limited to age, but that among the youth there is a visitation, and a call to tread the way of self-denial. If these will only abide under the preparing Hand, till fitted for service, I believe that they will be sent into the harvest-fields to labor, and that their labors will be blest.

I was pleased to hear that your Yearly Meeting

was favored, and I hope that that of Baltimore will be also. John Hunt has gone to attend it. Elisha Hunt and Sarah are visiting meetings, as way opens, within the limits of our own Yearly Meeting. I hope the Master will send thee and thy wife to visit these parts, ere long, and that He will give thee oil in thy horn for anointing.

Isaac unites with me in love, and in desires for your preservation. I remain

Thy sincere friend,

M. S. L.

TO THE SAME.

Ninth Month, 1868.

My Dear Friend: — The remembrance of former years, when we used to gather in social mingling and in religious fellowship, is not lost sight of; and mentally I often view thee in thy retirement and wonder how it fares with thee. With this memory and this view comes the hope that thy lamp may continue to be replenished with oil, so as to burn brightly till the close of thy pilgrimage. I am glad to know that thou art still able to get out to meetings, and to visit thy friends occasionally. I trust that the meetings now, as they formerly were, are seasons of Divine favor, in which Truth has the victory over all. Where the love of the Father flows unobstructed, it seems as though the whole soul is drawn out in thanksgiving and praise, so that the tongue has to give utterance thereto; not only to adore

his great and excellent name, but also to invite others
to come, taste and see that the Lord is good and gracious
in his dealings with the sons and daughters of men, in
order to lead them in the way of obedience. Surely
those who abide at the Fountain, and receive from his
bountiful hand, must feel ofttimes that their cup run-
neth over, and they have to hand out of its contents, for
the refreshment of others. The patriarch Jacob continued his labors till his close. His last benediction
was wonderful ere " he gathered up his feet into the
bed and yielded up the ghost." Was not this an evidence that God had blessed him all his days, and that
he had performed his vows, made at the time of his
deep trial, when he felt desolate and forsaken? Oh,
how many have given evidence of the plentitude of his
power, and of the increase of the Gospel stream, with
length of days, until its aboundings were continual.
When the physical powers have failed, the spiritual
perceptions have brightened, till, the outer world seeming to be shut out, the inner has become more glorious
than ever before ; and they could sound the Lord's
praise in one continued out-pouring of expression. The
evening of life, amidst the aboundings of his love, has
always seemed to me as the happiest period. The cares,
anxieties and turmoils, attendant upon our pilgrimage
journey being over, we have only to wait in quiet expectation that ere long a sweet voice will be heard,
saying, "Having been faithful in thy day, now enter
into rest." Happy indeed the latter days of those who

are thus awaiting their change, for they are assured of the crown immortal to be placed on their heads.

I trust that such may be thy experience, after a life of labor in the church, keeping in the harness until the journey is ended and the work done. When retired in stillness I often visit thee, and always with this feeling, believing as I do in the all-sufficiency of the anointing power to qualify in old age as in youth or in middle life, for preaching the Gospel in the demonstration of the spirit, and that the stream widens and enlarges according to our dedication and faithfulness.

As the infirmities of age multiply, there is, in our surroundings, less to interest us ; and as my dear mother, in her afflictions, used to say, "Nothing to bind me to earth."

I remain thy loving friend,

M. S. L.

TO HER GRANDDAUGHTER, E. L.

CAMDEN, N. J., First Month 1st, 1884.

My Dear Granddaughter :—While Daniel is out, and Isaac is with his aunts, I will write a few lines to thee to say that it was very kind of thee to be willing to spare thy husband and son long enough to make us a visit.

We do appreciate it very much, and we enjoy the precious boy as well as his dear father. If thyself and Richard had come it would have increased the pleasure ; but we hope *that visit* is in reserve. They seem to have enjoyed meeting their relatives, and Isaac has made friends with all, winning love and admiration wherever he went. We all think he is a very good boy, evincing the judicious and affectionate training of a mother's gentle hand.

Thy letter, which came yesterday, shows a brightness in the absence of thy dear ones, and a disposition to bear up in hope of their safe return, when Isaac will be able to entertain you with much that he has seen and learned. This trip and its incidents will not be soon forgotten by him, and his brother Richard may be made acquainted, by hearsay, with many things to draw his thoughts Eastward. What a halo children cast around the family circle. Especially is this the case when they are intelligent and inquiring.

This evening the dear ones are to leave us ; and we trust they will find safety and protection, in the keeping of that kind Providence that watches over us wherever our lots may be cast.

They found us much better in health, and I hope we may get out again if the weather should clear and the snow melt.

It will remain a great comfort to me that I have once more seen Daniel, and have also looked upon his dear son. If life be spared, I shall hope to greet thee and Richard some time. I know it is far to come from St. Louis to Camden, yet way sometimes opens for us, and is made easy, beyond our human calculations.

From what I have learned, I shall seem to see you, and almost to locate you in your own home.

May the Good Shepherd keep us, and aid us all in eyeing the hedge that encloses us in the sheepfold; and may He keep the lambs with us in our affections, and in our prayers enable us to give them to the Lord that He may bless them.

Farewell! Love to thy father and to little Richard.

Thy loving grandmother,

M. S. L.

DETACHED PARAGRAPHS.

FROM THE LETTERS OF M. S. L.

Where grace abounds it regulates all, and centres the mind, but where its offers are rejected, longer steps are taken in the broad way of so-called pleasure.— *No date.*

I know the lonely feeling of a young person for want of congenial society; for when in my youth I withdrew from the giddy round, I trod the loneliness of my way for a season. But, in his own time, my Heavenly Father made a way for me to mingle with those who loved Him, and who delighted in his commandments. —*No date.*

I feel to commend you in your efforts to educate your children; for with Job Scott I do believe that too much rusticity is *not* an advantage to a Christian.—*No date.*

At —— Quarterly Meeting Friends have certainly had the best of help to sustain them, and have known their heads to be covered in the day of battle.—*No date.*

Since our last Yearly Meeting I think we have cause to lift up our heads in hope; there was manifested there such a gathered feeling, such an increase of love and harmony, with an evident desire, on the part of many, to rally to first principles, even to those which brought us together as a people.—*No date.*

When the cares of this life press down the better part in us, we fall into a condition of spiritual lethargy from which nothing but Divine Grace can redeem us. " No cross, no crown "—how much is contained in these words.—*No date.*

Eternity seems very much nearer than it did when I was a child, and the dear departed do not seem very far off, only gone before to a better world, to an unchanging state. When we have finished our days in this lower world, may we be ready to meet those who are gathered into the Heavenly garner.—*No date.*

I am always interested to hear items of moment concerning thy family. I think it good for parents and children to remain together in one household, so long as they can rightfully do it, loving and companionable. Where this is the case the parents are affable to the children, and the children confiding in the parents; so as to be mutually helpful in the ascent and descent of the hill of life.—*No date*.

If we were satisfied with what is revealed to us, and to our children, I believe we should be willing to *leave* the secret things which belong to God. I want no strife of tongues, and have no interest in contention. To promote (as a very feeble instrument) Truth and righteousness, and to live in peace with all mankind during the time yet allotted me in this state of being, is what I desire.—*No date*.

There are many allurements in view to entice the young, but I have great faith in the endeavors of parents to keep the ground fallow, and to prevent the weeds from growing during the period of childhood and youth. Then will the children as they grow older (and especially if separated from the tender hands that reared them) feel urged to the same work—that of attending to the garden of the heart, to dress and to keep it. Early training does a great deal towards a right growth.—*No date*.

I felt it a great cross to give up the fashions and amusements that I had indulged in ; but I found a Power sufficient to remove every obstacle, and to make for me an easy and pleasant way within the limits of Divine love.—*No date*.

Oh, the Church! May strength be afforded your spirits to travail for its arising ; for its coming out of the wilderness into the clear light of the sun ! May we all seek for the spirit of prayer and supplication, to be

preserved from the temptations held out on every hand
to draw aside from the way of the cross! I feel, indeed,
feeble and of little account. Still I hope to be protected
to the end. Farewell!—*No date.*

Where Friends are few in number, if they meet as
they ought, they can have Heavenly Meetings. — *No
date.*

Many are the heavy-hearted in our Yearly Meeting,
in view of the state of Society; but I believe the only
way is to repair to the Fountain and there wait in all
humility, leaving the issue with the great Controller of
events. There seems to be a disposition to sustain *new
doctrine*, and this disposition causes many to suffer; but
good may come even out of the suffering.—*No date.*

In some of our smaller meetings there is manifested
a dull, drowsy spirit; and when this is indulged in, how
it lays waste the strength, and how it discourages those
who come to these gatherings to renew their covenants,
and to experience a being refreshed from the mingling
with exercised spirits.—*No date.*

The grandeur and sublimity of Nature's works in-
spire the heart with gratitude. Who can behold and not
admire the works of an Almighty Creator?—*No date.*

May the fathers and the mothers who cleave to the
law and the testimony be strengthened to distribute the
bread, with the Master's blessing. This bread will
satisfy hungry souls, and strengthen them to seek an
acquaintance with Him who gives freely to those who
ask Him, if they ask aright.—*No date.*

The *unsettlement* and *agitation*, in one place and another, are discouraging; and they cause the Lord's servants to go on their way mourning and heavy-hearted. —*No date.*

I am very favorable to Monthly Meeting Schools; believing that they will prove a benefit to the Society. —*No date.*

Our Yearly Meeting was large, and it proved to be a very comfortable and favored season. The solemnity was remarkable, and a precious covering was over us at the close. After the reading of the concluding Minute it was some time before any one seemed ready to rise.— *No date.*

There is much concern on the subject of education; but a good, substantial, guarded education is the kind to which I feel most bound; and it is to *this* that I hope I shall continue to look, rather than to the fashionable polish of the day, so long as I continue to be at the head of an educational institution.—*No date.*

I think the life of the religion of Jesus is very low, indeed; and I do not know whether there is enough of a willingness to go down into suffering, baptism, and death; so as to arise with Christ, and be able to hold Him up as the life of the "Christian Quaker." Surely we shall have to undergo a shaking, and a purifying, that there may be more consistency seen amongst a people making so high a profession as does the Society of Friends.—*No date.*

We think that the Discipline ought to be more

promptly attended to in cases of removal ; and especially that Certificates should go in a regular channel to the Monthly Meetings, and not to the individuals for whom they are sent. An attention to order prevents trouble. —1849.

After the interment of the body of our beloved friend Edward Hicks, we dined with a Friend who gave us a production emanating from the Meeting for Sufferings of Indiana Yearly Meeting. Not only is the language true, but the feeling on reading it was solemn ; for, like Gospel ministry, it is clothed with authority. —1849.

We lately visited our friend John Comly. He is better, and has been once out at meeting.—1849.

We have had a very acceptable and truly edifying visit from dear George Hatton, who attended our Quarterly Meeting last Fifth-day, and had an appointed meeting in our village that evening. His ministry is deep and powerful. He preaches baptizingly. I regard it as a privilege to sit under his ministry, and it is comforting to find that he stands upon that ground upon which stood our worthy predecessors. Like that worthy elder, George Fox, he is firm in the faithful support of our wholesome Discipline, and comely order. My husband and myself took him to Bristol, Pa., on Sixth-day, where he had an evening meeting, which was well attended and highly favored, for he had good service therein.

Next day we went to Byberry, to the house where

our valued friend, John Comly, recently passed away. We passed two days with his children, and attended Byberry Meeting on First-day. It was a season to be remembered; the doctrine plain and close, flowed freely and largely. Not a feeling could arise to obstruct the Gospel stream; and I thought we could say, "Sing ye unto the Lord, for He hath triumphed gloriously," &c. After a solemn opportunity at the house of Sarah Comly we separated; Nathaniel Richardson taking George to Newtown, and we returning home, with the sweet reward of peace.—1850.

From Baltimore Yearly Meeting we have favorable accounts. A good meeting, and several strangers in attendance; amongst them dear John Hunt.—1850.

I may suffer loss in best things, and sometimes I fear that I do, by not attending to small duties from home. Obedience is everything: you know this, dear Friends, and though I may be slack, yet would I encourage *you* to let obedience keep pace with knowledge, that your day's work may be going on, in the day-time, a peaceful evening succeed, and at the end the reward of " well done " be yours.—1850.

Some Friends do not agree with me in my opposition to divorces. I disapprove of receiving any one into the Society who has been divorced and remarried.—1850.

Too few of the older people seem to manifest that tenderness and humility which are so convincing, and so encouraging to those who are younger in life, as well as in religious experience. Has our love waxed cold, or do the cares of this life choke the seed, and render it unfruitful? There must be some cause for this state of things among us. But I suppose we must look ahead; believing the Power is the same that ever it was, and that the great Head of the Church is able to build us up, and establish us upon that rock against which nothing can prevail.—1852.

Oh! when I look back at Society, as it used to be, in the days of my youth, how bright it appears. I hope to see a rallying, and an arising in brightness, before I leave the world. I hope to be more faithful and obedient myself, that I may contribute my mite towards a restoration.—1852.

Our granddaughter is to be married on Fifth-day, at the house of her father, Granville S. Woolman, which is on the old "plantation" where John Woolman lived, and where he *killed the robin.*—1852.

My husband has felt very desirous that thy faith may not fail thee; but that by obedience and faithfulness in all things, thou may be able to keep on with the work required of thee, turning neither to the right hand nor to the left, nor shrinking from any duty.—1853.

I was pleased to hear from you, through Sarah Hunt, and was glad to hear that she homed at your father's. Mary G. Allen was here, not long since; though her physical health is frail, she is lively in spirit. John Hunt has gone to the meetings in the limits of Nottingham, and Southern Quarters, and Ruth Pyle and Mary Pike to Bucks Quarter. They are all dedi-

13

cated servants, and I am glad to hear of such being out on religious visits.—1853.

I think it is much more desirable to increase the size of your farm, than to let the young people squander to find other business. How many, on this very account, have left Friends. How few of our young men are found pursuing the path of humble industry on their farms, and yet what business life is more pleasant than an agricultural one.—1853.

I felt near unity with thee when first I met thee, at Westtown. I have never experienced any diminution of this feeling, and I hope I never may.—1853.

I am fond of school and of the society of the young, also concerned that they may have a guarded education, and one that will not puff them up or place them above the swift witness for God in their own souls. It is also my aim to keep them from indulging in such *amusements* as I consider out of the simplicity of the Truth. I am also opposed to their reading works of fiction. I find that of those under my care there are many who respect my views and sympathize with my feelings, so that counsel on these subjects may be comparable to bread cast upon the waters.—1853.

Oh! that the *qualified laborers* may go into the harvest field and thrust in the sickle, that the harvest may be gathered.—1853.

Oh, that we may all keep humble, in the nothingness of self! then, though the potsherds of the earth smite together, we shall not be hurt.—1853.

The disciples of Jesus were always a despised few; buffeted, reviled, spit upon; but strength has ever been given to endure all things, and suffer all things, that their joy might be full.—1853.

We attended Baltimore Yearly Meeting, which was large, and for the most part favored. Latterly some of their pillars have been removed by death, which deprivation they sensibly feel.—1853.

Dear John Jewett seems meek as a child, and Susanna is very much missed. Nicholas and Margaret Brown are in *good keeping*, cheerful, yet feeling much concerned for the welfare of Society. They expressed their near and dear unity with thee. We made them a visit last summer, and a very pleasant one it was, being the fulfilment of what we had long desired.—1853.

Restore S. Lamb is in the Southern States on a religious visit. We have a letter from him written in Richmond, Virginia, in which he speaks of having been kindly received. He has had a number of interviews with ministers of other denominations. He thinks that the way to effect the great work of emancipation, would be to go *among* the slave-holders and expostulate with them.—1853.

We consider ourselves of too little account, and too weak to strengthen the hands of a dear, tried brother, to whom we feel knit in the fellowship of the Gospel of Christ.—1853.

I do not marvel that there are few so devoted as were our early Friends. So many have cumbering

cares, whereby to plead, " I pray thee have me excused."
I think, however, there are many that love the principle,
and some that are even willing to bear the cross.—1853.

The world's polish makes a beautiful outside ; and
carved work, in this " refined age," is more admired than
substantial material. But what would the carving be
worth if the substance upon which it is wrought be of
no value.—1853.

Nothing can preserve us, as a religious body, but
the Truth, plain and simple as it is, uncouth as it may
sound to the worldly ear.—1853.

How happy those who can keep in the peaceable
spirit of Jesus, firm and steadfast, but meek and patient.
The lion and the lamb shall dwell together. I am
thankful that my lot has been cast amongst Friends ;
yet I mourn over our Society, seeing that our faith
appears to be too nearly allied to that " which is overcome
by the world." As the world takes possession of our
hearts, we run out into its spirit, into pride, high-mind-
edness, covetousness, and into many new and foolish
notions and speculations.—1854.

Mind the Light, a light that shines within, en-
lightening the conscience until the day dawn, and the
Day-star arise in the heart, and direct us to the Young
Child, who is the Son of promise, to sit upon the
throne forever. The Light gives " certain evidence of
Divine Truth"—not speculative notions and theories,
nay, verily ! but a clear sight of spiritual things, and a

true discernment of the spirits of those who promulgate
them.—1854.

The late Yearly Meeting in Ohio, though weak as
to numbers, afforded some encouragement ; for a solidity
was present which furnished evidence of a travail in
Zion.—1854.

I am pleased to find that there is a general interest
and concern on the subject of education, and a desire
that our schools be taught by those are not merely
members, but who are consistent Friends. Early impressions are lasting, and the example set the children,
and the influences surrounding them, are likely to oper-
ate either favorably or unfavorably. Hence the importance of their receiving moral and religious training
along with the intellectual. Too many disregard our
testimonies in favor of plainness, and the avoidance of
amusements, &c., thus making it difficult for those who
are concerned on these points to have our schools carefully guarded against innovations. Of course there is
no objection to innocent childish sport, either at school
or at home. Play is natural to the young, and we would
not forbid, but carefully regulate these sports. In our
Yearly Meeting, we are encouraged to persevere in establishing Friends' schools.—1854.

Friends were raised up to be a peculiar people ; a
plain, self-denying people, led and guided by the Holy
Spirit into a spiritual and heavenly way. —1854.

Many are like the dove going forth from the ark,
and finding no rest for their feet, because the unstable

element covers the earth. The waters have not subsided, but are agitated by every wind of doctrine. Oh, when, to these unsettled ones will the solid land appear? When will they be drawn to meet together and worship around the Son, each sitting under his vine, and under his fig-tree, where none can make afraid?—1854.

If Friends who are *real* Friends would only be firm, a better time would soon come; because that which is of man would be judged down, the power of the Highest would be sustained, and his devoted servants would be sustained *in* that power.—1854.

None but the redeemed of the Lord can support our testimonies in their integrity. None but those who have obeyed the call to come out of Babylon.—1854.

We were glad to hear of your welfare, also that you were favored with a comfortable Yearly Meeting. The many deficiencies cause the Lord's servants to go on their way mourning; yet, we find that there are still those of the true seed whose faith remains unchanged, and this is cause for encouragement.—1854.

The outlook toward your place is pleasant, for we think that the Light is shining there; and that it will yet shine brighter, causing an increase, and an in-gathering.—1854.

We had a very large and interesting Yearly Meeting. Greater solemnity and harmony, perhaps, have not been known within our recollection, throughout all the sittings. We have cause to feel gratitude to the great Giver of all good.—1855.

I believe if we know the Father and the Son, and *own* them; we shall also know the purpose of Christ's coming in a prepared body.—1855.

If parents would come into simplicity and self-denial, then I believe the dear children would be gathered, and turned away from seeking enjoyment in those alluring things which are so fleeting and uncertain. —1855.

Your epistles always meet with a cordial welcome, for they convey the evidence that you are of the household of faith. Yea, of that faith, not only *once* delivered to the saints, but that continues to be delivered in every age and generation to the saints in Christ Jesus.—1855.

We have *reason* to comprehend the things of a man; but a *spirit* in man by which to know the things pertaining to God. The attempt to substitute reason for revelation, is the result of man's having partaken of the forbidden fruit.—1855.

How serious, how weighty is the consideration of the many sayings uttered by the blessed Jesus, concerning those who would *not own* Him.—1855.

Friends have always acknowledged Christ, the Head of the Church, the Light and the Life.—1855.

I think it is a privilege to move in a *plain way*, even in school; teaching only those branches that are useful and substantial.—1856.

It takes many baptisms and deaths, before we become regenerated and born again, and know of a certainty that we have passed from death unto life, because we love the brethren. It is only after this regeneration that we can "bless them that curse" us, and pray for them that "despitefully use" us. This is what I desire to attain to, and to be established in.—1856.

Did you see the account of the burning of the ferry-boat on the Delaware River? So many lives lost, so near to the shore, it seems almost unaccountable.—1856.

Dear Friends, my love flows toward you, with desires that the Lord will bless you with the continued incomes of light and life into your souls, to make you "fruitful in the field of offering, and joyful in the house of prayer." "Greater is He that is in you, than he that is in the world."—1856.

The tide of fashion runs strong and swift, threatening to overwhelm all; but there is a Power that can stay its mighty waves. There is encouragement from beholding the number (even in the younger walks of life) who love our meetings, and manifest an interest in our principles and testimonies, including the one in favor of plainness of speech and apparel. If these keep their places they will be first stripped, and then clothed with the whole armor of light.—1856.

I suppose the privilege with you, in your meetings, as with Friends elsewhere, is to suffer as well as to rejoice; for the seed is under suffering, and is pressed down, "as a cart is pressed that is under sheaves."—1856.

We desire that you be faithful and obedient in all things; remembering that strength is furnished according to the need. The *reward* for obedience and dedication is sweet peace even while in this life, and in that which is to come, "Joy unspeakable."—1856.

Oh, that I may stand upon the watch-tower, and keep in a prayerful state, that I may be preserved in humble estimation of self. I have none to fear so much as myself.—1857.

We had a large meeting yesterday, and both sittings were much favored. They seemed like good old times when "they that feared the Lord spake often one to another, and a book of remembrance was made." Harmony and sisterly love seemed to abound, and the solemn quiet gave evidence that the good Shepherd had us in his keeping.—1857.

Our friend Jacob S. Willets (son of Samuel) was bitten by a rabid dog on the first of Sixth Month. About a week ago he died of hydrophobia. It was a distressing case.—1857.

My husband's health is very poor; he has been ill several times within the past two months. He is advised to go to the shore (should he get able), and even if not strong enough to take a surf bath, the inhalation of the salt air, it is thought will invigorate him.—1857.

Elisha Hunt is rather better. Sarah went to Genesee Yearly Meeting, but hastened home, not feeling easy to be long absent from her husband. The aged are passing away, and some of those who remain are quite feeble.—1857.

My husband has been more comfortable during the

past few weeks; he is now better than his friends ever expected to see him again, and as he has survived the summer, he may continue awhile longer. He gets out to meeting pretty regularly; and frequently takes a short ride in the forenoon, when the weather is pleasant. His brother Abraham Lippincott, and his nephew Peter Lippincott, both died recently; the latter very suddenly in Cherry Street Meeting. Many, very many, of our dear relatives and friends, are passing away, and oh! what a change it makes in the social circle, and in our religious meetings. But this is a changing state. To be ready and willing to go hence, when the time comes, is of all things most to be desired.—1857.

Oh! how I desire that Friends may draw near to the well of life, and there wait, to receive from the Master living water, and to dispense only what they receive from Him; that when they invite, it may be to "Come, see a man which told me all things that ever I did." —1857.

Silence has held dominion over my pen, but it is not an instance of "affection's stream arrested in its course." I have been too much occupied to write to my friends, however much I desired to do so. Oh, how the world engrosses me! Even when I feel as though it is all as nothing to me, and when I seek retirement and seclusion, I have to be conspicuous. But perhaps it is all right; for I was not created for myself alone.—1857.

It seems as if a great deal has occurred since I last saw thee; and though much has been done, yet I hardly

know how to refer to it, to any advantage. But to poor
self I *can* refer, and tell thee that the old Reasoner has
made me a good deal of trouble, in persuading me that
I could not leave home to finish my visit to the meetings
of Bucks Quarter. Oh, what poverty of spirit is the
result! or has been, until it seemed as though all good
was gone, and I was left as in the barren desert. By
suffering I have been made willing to go and finish this
work; after which I trust I may be permitted, for the
present, to stay at home and attend to my temporal
concerns. I have been feeling greatly discouraged, and
sometimes almost ready to give out by the way.—1857.

Our school is full, and we could not accommodate
all that applied to enter. We have a very pleasant
company of pupils, and get along satisfactorily in every
department. When a load is ready, and there is force
enough applied to start the wheel, it will roll around
with apparent ease; so we find it to be in this establishment. I do love school, and love to mingle with the
young. We have one pupil (about eighteen years of
age), who wears a plain silk bonnet. She is a lovely
girl, and quite a favorite with the others. I have not
heard of one passing remark that was unkind or unbe-
coming, having been made by her schoolmates concerning her. This, I think, is an evidence of the respectful demeanor of our pupils. I hope that this feeling
may continue, and that the young members of our Society
may come to see the propriety of a simple dress and of
its consistency with our profession. Oh, how well do I

remember the cross I had to bear, when, for the sake of peace of mind, I had to put on a plain dress, and become a subject of remark, and sometimes even of ridicule. But there was a sustaining Power that enabled me to despise the shame, and that became to me *far more* than any worldly enjoyment.—1857.

I feel it obligatory upon me to observe plainness and moderation, and it has become easy to me to do so, only by *bearing the cross*. I think that examples in these things (economy, as well as the cut and shape of the garment) are abundantly wanting in this day, when luxury and superfluity are so much indulged in, and when many plume themselves, and seem ready to fly off into the air.—1857.

Ah! there is but one way for Friends, and that is the good old way of implicit obedience, of a submission to the cross of Christ.—1857.

Isaac has been more poorly, and he has again very wearisome nights. He has been much resigned to his sufferings, and to the prospect of not being a great while with us ; but satisfied, I think, to leave all to the great Disposer of events, believing that He doeth all things well.—1857.

In wisdom are the ways of Providence, and He worketh wonders in the deep. Finite beings cannot scan Omnipotence, neither can they comprehend his mysterious workings, nor search into the secret things which belong to God. It is enough for us to know and believe that He is good, and that He designs to bless the inhabitants of the earth, and to bestow happiness upon all the rational family upon these terms, that we repent and be baptized with the baptism of the Holy Ghost and of fire. Did we not believe in God, manifested in Jesus Christ—did we not believe in a Saviour and Redeemer, ever present and ready to save and to help, where should we flee in time of trouble? To whom should we look when every earthly dependence fails?—1858.

Dear Cousin S! How often have I thought of the sweetness of her spirit, and especially so since her last visit to us. Well, she lived a very innocent, and as I think, happy life. She had an affectionate husband and kind children, and lived, we must believe, the time allotted her in this state of change; and now, we trust, she has received a crown immortal and unfading. Her precious spirit was covered as with a mantle that in its descending may rest upon those who beheld her departure. May the everlasting Arm be made bare to uphold thee, and to encircle thy precious offspring.—1858.

In my stripping and loneliness I feel poor, unworthy of the least favor, and not qualified to give even a cup of cold water to the thirsty traveler; yet since the reception of thy kind and deeply interesting letter, I have felt more than I can express, and I thought a little reply might not intrude upon thy quiet meditation. —1858.

During the last two months of his life, my beloved

husband was able to say that his work was done; that his greatest desire and concern through life had been to serve his Divine Master; that he had endeavored to be faithful, and for months, by day and by night, he had enjoyed continual peace amid much bodily suffering. To be thus sustained at the last is what I greatly desire for myself and for others.—1858.

In pondering over the mysterious formation of man, I cannot but believe that he is designed to be as happy *here*, as his capacity will admit, and that nothing is wanting to the perfecting of this but entire resignation to the Divine will. A willingness to be led and guided by the unerring spirit of Truth will lead by rivers of pleasure that water the earth, as they flow on to the Infinite Sea, where death is swallowed up in immortality. —1859.

Though surrounded by a large and interesting family, I often feel lonely for the want of some one to confer with, who would be interested, as I am, in things nearer and dearer to me than are the affairs of this life. I pass very many such lonely hours, and trust that I am *resigned* to pass them; believing it may prove to be for my greatest good. My children, teachers and pupils are very kind and attentive; and Friends, too, remember me, and many of them visit me in love. Yes, I have many favors for which I am thankful, though there is a void left, by the removal of my dear partner, which none can fill. I have, however, the sweet consolation that he rests in peace, and this reconciles me to the separation, and raises me above drooping in sadness, as I otherwise should, without my outward armor-bearer.—1859.

Our dear friends Nicholas and Margaret Brown, made their home at our house, while attending our Quarterly Meeting. They are green in old age, and stand upright in support of the good old "Quaker" doctrine and Discipline. They are quick-sighted to discover error, and way is wonderfully made to receive their testimonies.—1859.

We have had too much oratory and head-knowledge in the name of religion; and the people have (some of them, at least) been carried off into speculation. From this there is a warning voice to come away and be separate, that the garment may be undefiled, the heart made pure, and a *heart religion* be ours. Absolom had a beautiful head of hair, and great account was made of *polling* his hair, but when he was about to be proclaimed king, his locks proved to be the cause of his destruction, and the people whose hearts he had stolen away, returned and gave their allegiance to the lawful king. Things transpire alike in different ages. Man is vain and imaginative; but when he becomes lifted up in his haughtiness, there is a Power that can intercept his course and thwart his plans. None are safe, but as they continue in a state of watchfulness unto prayer.—1859.

I have my hours of loneliness amid the young and buoyant, who are looking forward to an auspicious future in this life. They behold a beautiful world before them, unfolding joys that gladden their hearts and cause them to delight in existence. Oh! did they always keep so in the innocency as never to mar the Divine impress, how would the waves of happiness roll on in due succession, without anything to arrest their flow. Even the probations, meted out to sentient beings, would increase the happiness, for each new trial would loosen a link in the chain that binds to earth, and rivet one in that which draws to Heaven.—1859.

Your letter was both fresh and cheering, as an emanation of Gospel love, comparable to a messenger bearing glad tidings from the good Land.—1859.

The ornaments of dress, where there is a fondness for them, are comparable to the little foxes that have their hiding-places from which they come out to hurt the tender vines. How I long to see the sweet-spirited young men and young women, very many of whom are near and dear to my best life. Coming under the preparing and forming Hand, and thus being fitted for usefulness in the Church.—1859.

My Heavenly Father found me, in early life, exposed to snares and temptations; and often when I was in the depth of sorrow, known only to myself, He kept the guardian angel of his presence near, and wonderfully made a way for my preservation. Though I was often rebellious, yet before my twentieth year I renounced the world, with its pleasures, its gayety, and its vanity; and endured the cross, despising the shame. I have never had reason to regret this renunciation, having found so much solid comfort and satisfaction, and believing that all my trials have been blest to me. Such would be the case with our young people now, if they would only submit to the yoke of Christ, though I would' have them be more faithful than I have been. But how many we see, even till middle life, who flit like the butterfly in the summer sun. These, peradventure, will yet be gathered in the Heavenly enclosure and come forth in brightness, after some of our heads have been laid low. Such, at least, is my hope.—1859.

I am obliged to R. H. for the part that he is taking in preparing for the press a revision of Murray's Readers, than which none have ever better suited me. I find it difficult to procure books in which the plain language is adhered to. Even our grammars depart from it, though I try in my teaching to sustain it.—1862.

With all its imperfections, I hope our Society is gaining ground. Our meetings are increasingly solemn, as well as large, though the mid-week meetings in some places are not so well attended as they ought to be. Many valuable Friends have been gathered to their fathers, and we feel the stripping ; but we hope that others are under the preparing Hand, and that in time they will come forward for service.—1864.

Elisha Hunt and wife, and William Folwell and wife are still able to mingle with their Friends. My dear husband's brothers are all gone. How I miss him and them ! They were happy, cheerful men. Restore S. Lamb is feeble, as is also Mary G. Allen. Other

14

Friends, hereaway, are mostly in usual health, though many are growing old.—1864.

I would that the mourners in Zion might multiply. Their prayers are not offered in vain, neither are their tears shed for naught. My spirit salutes the Lord's servants, and desires their health and prosperity.—1864.

Among the absent ones whom I often visit, in thought, is your venerable father—my long-tried and beloved friend in the fellowship of the Gospel. His voice fell sweetly on my ear, and the message reached my heart, in my youthful days, when I was fervently engaged in seeking the pathway to Zion. Never *less dear* has he been to me, as a father in the Church, and I trust a pillar in God's house.—1865.

I should love to meet you often during our earthly sojourn; but if we cannot meet face to face, I hope our spirits may often mingle in the holy sanctuary, where there is a communion, which the commotions of the world cannot disturb, and where strength is furnished to move upward and forward towards that Land of rest, whither I trust we are wending our way, and where we shall meet to part no more.—1865.

If thoughts could write, I do not know how voluminous would be the packages received by my absent friends.—1865.

When I call up, and view on memory's page, a host of worthies, both those in this world and those in the world to come, they seem to pass in review before my mental vision, to gladden my solitary hours. It is good to see them thus, to know that such have been, and some yet are, walking on this goodly earth of ours, as pilgrims seeking a far-off country where change is not, and where trials never come.—1865.

By strong cords of affection, I am bound to the human race; and the farther I advance towards the termination of all things here below, the more is my heart enlarged in feelings of kindness, tenderness, compassion and sympathy, towards dear friends, and towards erring, wayward brethren and sisters as well; so that my heart breathes forth spontaneous aspirations on behalf of all. Without the guidance of the Holy Spirit man is frail and prone to do evil; but when obedient to the still, small voice, he is only a little lower than the angels.—1865.

Oh, that the Spirit that covered our forefathers might cover us of this generation! that we might, as a Society, put our hands to the plow and not turn back. If we would only draw more and more together, around the one Head, Christ, and learn of Him, not attempting to lean upon our own understanding, I believe we should yet be a blessing to the world.—1866.

Friends mingling in visiting families, neighboring meetings, &c., *under a concern*, has I think, a salutary influence in binding more closely together, and in awakening a desire to be more diligent in the attendance of mid-week meetings, and in the support of other testimonies. But everything promotive of advantage must be done through a *right concern*. I have, for some years past, had a First-day school for my pupils, which I trust has proved profitable to them, and I have myself been instructed. It brings me much with them on that day, and ofttimes opens the way for me, as I feel it, to hold up the religion of Jesus Christ, and the confirmation by the New Testament, of the Truths stated in the Old. —1867.

When the infirmities of age overtake our parents, and other aged ones, we should be patient with them, and tender as they were of us, in the days of our childhood. Several who remain in mutability are feeble, bodily and mentally; but I trust that the *better part* is in safe-keeping.—1867.

I accompanied my brother and his wife to their Quarterly Meeting, held at Fallston, Maryland, having obtained a Minute for that service. I believe I was in my right place in going, and I was abundantly helped, to my humbling admiration, to show what constitutes a *true Friend*, what are the duties of such a one, and whence comes the qualification to discharge these duties aright.—1867.

As many, and some of these among the young, see the evil tendency of this *restless spirit*, we have hope that deliverance will come, and that there will be a coming up out of the mixture, in our ancient beauty and clearness. The love of the world's maxims, customs and policies has caused our leanness, and hindered our advancement. So much lecturing, oratory and running to and fro, that the time for silent meditation seems to be placed afar off. Silence is the state in which to learn wisdom; indwelling with the Holy Spirit, waiting to hear and obey.—1867.

I often visit, mentally, my many Western friends, and feel fervent desires for your encouragement in the right line. Faithfulness brings its reward, though little *fruit* may appear. "Be thou faithful unto death and I will give thee a crown of life." Oh the crown, the glorious crown! How we desire it for ourselves and for our dear children. Yes, the dear children claim our constant anxiety and concern, even when they are comfortably reposing in sleep. This concern, I believe, is not lost, though at times we may see no good effects. Let us trust and hope for the future. There is tenderness in many of the young, and in time they may be broken in upon, with a Power which they cannot withstand. A time of gathering may come, ere our bodies are laid in the silent grave.—1867.

Elisha and Sarah Hunt are in usual health, though the former goes out but little, owing to his age and a stiffness in his limbs. He is very bright mentally and tender spirited.—1867.

I have recently attended the funeral of the wife of Joseph Horner, a valued Friend ; also that of my dear cousin, Dr. N. Shoemaker, of Philadelphia.—1868.

In our Yearly Meeting we are often burdened with much speaking, but this year, in both Philadelphia and New York, I thought we had favored periods of solemn silence.—1868.

I have thought for years past, that in some places the removals from country neighborhoods to cities have been a serious disadvantage to our Society, having led out of a plain way of living and a plain way of preaching.—1868.

Hannah Stephens died suddenly, at her nephew's, near Mt. Holly, where she and her sister were making a visit. Last Seventh-day I saw her niece, who said that aunt H. had not been very well, and that she would be unable to attend Yearly Meeting. She was a valuable Friend.—1868.

Where children do all they can to help and comfort their parents, how much they can lighten the burdens of age and infirmity.—1868.

I recently wrote to our aged Friend, George Hatton, whom I have regarded ever since my youthful days, as my valued friend and counselor in spiritual things. How often has he sounded the Gospel trumpet in large assemblies, to the warning of the rebellious and wayward, and to the comforting of the mourners in Zion, and the heavy-hearted in Jerusalem.—1868.

I did not suppose that ——— would be a desirable place for you to choose as a home. Friends there have decreased in numbers, and the cause of this decrease may perhaps be attributed to three conditions, one being general and the other two special : unfaithfulness, the environment of slavery, and the desire to grow rich.—1868.

There are some who are learned and wise in the

world's philosophy, who undertake to *instruct* in our religious meetings, to the grief of the sincere-hearted, and the suffering of the true seed.—1868.

The new birth must be known, ere valiants can come forth as did the sons of the morning in our religious Society, bold as a lion, meek as a lamb, and bearing testimony that none could gainsay.—1870.

Since we opened school in the autumn, I have lost a number of relatives. A brother-in-law, two nephews, two nieces and some cousins have been removed from earth. The great business of life is to lay up durable riches to last us forever. This is my understanding of things, and if life is rightly occupied we shall use and enjoy the good temporal gifts bestowed for our comfort and convenience, and love and adore the Great Giver, rendering to Him the greatest of our possessions—even our *whole heart.*—1870.

There seems to be an increased interest among the younger members of our Society in becoming familiar with the ground of our testimonies and the principle from which they have sprung, as branches from a root. This has brought our members of different ages together in a common interest.—1870.

The more Friends mingle together socially, the more are we drawn together in love, and the more favored are our religious meetings. I often think how the early Friends went from house to house, encouraging, instructing and strengthening each other.—1871.

CHAPTER IV.

REFLECTIONS, ETC.

A WORD OF EXHORTATION TO PARENTS.

The query which has presented itself to the minds of concerned parents, not a few, is adverted to in to-day's *Intelligencer*. While reading the remarks in that paper I was reminded of the sentiments expressed by Nicholas Waln in a letter to his aunt Shoemaker. This letter was written in London, while he was pursuing his studies in that gay metropolis. The gratitude which he felt for the care of this aunt, who had supplied the place of a mother to him, and the impression that her advice had made upon his mind, may be inferred from his Scripture quotation.

"Train up a child in the way he should go, and when he is old he will not depart from it." Though he may depart while he is young, yet when he is old it will be like bread cast upon the waters—found after many days.

Although she had mourned over his wayward course, feeling that her affectionate counsel had been disregarded and that the labor and attention which she had bestowed upon him were of no avail; yet this letter proved that such had not been the case.

Being now in a foreign land he remembered her with tender affection. The sweetness of her voice seemed

to fall upon his ear, and her counsel, which arose atop
of all, was as the bread of life to his hungering spirit.
Then it was he penned these words of encouragement
for her to pursue the tenor of her way with a feeling of
confidence that her labors would be blessed. Heretofore
the instability of his conduct had been comparable to the
boisterous ocean, which in its heavings and surgings
threatens to ingulf everything cast upon its bosom;
but now a change had taken place, and her solicitude
for his welfare met a response in the acknowledgment
that her counsel had taken hold upon him, and might
prove to be the means of his preservation.

Parents, remember this one instance and take courage; withholding neither hand nor voice from every
effort in your power to direct and to save your precious
offspring while they are treading the slippery paths of
youth—paths which are overhung with temptations, and
thickly beset with snares.

Your words may seem to fall upon heedless ears,
but the precept, the exhortation which they convey may
find a place in the memory of your child, and may serve
as a watchword to him when danger threatens and when
the jaws of death seem to be opening to receive him.
Then the wisdom of a father's counsel, the tenderness of
a mother's care, and the earnest pleadings of both, may
come to the rescue and turn him from his wayward
course to a path of safety and of peace.

In the aboundings of love for the dear ones for
whom you would sacrifice so much, put up your peti-

tions to your God and Father, that He will not let his eye pity, nor his hand spare these, till he has brought forth judgment unto victory.

FOR "THE JOURNAL."

The axe must be laid to the root of the corrupt tree if we would have no more *poisonous fruits*. Is not the tree of intemperance a corrupt tree, and is not the fruit it yields poison? Do not those who eat thereof inherit the curse of death to innocency? If we will look around shall we not see multitudes going a downward course into degradation and misery, throughout the length and breadth of our land? Men, made but a little lower than the angels, coming to an untimely end; their sun, once bright, setting under a thick cloud of darkness, their families pining in wretchedness and poverty!

What is to be done? Am I my brother's keeper? And who is my brother? He is our brother who has wandered in a forbidden path; and, being tempted by taverns and drinking saloons so thickly crowded on his way, has been wounded, robbed, and lies weltering in his blood. Let us turn aside and dress his wounds, and then wield the axe to destroy the root, that the corrupt tree may wither and die. Take away the license! Refrain from the wine and the beer cup, &c., and then have faith that by prayer and fasting—total abstinence —we may, with Divine aid, cast the demon spirit out of our midst. Rather than place a stumbling-block in the way of a weak brother, let us drink no strong drink while the world standeth.

If we can arrest the flood of intemperance, other evils, those which follow in its train, may be subdued. Smite the giant and his hosts will be scattered.—1873.

A FRAGMENT.

The heavens and the earth speak forth the praise of their Creator.

What harmony! What regular progression — all moving in their appointed courses, without a jar! What a lesson should they teach to the beholder! Did we move in the line of Divine appointment, each filling the place he was designed to fill, the same harmony would be displayed in our movements through the world, and one would not disturb another in his onward course. As travelers on a life-long journey, prompted by both interest and inclination, we should move straight forward toward that habitation appointed for our home, after a well-passed life in this state of being.

Then why is not man happy while here? Why does he not find this life to be a blessing? Ah! by disobedience he has forfeited his inheritance, and caused the earth to bring forth, for him, briers and thorns. Yes, it is disobedience that makes man the author of his own and of his neighbor's woes.

Is it not surprising that with all this knowledge, rebellion should still mark the pathway of the unregenerate man?

PASSING TIME.

"The lust of the flesh, and the lust of the eyes, and the pride of life." What a round of pleasure-seeking there is. What a running to and fro. What an expenditure of time and of money to gratify these desires, when lo, man is like a shadow that soon passes by. No earthly thing can he hold securely, even with his closest grasp; and as for those glittering *amusements*, which fill up the passing hours, they are like the bubble that expands with beauty as it escapes, but if it be touched it bursts asunder, and is not.· Many and complicated are the devices resorted to, to speed the moments on their course, as though time in this life were to continue forever—when lo! it passes more swiftly than a weaver's shuttle, and is bearing us onward to a never-ending eternity.

Oh ye who frequent these places of amusement! Have you no responsibilities? Have you no work of greater moment than the gratification of your senses, or than mere entertainment to fill up the blanks (?) of time? Are you placed here for no other purpose than to shine forth as the brilliant butterfly—flit about for a short season and then depart? May you pause and consider. Wise would it be for those who thus spend their precious time to pause long enough to ask themselves the solemn question—what is life? Why was I invested with this responsibility? I have been gifted with physical and intellectual powers, and with an innate thirst for happiness. Am I sufficiently grateful for these gifts, and am I answering the end of my creation? Do I devote a due portion of my time to holy, spiritual communion, and is that communion as full and as free as it should be, or is it interrupted by the vain thoughts which have found a lodging-place in my mind, and which have been nourished if not engendered, by my attendance at places of amusement?

Till these inquiries are searchingly made and honestly answered, man will not be likely to find his true position; but he will remain, so far as his spiritual condition is concerned, but little above the brutes that graze the mountain-tops. His thoughts will tend towards *this* world, and when the time shall come for him to leave it, to what can he look forward?

His diversions have been his idols, and when removed from these, what will he have to depend upon?

HONOR AND DUTY.

Men are disposed to honor those who accomplish deeds likely to find a place on the page of history.

The warrior who has led his armies into the field of battle, and there has slain hosts of enemies (so-called); the statesmen whose influence regulates the laws of the land; the orator whose eloquence wafts the sentiments of his hearers in unison, as does the gentle breeze the tree-tops of the forest; the philanthropist, whose efforts are exerted to assist the widow, to protect the orphan, and to relieve the oppressed; the emancipator who would elevate the down-trodden sons of Africa from the degraded position in which the avarice and tyranny of their white brother has placed them :—these severally receive honor from the multitude according to the different stand-points from which their acts are viewed.

But worthy of double honor, and indeed *doubly honored* in the sight of Jehovah, are those who have dedicated themselves to his service, be that what it may.

These will be found trying to preserve men's lives, not to destroy them. They will also enter into sympathy with the oppressed, and with the suffering of all classes. Some may be called to administer to an oppressed race the comforts of the Christian religion ; telling the poor captives that the Great Creator loves all those whom He has made in his own image, and designed for eternal life. They may have to proclaim to the Ethiopian, or to the Red Man of the forest the glad tidings of the Gospel of peace and salvation, directing him to a light within himself that will show him the path of virtue in this life, and lead him to a happy home in the next. That Christ is able to save all those who trust in Him, and that He offers to man the free gift of his saving Grace, without money and without price. Gospel streams flow abundantly as the waters of life, and all are invited to come, drink and be refreshed.

The messengers of this Gospel may be disregarded and even despised by the multitude ; or they may cause the inquiry to be raised, " Whence hath this man this wisdom, and these mighty works ? " But however neglected, derided or contemned, these dedicated workers, if faithful to their calling, will receive a reward more lasting and of far greater value than all the honor that the world's votaries could give.

THE OLD MAN'S SECRET FOR HAPPINESS.

If we believe the oft-repeated assertion that the seat of happiness is in our own mind, we must admit that to every member of the human family this boon is freely offered.

Then why are we not all happy? Why do we behold the multitudes of plodding, care-worn inhabitants of this goodly earth of ours in a state of wretchedness, sighing for deliverance from that which makes life so oppressive as to be like a peddler's pack that bows the bearer down? Is it not because their thoughts tend downward; and they seek delight either in sensual gratifications or in worldly vanities?

"Too low they build who build beneath the skies." They seek to gratify the body or else to store the mind with that which is as different from wisdom as dross is unlike gold, and which leaves them as far from contentment as the equator is from the pole.

Finding that they have missed their aim they feel an inward pain, as if a canker were gnawing at the root of their peace.

Where, then, does lie the secret of man's happiness? What *can* satisfy him in all the vicissitudes of life? What *can* enable him to receive with equanimity prosperity and adversity, and cause the stream of peace to flow in an uninterrupted current?

I reply in the language of an aged colored man who, when asked what made him so happy at all times, replied, " I have always tried to keep my mind easy."

Try this, and the secret is discovered. The mind makes the man; and if the affections are placed upon Him who created us, and bestowed upon us our mental faculties as well as our physical being, if we regard Him as Sovereign Lord of all, and ourselves as his servants, we shall be ready to move at his will, obey his commands, and ask counsel of Him to direct us in the Way Everlasting.

When man comes to be thus directed, his corporal wants will be made subservient to the intellectual, the intellectual to the spiritual, and the care for the safety of his never-dying soul, paramount to every other consideration.

Then he will know what it is to be raised from the grossness of sensual indulgences, to be extricated from the maze of worldly vanities, and to be established in a place of habitation secure from danger. All forbidden guests will be debarred an entrance into this peaceful abode, in the inner sanctuary of which sits Happiness, enthroned and undisturbed.

Keep the mind easy by doing what is right; then if we love our Creator, and live peaceably with all men, we may acknowledge that we have found the secret of

happiness, and that we can subscribe to the sentiment
expressed by the poet,

> " None are unhappy—all have cause to smile,
> But those who to themselves that cause deny."

THE RELATION OF A MEMBER TO THE BODY.

I feel that in the liberty which the Truth gives, I
may offer my opinion, present my view on a subject
which is both interesting and important to the Society
of Friends. While considering the matter, since a recent
interview that I had with some Friends, I have consulted
neither book nor person, but have endeavored to keep
in the quiet, that I might know the mind of Truth in
relation to it.

After thus deliberating, I feel free to say that I believe the Society is constituted as are our bodies; that no
member is independent of the other members, or of the
body, but that where one member is diseased the whole
body is affected. If the Church is composed of living
members, and if Christ is the Head, then does his Spirit
flow through the whole body, reaching every member
thereof. If one member is unfaithful in the support of
our testimonies, then must all the other members—the
whole body—suffer for the unfaithfulness of this one;
and the suffering must continue until the offending
member is restored to a healthy condition.

If one member should claim the right to indulge in
certain amusements, or to engage in certain practices,
because *he* sees no impropriety in so doing (so long as

15

he keeps within the bounds of the moral law and leads a reputable life), although his course of conduct is in open violation of some of our cherished testimonies— then does he not separate himself from the body by being out of unity with those who are faithfully supporting the law and the testimony ?

If each member is to decide for himself which of our testimonies are unimportant, because they seem so to him, then shall we not soon be landed in that chaotic state where organization is no longer a benefit, and scarcely a possibility.

Yes, Friends, we must *unitedly* support our testimonies, or else they will fall to the ground. Where one member errs, the body errs with it, and all are turned out of the way.

When the disaffected member shall become sensible of his error he will be brought into suffering, in which the body will participate. Oh, then what kindness, what tenderness, what humility, what love, what deliberation should there be in every movement of the body, that the mind of Truth may be known, and that that which is lame may be healed. A living member must *suffer* before he can properly deal with an offender.

THE FRIENDS.

Our worthy predecessors, being of one heart and of one mind, drew together in the fear and the dread of the Most High God, to worship Him in spirit and in truth. The light within taught them that God is a Spirit, and

that He required of them spiritual worship. And in
their assembling for worship they realized the promise,
"Where two or three are gathered together in my
name, there am I in the midst of them." These could
acknowledge, from experience, that it is life eternal to
"know thee the only true God, and Jesus Christ, whom
thou hast sent." The Son was revealed in them, as the
only way to the Father—the way into the kingdom of
God, and of his Christ, as a Saviour to save them, a
Redeemer to redeem them, a Mediator and Intercessor
with the Father. Thus they came to sit together in
heavenly places in Christ Jesus, where none could make
them afraid. These formed the Society of Friends, a
militant Church, with no Head but Christ. "One is
your Master, even Christ, and all ye are brethren."
"Ye are my friends if ye do whatsoever I command
you." They beheld the beautiful order and wise economy
of the visible church, where the head of the woman is
the man, the head of the man is Christ, and the Head
of Christ is God. They understood that the children of
the Lord are children of the New Jerusalem, which is
from above, and is the mother of us all.

Their knowledge of these things was received by
revelation—no man could teach them the things pertaining to the Spirit. They fed upon the Bread of Life,
which Bread, says Christ, I am. They drank of that
spiritual Rock that followed Israel, and that Rock was
Christ, "Jesus Christ, the same yesterday, and to-day,
and forever."

OUT OF MY PLACE.

For the sake of others I consented to go on this trip to Montreal and Quebec. Though I say it not to my companions—for I desire not to mar their enjoyment—yet I still feel that home would be the proper place for me at this time. I have no life in a pleasure trip, feeling that I have no spare time to pass in this way. I feel that I am out of my usual course, out of the way of any useful business for myself or for others, and being poor mentally, as well as spiritually, I am not keeping any record of this trip. I hope that we may get home safely, and that in future I may profit by this experience, so that when a trip is to be taken for sight-seeing, I may be excused from joining the company.—1853.

MY DAILY DUTIES.

Why is it that such a poor, unworthy creature as I am, should have to preside over such a family (ninety in number), to be in some measure responsible for them, and to set them an example worthy of their imitation? It is an humble station, and one in which I feel that I have need to keep in a state of watchfulness unto prayer. I travel through the deeps, and tread the loneliness of my way, when there is none to look to, but the Lord alone.

A CONTRAST.

Oh! how bright is the halo that surrounds the Christian's death-bed. How radiant are the beams of his setting sun! Long, long is it ere that brightness fades away, and is forgotten by those who were privileged to witness the closing scene.

Is there no difference experienced at the close of life, between the man of the world and the Christian? I mean the regenerated, self-denying Christian, who bears his cross and patiently awaits the immortal crown. His is a hope that fails not—a faith that neither heights nor depths can disturb—for he keeps the end in view, and when the time for his departure comes, he peacefully passes away to receive the reward of *well done*.

Surely there *is* a difference between the end of such an one, and that of him who has lived a worldly life, and whose only treasures have been laid up on earth.

Some Account of George Parker, deceased. Formerly a Slave.

"Of a truth I perceive that God is no respecter of persons; but in every nation he that feareth Him, and worketh righteousness, is accepted with Him."

I deemed it proper to keep some account of the expressions of resignation, and of the peaceful close of our dear young friend, George Parker, who died at our house, of pulmonary consumption, on the 28th of Third Month, 1854, in the twenty-second year of his age. His parents, with their children, were slaves belonging to —— Fitz Hugh, of Virginia, till 1851, when they were manumitted by a provision left in their master's will, made some years before. George, with an older brother and a number of others, came to Philadelphia and procured homes in and adjacent to the city. His mother, of whom he was the youngest and darling son, and a sister remained in Alexandria, Virginia, with their former mistress.

George entered into service with us in the latter part of Sixth Month, 1853. His brother being near by, they had the opportunity of being often together, which contributed much to their happiness, as they were closely attached to each other. George continued faithfully and honestly to discharge his duties, at all times, till sickness disqualified him for labor. He was kind, obliging, and remarkably polite and respectful to every one with whom he had intercourse. Being of a quiet and amiable disposition, he lived in great harmony with his companions in service, frequently admonishing them if they neglected their business or indulged in rudeness, but evincing so much kindness and good feeling as to endear himself to these co-laborers, as well as to the rest of the family. As he could not read, he appeared to enjoy himself in quiet reflection ; and many evenings were passed mostly in that way.

During the summer and autumn he enjoyed his usual health, though always delicate, for he was of a scrofulous habit. In the early winter he began to suffer more ; so that for about a week he was laid by. Soon after getting out again he took cold, and was attacked with a hard cough and pain in his chest. Sometimes the remedies employed, and fair weather, would partially restore him, then again he would be more poorly. The severely cold weather in Second Month, however, proved to be too much for his enfeebled frame, and his cough increased and strength diminished quite rapidly. He felt that he was sinking, and yet his patience and cheerfulness were remarkable. He stayed mostly by the fire in the day-time, and often during the latter part of the night, for his cough was troublesome when he was in bed, and the oppression greater than when sitting up.

Our faithful physician, Dr. Stokes, attended him, but could do little for him except to alleviate the suffering. George co-operated with his efforts, being always ready to comply with his wishes, and to follow the directions given. But notwithstanding all efforts to check the disease, it made rapid progress. Thinking that a change might prove beneficial, he went to pass a few days with a friend; but finding himself fast declining, he was anxious to return home, and being favored to do so, he expressed much gratitude, seeming as if he could scarcely be thankful enough. He continued to go about the house and sometimes out of doors, until within five days of his death. Then he was suddenly prostrated, and became so ill that we had him moved into the nursery, where I could attend him during the day, and his brother be with him at night.

He expressed a wish to see his mother and sister, and requested me to write to them, thinking that his sister could come on.

When I would leave the room I could hear him

engaged in prayer, so that I perceived he was aware of his critical situation. Though his sufferings increased he seemed to be in a Heavenly frame of mind—all peace and serenity.

Upon my return to him after a time of absence, he said, "I have had a suffering time. I am in much misery, and I have not been able to lie down." I told him I was sorry that I had to leave him, and that I had felt anxious about him. "I know it; I got into a little doze, and dreamed that you had come," he replied, with emotion. I then said, Does thy mind feel comfortable? "Yes, yes," was his reply. I told him I thought he had always been a good boy, for he had been dutiful and faithful while living with us. To this he assented with tears.

He often addressed his brother in terms of affection, such as "John, you are such a comfort to me."

One morning he said, "Oh, I have had a wearisome night, 'wearisome nights are appointed unto me.'" After the visit of the doctor, on that morning, he inquired, "What does the doctor say?" I answered, "He says both of thy lungs are diseased, but he and we will do what we can to make thee comfortable." "All has been done," he exclaimed, and then, after a solemn pause, added, "I can't stay long; I am so weak I must go soon. There are a good many that I should like to see. Has some one written to my sister? Then I want to see William and Lilly and other cousins living in Philadelphia." He also wanted to have his love sent to his former mistress, Fitz Hugh—for whom he expressed great regard—to his mother and other relatives and friends, adding emphatically, " yes—to everybody." His feelings seemed to be expended in love. Quite frequently he uttered ejaculations, such as " Mercy ! Mercy ! Oh, Merciful Father, O Lord, save my soul ! I can't live long. Oh, take me home ! " Then he would turn to his brother and say, " Oh, John, don't grieve for me. Don't grieve ! I can't stay long with you." After one of these injunctions he said, " John, you will find my knife and some other things in my pocket."

To me he said, " I am afraid you are doing too much. Can't some one take your place and let you go to the table at meal times ? " Being assured that it was agreeable to me to wait on him he looked around and smiled.

When his cousins who had been sent for, came into the room, he looked at them calmly and said, " I am so glad to see you; I want you both to stay all night. I can't live long. I may live till night, but I think I cannot till morning. I have often asked that I might be blessed in sickness." I told him I thought he had been blessed, and I trusted that he would find rest in the end. He replied, " Yes, yes, O Lord, save my soul ! " Next morning the pains of death appeared to be coming on. He several times looked affectionately at his brother, and said " Oh, John, don't hold me ! Don't hold me, but let me go." Once adding, " I want to go home, to the other world, where I came from. Oh, I want to go to rest!" The expression of his countenance gave evidence of the sweet frame of mind that he was in, and of his resignation to the Divine will.

He wanted to have a hymn sung, but thought it was *almost too much* to ask. I told him his cousins might sing. After the hymn I told him that I had prayed for his easy passage out of time ; and that I trusted his change would be a happy one, for it had appeared to me that his soul was pure and spotless; and that I hoped those of us who were spared a little longer might so live as to meet him in that happy state where there shall be no more parting, and where all tears shall be wiped from our eyes. He serenely gave a look of sanction to these words.

The oppression became so great that the windows had to be raised, cold as the weather was, to enable him to get a little more breath. His expression was, "to get a little breath pains me through my whole body." Some of his friends coming in, he said to one of them, " Henry, won't you sing a hymn for me ; I am almost gone ? " In a short time the doctor came, and found him sinking. After a slight struggle he leaned over against his brother and calmly breathed his last, like one falling into a sweet sleep.

Thus passed away his spirit from its earthly tabernacle, and entered, as we reverently believe, into that rest prepared for the people of God.

Many of his friends; and of our friends and neighbors, attended his funeral—about fifty colored persons were there—when, after a solemn season, his remains were deposited in Friends' Burial-ground at Westfield.

I think I shed tears enough for both his mother and sister, who were far away and could not be present; they were tears that would not be kept back, and were accompanied with gratitude for his peaceful close.

It seemed as if our family felt the prevalence of love; no lonely feeling, no terror in the house while the corpse remained there. It must have been because of the quietness of his close. Surely there is a Power, all love, to keep us tranquil in times of trial.

TO THE YOUTH.

[Published in *Friends' Intelligencer*, vol. XIII., pages 164-165.]

" Be ye also ready, that though called early, ye may go in peace."

Died, at Colerain, Ohio, Fourth Month 22nd, 1856, of consumption, Anna B., daughter of Isaac Wells, aged twenty-three years.

She was for several years very delicate, yet, having a great desire to be a teacher, applied herself closely to the cultivation of her mind, and (self-aided almost) made such progress as enabled her to instruct in the primary branches. After being engaged for some time to the satisfaction of her employers, she believed it right to spend a few months in a boarding-school, that she might become better qualified for that service. She entered in the autumn of 1854, and though often feeble, pursued her studies as diligently as her bodily strength would allow. Being of an amiable disposition, she established herself in our affections, and we were willing to hope that she would enjoy better health. In 1855, she attended Philadelphia Yearly Meeting, at the close of which she walked in the rain to the ferry, and rode in the stage without drying her shoes. She contracted a heavy cold, and her health declined, though (for two weeks), she was able to attend school part of each day, but, at length she had to relinquish her intention and return home. A few weeks after, she wrote to me for a *recommendation*, intending to take a school; so lively was her interest in the children of their neighborhood, whose opportunities were very limited, and her concern that they might have a religious, guarded education. At length she felt the disease, which had been *slowly* progressing, was *rapidly* gaining ground; and she could labor no longer. In quiet resignation she yielded. She was not surprised nor alarmed, for it had seemed for years, that " death was in all her thoughts." She expressed much to those around her while on a bed of languishing, of the fulness of peace in prospect before her, in view of her release from this world of trial and change.

A few days before her close a well disposed neighbor inquired if she would not wish to converse with a minister about spiritual things. She replied, " It matters not—my mind is fixed, my peace is made. I fear not death. I only crave my departure may be easy.

Death has no terror, the grave no victory ; for my soul triumphs over death, hell, and the grave."

She told her dear parents not to think hard of her because she went to boarding school (they having discouraged her on account of her feeble health.) "My peace," said she "seemed to be in it. I am glad I went." The evening before her close, she called her brother William to her and addressed him — "Dear brother, do not hold me; let me go to the realms of bliss above, beyond all pain and suffering. Pray for me to be set free this very night if it be my Heavenly Father's will." To her father she said, "I feel my end approaching," and then appeared in fervent supplication, "O Lord Jesus, receive my spirit! yea, Lord, this *moment*, if such be thy will; nevertheless, not my will, but thine, O God! be done." After this she suddenly revived and said, "I have something on my mind for *some* present—all sit down—my blessed Lord has prolonged my life one night more." Then told her brothers her wish, and requested a private interview with her father, to whom she relieved her mind — asked her brother Levi to read several chapters in the New Testament, and remained very cheerful and easy till daybreak. Then asked for a basin of water, washed her hands and face, adjusted her hair and cap, and folded her hands, saying, "Now, Lord, I am ready and wait thy will." She continued in supplication, and passed so quietly away that none present could discern when the vital spark fled. Her brother, in his letter to me says : " So easy, so tranquil, so triumphant a death none present ever before witnessed."

M. S. L.

MOORESTOWN, N. J., Fifth Month 12th, 1856.

[An account of the illness and death of her husband. Taken from a letter written to her valued friends Robert and Susanna Hatton.]

Second Month 21st, 1858.—I write to inform you that my beloved husband has been removed from our midst, full of years, ready and patiently awaiting the appointed time for his change. For several months his suffering was very great, but his patience, cheerfulness and resignation were remarkable. His faithful attendance of our religious meetings, and his solid, weighty deportment when there gathered with Friends (even after he was unable to sit up long at a time, being mostly in bed save while at meeting), is also worthy of remark. Six weeks before his death, when he was, with full unity, replaced by the meeting in the station of Elder, he told me he felt no desire that it should be so, as his work was done ; adding that he felt sweet and continued peace for his faithfulness, and the assurance that he had, through life, endeavored to serve his Divine Master. Though he felt that he had done very little good in the world, yet he had, according to his convictions of right, endeavored to perform his duties, and was now being rewarded with a feeling of continual peace.

He was sustained through great bodily suffering, and preserved in clearness of mental faculties, till a few hours previous to his close—the change taking place gradually. When the heart refused to receive the returning current, he had a spasm. After this had subsided he breathed quietly for about five minutes, and then calmly passed away.

After death the countenance retained its serene and pleasant expression, looking as though in a sweet sleep.

For about thirty-six hours before his close, his throat was so sore, and the oppression was so great, that he could not lie down.

He took entirely to his bed on Sixth-day, and died the following Third-day, ninth inst., at half-past five in the afternoon. He was so emaciated that he desired not to keep his bed, so long as his strength would admit of his reclining in an easy chair.

Very many of our friends and relatives called to see him, and to aid in waiting on him, during the last few days. To these he spoke occasionally, though with great difficulty, telling them of his comfort and his confidence, saying that he had placed himself in the care of the Great Supreme. When looking around upon some of his nieces and nephews, he said to them, "These feelings you must all know."

His serene countenance lighted up with a smile as he looked at us in his agony, to assure us of his happiness. Oh, may I ever retain and keep fresh the remembrance of this look!

During the last few weeks, when he plainly saw that the end was drawing near, he had everything made ready, so far as practicable, that he might leave all as easy for us as was possible for it to be.

As time passed on he desired more and more to be in the quiet, and though pleased to see his friends, he said but little. He enjoyed having his family with him, in silence, and wished especially that *I* should be near him. Much of the time he was engaged in prayer, and not for himself alone but for others also. The young people were especially the objects of his solicitude, that they might love the Truth and not care so much for dress and fashion. The Society of Friends was near his heart, its testimonies and its principles, its order and its *sound doctrines.* I trust that his precepts, strengthened as they were by his example, will not be lost.

On the day of the funeral the weather was clear and cold, and the company very large. There was a solemn hush over all. It was the first coffin and the first grave that ever looked to me like a comfortable home for the earthly tabernacle. Powerful testimonies were borne by several Friends—J. H., and J. T., among others, speaking of his uprightness as a pillar in the Church, as a neighbor beloved, as a devoted friend to the poor, as well as a tender, loving husband and father.

His was, indeed, a long and useful life. He gave away hundreds of dollars to the poor; and even when in straits himself he divided his means with others.

There was no bitterness in his heart against any ; as he said, " To his own Master every man must stand or fall," adding, " those who are in the Truth shall stand ; but those who are fighting against it, must fall."

We shall feel our stripping very much indeed, for we have lost a dear friend and father ; but we have a Father in Heaven in whom we trust, and whose goodness and mercy still endure. The continued assurance that the dear departed is in the full fruition of bliss, rejoices my soul.

We enjoyed our life together, checkered though it was, for we were joined in that union that death cannot dissolve ; and I look toward meeting him where parting shall be no more.

May the blessing of preservation attend us all through life, is the desire of your friend,

M. S. L.

[The following extracts from two letters to her grandson, give the only account that we have from her pen, of the last days of her daughter Jane.]

Second Month 13th, 1885.—She is still living, but very low. She has been a great sufferer, and still suffers much at times, and is very, very weak. Mentally she is bright, entirely resigned, and desirous to be released at the right time. Indeed, for the past five years, since she has been sick, and often a great sufferer, she has known what the result would be. Several weeks ago, knowing that she was failing, she had all

16

her affairs arranged, and has since given directions for funeral, interment, &c. She has requested that all be *plain* and *quiet*. Thy aunt Phebe is with us, and expects to remain until after the change. To her, Jane made known her wishes as to the arrangements after death, and then as if turning her mind from earthly things, she said to the doctor, "Everything is now ready, and I can die in peace." Every day she looks with hope toward the close, though she desires to be patient, as has been the case during her long illness, which she has accepted so cheerfully. She has, as is not unusual with consumptives when near their close, a dread of strangling or choking with phlegm, but the doctor soothes her by telling her that he thinks she will pass off easily, as was the case with thy father.

Many of her friends and relatives have visited her, and much kindness has been manifested by bringing or sending delicacies to tempt her appetite, and beautiful flowers for her to look upon. For the past few weeks she has not been able to see much company, and now she can see scarcely any, without increasing her suffering.

We are so glad that thee and Isaac came last winter, when she was able to enjoy your society. We knew then that she could not live a great while; and now, though a close trial to part with her, yet we are thankful to have had her spared so long; and still more so, to see her aware of her situation, and yet resigned and happy. We feel that we cannot ask to have her live, if she must continue to suffer.

She would have been glad to see Lizzie and Richard, but now she can only send love, with desires for your welfare, in which we join.

Second Month 22nd, 1885.—I write to thee as soon as I feel that I can. We should have been comforted to have you with us, but knowing that you could not come, we did not expect you. That our feelings were together we well knew; and this helped to compensate for your absence in person.

Jane's sufferings for most of the time after the first change—about forty-eight hours before the final one— were very great, but with wonderful patience she bore all. Her resignation and peace continued, and she made a touching appeal that our prayers with hers might ascend for her *release*, if to her Heavenly Father it should seem right to grant this request.

From the frequent accumulation in her throat, and her inability to raise much, on account of her weakness, she dreaded strangulation.

The last night was, indeed, severe, and it was hard for us to witness her suffering, which we were unable to relieve, and we could only try to comfort her. Several times she spoke of the lightness of her afflictions when compared with those of the blessed Jesus, both in the Garden and on Calvary.

About day-break she experienced a little alleviation of her suffering, but the change that was coming came fast: she passed quietly away, sensible and clear in mind, till her hand dropped from Margaret's.

Everything had been said, done, devised and made ready, as clearly and calmly as if about to start on an earthly journey. For several years she had known what was coming, and felt resigned to the event, though she said if she could be well she would like to stay with us, for she had such a happy life, and so loved her family and her friends.

She was the recipient of much kindness and attention from our friends, and everything that it was thought might aid or comfort her, physically, was furnished. Her love and gratitude seemed abounding; and after her other messages had been left she said, "Mother, give my love to everybody."

Just at the last, dropsy set in, which caused a slight swelling of the face and made the corpse appear very life-like.

Everything in connection with her burial was done in accordance with the directions she had given. The funeral was large, both here and at Moorestown Meeting House. Phebe and myself did not go out, as we both were somewhat ailing.

The body was laid in the Friend's ground at Moorestown, where those of thy grandfather, thy father, our other children, and many near and dear ones repose. Their *remains* lie there, but we trust the immortal souls are at rest—so many gave full assurance thereof, and were favored to die in peace. Should the same be *our* portion, we shall reunite. The future is a promise of bliss, and this at the end crowns all.

You may judge of our trial and bereavement ; but we resigned the dear one, and did not desire to have her suffering prolonged. She was so happy, having neither doubts nor fears to disturb her, that we can only feel as if our loss is her eternal gain.

M. S. L.

CHAPTER V.

VERSES.

AN ASPIRATION.

POOR and distressed, I inward turn,
    To muse upon my woe ;
I feel depressed and deeply tried, -
    Oh ! whither shall I go?

To Thee, Great God ! my spirit turns,
    My soul in secret prays,
That Thou may keep me safe from harm,
    And shield me all my days.

I know I've grieved thy own dear Son,
    By turning back again,
From journeying in the narrow way,—
    Then why should I complain?

How raise my voice to Thee, and crave
    Thy mercy and thy love ;
When I so often turn aside,
    And disobedient prove?

Yet, I will raise my feeble voice,
    And for forgiveness pray,
That I may make thy will my choice,
    And own my devious way.

Mary S. Lippincott.

Be pleased, Almighty God ! to hear
  A trembling sinner's cry ;
Whose heart, once more, would turn to Thee,
  And on thy grace rely,

For daily strength to do thy will,
  And ne'er from Thee depart ;
Whose light can make the pathway plain,
  Whose love can change the heart.

Admit me into thine abode,
  To be a servant there ;
To go or come at thy command,
  And make my life a prayer.

1822.

THE STRUGGLE.

OH, how can I obedient rise
  To voice my Maker's praise :
How shall I ever bear the cross
  To tune *aloud* my lays?

In solitude I'd rather dwell,
  In dark oblivion's vale,
To view the face of man no more,
  Nor tell my piteous tale,—

Rather than face the multitudes,
  And preach the word of life :—
My human nature weakness pleads,
  And hence the constant strife.

One spirit says, "Give up, my child,
  And thou the way shalt see :"
The other,—"No, thou canst not preach,
  So come and follow me."

Sometimes, the first—which plainly speaks—
  I'm ready to obey :
Then comes the Reasoner, weakness pleads,
  And so I shrink away.

I'm tossed and whirled from side to side
  And ofttimes fear a fall ;
But still I find a Saviour near,
  Whose voice renews the call.

When shall I know a heart resigned
  To yield my stubborn will ;
To cast me down at Jesus' feet,
  His purpose to fulfill.

OVERCOMING TEMPTATION.

NOW let me count his mercies o'er,
  And praise my Maker's name ;
Rely on Him, forevermore,
  Whose power is still the same.

'Tis much I try my thoughts to guide,
  My passions fierce to curb ;
That I in meekness may abide,
  Where nought can peace disturb.

Yet still the tempter's baits are set
  To lead my mind astray,
To tangle me within his net,
  And drag me far away.

But oh! may He who reigns above,
  Still listen to my cry;
And, with a Father's tender love,
  Abounding grace supply.

In Him my hope is centered all,
  To Him alone I look,
To have transgressions washed away,-
  Sins blotted from his book.

Oh! will He hear my piteous cry?
  To me will He attend?
Will He extend his arm of love,
  And guide me to the end?

Poor and unworthy as I am,
  He does not me forget;
Tho' of his love I *feel* bereft
  He does not leave me yet.

My wanderings in a desert are,
  Where drink is hard to find;—
For Marah's waters taste of gall,
  With wormwood seem combined.

Yet still I hope to journey on,
  And reach that happy land
Which all the wandering pilgrims found,
  Who heeded *his* command.

Twelfth Month 29th, 1823.

Life and Letters of

REFLECTIONS.

On seeing the morning clouds disperse.

I SAW the clouds disperse in air,
  The sun break forth and shine ;
And thought the morn so fresh and fair,
  That pleasure would be mine :
      But ah ! for me, 'tis vanity
To hope for scenes so bright ;
      My joys have fled, in haste they sped,
And left my saddened soul in gloom of wintry night.

Days of my childhood, ye were sweet !
  My brother, thou wast dear !
How oft we joyful used to meet,
  Nor dream of trouble near.
      We little knew, the word adieu
Should pass our lips so soon,—
      In early day, thou fled away,
Like as the morning dew, gone long before the noon.

Thy transient tarriance, here below,
  Oft fills my heart with grief ;
But while I weep, I'm brought to know
  Wherein to seek relief.
      There is a God whose chastening rod
His children all must feel ;
      That they may find true peace of mind,
Which to devoted ones He will, in time, reveal.

Then, since 'tis thus, dry up, ye tears !
  Ye sighs, be heard no more !

Begone, afflicting, troubling fears !
  Gone with the days of yore:—
    I'll strive to raise my heart in praise
To God, who gave us birth ;
    This troubled mind, then, then shall find-
The fountain of true peace flows pure from Heaven not earth.

First Month 16th, 1825.

NATURE.

AND what *is* Nature? Can the mind of man
    With all its boasted powers, the word explain?
Dare he presume its mysteries to scan,
    That so no shadow of a doubt remain
    How aught was formed, and nothing formed in vain?

And what *is* Nature? Is yon blue expanse,
    Spread like a canopy our heads above,
Besprinkled o'er with sparkling gems to enhance
    Jehovah's goodness, and Jehovah's love, —
    The source of life, the spring which all doth move?

And what *is* Nature? Do the trees that wave
    Their branches in the breeze that gently blows,
Know more than we the Almighty Power that gave
    Them place on earth to flourish and repose :—
    Are not all these effects, his bounty to disclose?

Ah, yes ! And man their beauties may survey,
    Admire the graces in each form combined,
And learn the genuine cause of this display—
    Though Nature called—is God, forever kind
    To impart instruction to the inquiring mind.

TRUTH.

WHAT is that orb of radiant light
  Whose rays dispel the gloom of night,
      And gild perpetual day ;—
Is it the sun our eyes behold,
Each day his bright'ning beams unfold,
Round which this earth so oft has rolled,
      And still rolls on her way?

Ah, no ! More glorious 'tis, by far,
Than is that brightly beaming star
      Which shines upon our sphere.
'Tis Truth dispenses light and heat,
And clothes, with panoply complete,
Our minds, that thus enjoyment sweet,
      The passing hours may cheer.

Truth, from the fount of Heavenly joy,
Its crystal streams, without alloy,
      Shall in our bosoms pour—
As we are zealous to prepare,
Now, in our youth, a channel there,
'Twill free from harm and every snare,
      And fit for Canaan's shore.

RENSSELAERVILLE, N. Y.

Mary S. Lippincott.

HYMN.

TO Thee, O God, I raise mine eyes !
　Be pleased to hear my feeble cries ;
Look down with pity from above ;
And fill my heart with Heavenly love !

'Tis much I need a Saviour's smile
To keep me free from Satan's wile,
Preserve my heart from wilful wrong,
And safely, gently, lead along.

Oh leave me not, my Guide, my love !
But try me oft, my heart to prove,
And bring me nearer home to Thee
Where I shall be forever free.

Teach me to do thy holy will,
All thy Divine commands fulfill,—
To spread thy glorious truths abroad,
And turn the wanderer's heart to God.

I have not kept thy Word alway,
But turned aside from day to day ;
Have wandered from the path of Truth,
And been a proud, rebellious youth.

But now to Thee, O Lord ! I turn,
And while my lamp holds out to burn,
I'll seek forgiveness for the past,
And strength to serve Thee to the last.

Be Thou my hope, my strength, my shield,
Then, with thy aid, my heart I'll yield ;
I'll journey on my Heavenly way,
And bear thy yoke from day to day.

HYMN.

THOU only knowest, God of love,
How vain, how foolish, I should prove,
    If left to choose my way ;
Be, therefore, pleased to keep me low ;
Keep me from wandering to and fro,
When much I strive and fain would go
    Far, far from Thee astray.

Be pleased to guide me, all my days,
And teach my voice to lisp thy praise,
    My heart thy will to do :—
No more I ask, no more I crave,
Than this to know, to feel I have,
Thy presence near, thy arm to save
    Thy love my soul to woo.

———

TO A. J. T.

FEW are our pleasures here below,
    And quickly they must pall ;
The world appears a beauteous show,
But those who view shall surely know
Its dazzling splendor is but woe,
And darkness brings on all.

In early life my fancy viewed
A scene of perfect bliss,
Within this dreary solitude,
This wilderness so wild and rude,
I thought no grief would e'er intrude,
To blast my happiness.

Mary S. Lippincott.

But, ah, how soon the vision fled ;
I disappointment found ;
My cheerful moments from me sped,
And with them joys my heart had read,
And hopes that had profusely spread
My youthful bower around.

A gloomy aspect then
    All Nature seemed to wear ;
I looked toward Heaven, and sighed
    For early entrance there :
Then, humbled and resigned,
    I felt a Father's love ;
A holy quiet clothed my mind,
    Which came from God above.

And though we taste of deep distress,
May we not dare complain ;
For He who wounds intends to bless,
If we our griefs sustain.
And now, farewell ! Time hastes away ;
Its sands will soon be run ;
Then may our Saviour sweetly say
" Rest—for thy work is done."

A PRAYER.

THOU, Great, Supreme, Propitious, Merciful,
    Whose smile is ecstasy, whose frown is grief !
Why was my soul so bowed ? Spirits depressed ?
Have my vain, wand'ring thoughts unbidden trode
Imagination's round ; and with a zest,
Unseemly in thy sight, indulged in themes

Unripe for contemplation, and forbid
Yet to be nurtured in affection's soil,
While doubt and darkness veil the future scenes?
If so, O Lord, forgive thy erring child !
Restrain my ardent feelings, and confine
My thoughts within the limits of thy love !
Oh, teach my heart, in Thee alone to trust ;
To fix its purposes and rest its hopes !
For all on earth is restless as the waves
That rise and fall by agitating winds,
And bury in the deep man's fondest hopes,
Ingulf his treasures, and frustrate his plans.

—

LINES ADDRESSED TO R. S.

MY heart with sympathy afresh doth glow,
        And gladly would the healing balm bestow ;
If thou art free to tell me thy distress,
Perhaps thy cup of sorrow will be less :
Thy throbbing breast may feel a calm relief,
By thus imparting to a friend thy grief.
And oh, dear sister ! there is One on High,
Whose ear is open to each secret sigh—
He knows thy state, remembers thee in love,
And He thy never-failing Friend will prove.
Be not dismayed, for there is nought to fear ;
His guardian-angel presence still is near.
For his pavilion is a refuge sure,
And in it all his children dwell secure.
Though waters rise, and howling tempests blow
Around thy dwelling, threat'ning to o'erthrow ;

His Holy Hand is underneath to save
Thy soul from sinking in the watery grave.
Then courage take, and to the port of peace
Press on with faith, and strength will yet increase;
Thou'lt reach the goal of rest beyond the skies,
Where holy anthems to the throne arise;
The face of God, there ever to behold,
And rest with angels in thy Shepherd's fold.

PARTING LINES.

Addressed to a Companion at Rensselaerville.

THE approaching hour is near,
    When thou and I must part, perhaps forever.
Sad, solemn thought! yet should it be e'en so,
That observation ne'er again shall bring
Thy form to view; still there exists
A precious cement in the hidden life,
Which even gray old Time cannot dissolve.
Though his destructive scythe may sweep away
All sublunary grandeur; level down
The pomp of monarchs and the pride of men;
Our love shall change not, if we keep in view
The goal of peace beyond this fleeting scene,
And fix our hopes on High. For from the fount
There flows a gentle stream of love Divine,
Binding together, as with silver cords,
The spirits of the righteous, even here,
Before dismantled of these robes of clay.
I leave, but not forget thee. Thou shalt still—

At seasons when all Nature's hushed around,
And silence reigns—fit time for contemplation—
Have place in memory of thy distant friend.
Fond memory shall, well pleased, recall the hours
Which we, in converse sweet, together passed,
Beneath the roof of our parental friend
Whose love extended to his little flock,
And from his lips sweet counsel ofttimes flowed,
Which raised our spirits when sore prest with care.
O sister! may we nevermore forget
Favors which boundless Goodness has bestowed,
When, in his love, He made our cups run o'er,
And gave us joy for sorrow, bliss for woe!
Farewell, dear friend! I go : from loved ones go ;
The many who my fond affections share.
I go to kindred, friends of early days,
A mother—sweetest friend this earth affords—
From whose sweet lips dropt ofttimes out
The comprehensive words—"Be good, for that is all ;
All, my dear children that I ask of you." * * *
May choicest blessings rest upon thy head,
Pure from the unmeasured Source of life and love,
Forever be thy heart the Lord's to do his will :
So, when a few more years have rolled around,
And Nature's powers have waned, their vigor spent,
Then may thy sun go down without a cloud,
And thy enfranchised soul, from earth released,
Soar far away into the realms of light.
There we may meet, if hand in hand we go,
(Though distant far our fragile frames may be
One from the other) as hopeful pilgrims to
A far-off land, to join our Master there.

A THOUGHT.

WHY have I left all serious thought,
    To seek those pleasures dearly bought ;
And which, ere this, I have been taught
        Are nought but vanity?

Why have I not my will resigned,
And left all foolish things behind ;
Seeking to God for strength of mind,
        In true sincerity?

'Tis in that state we're brought to know
The vanity of things below,
So as with joy to let them go,
        For pure simplicity.

AN ASPIRATION.

TO Thee, my God, this morn I raise
    My voice, thy glorious name to praise,
        And tune anew my lyre ;
Be pleased, once more, to condescend,
And to my feeble cry attend—
Be Thou my Father, Guide and Friend,
        My inmost soul inspire.

This heart has oft been known to stray :
Has deviated from thy way,
        More times than I can tell ;
Yet still, with faith, I look on Thee.
Poor and unworthy though I be,
Desiring Thou wilt chasten me.
        Till fit with Thee to dwell.

BLESS US, O FATHER, BLESS!

Written, probably, on the day of her Marriage.

THEE we adore! Thy presence now we seek,
　To strengthen and sustain, for we are weak;
Though bound by love to join in wedlock's bands,
Yet to confirm the pledge, strengthen our hands.
Oh, raise our hearts by faith to trust in Thee,
That kind and faithful we may ever be.
Should joys attend us, may our prayers ascend,
As incense offered to the Lord, our Friend;
Or, if affliction be our portion here,
Still grant us grace, thy goodness to revere:
No less our Friend when sorrows bow us down,
Than when the stream of joy flows smoothly on.
Be thou our light, to guide us on our way
From earth's bewildering shades to endless day.

TO MY HUSBAND.

THOUGH trials are our portion while passing through this
　scene,
They sometimes are permitted, our love from earth to wean.
Thou feelest desolation pervade thy troubled breast,
While harrowing cares and hopes destroyed disturb thy wonted
　rest.
Thou travelest in secret, along thy lonely way,
Desiring still to keep thine eye upon the star of day;
And oh, dear one, be not dismayed, nor yield thou to despair,
But know in all thy trials sore my soul doth freely share.
I've drunk of sorrow's bitter cup, have felt some poignant
　grief,

Yet on my Saviour's bosom I have always found relief ;
And there, my dear companion, let thy fond hopes be stayed,
Then, of the storms and tempests thou need not be afraid.
Although thou dost not feel it, thy God is with thee still ;
Preparing thee more fully to do his holy will ;
He's drawing thy affections, from earth's bewitching ties,
And staining all their beauty in thy *now anointed* eyes ;
That thou mayst view the glory, reserved in Heaven above,
And, numbered with God's children, be sealed with holy love.
Though adverse winds may raise the waves that threaten to
    o'erwhelm,
Keep faith and hope in constant view, and thou the tide shalt
    stem.
A language of encouragement I feel to thee is due,
As is thy day, thy strength shall be, thy journey to pursue.
Within the mighty waters his chamber beams are laid,
So, though thy bark be tossed thereon, thou need not be
    afraid ;
For He'll arise from slumbering, and bid the tempest cease,
Then steer thy course for Canaan's shore, the only land of
    peace.
He'll give, in place of sorrow, those joys that perish not ;
And thus thy former trials will almost be forgot.
Whom the Lord loves He chastens, now as in former days,
For which, in times of favor, we oft are filled with praise.
I do believe, my cherished one, the Lord is choosing thee,
A vessel stampèd with holiness, within his house to be.
Oh, my beloved companion ! may we again renew
Our covenants, our confidence, and then our way pursue ;
The way to Zion's holy mount, to offer incense there,
And to pass our fleeting hours and days in deep and fervent
    prayer ;

With our tent spread in the valley, where Heavenly dews de-
　　scend,
With Jesus for our constant, and our never-failing friend ;
For under his pavilion, no foes can e'er prevail,
Although they may encamp around, and threaten to assail.
Then though the world against us, with hostile arms arise,
It shall not e'en disturb our peace, for God can hear our cries.
Then may the Lord, in mercy, be with us, day by day,
And give us strength and courage to drive all our doubts
　　away.
Farewell, by pen and paper ! Oh, Lord ! our souls do keep :
Until at last we slumber, in unawakening sleep ;
Then bear us to a mansion safe, of never-ending rest,
And bid us join triumphant, the number of the blest.

CHESTERVILLE, N. J., Third Month 1st, 1830.

"THE STAR."

A Periodical, edited by four boys; brothers.

A STAR announced the Saviour's birth,
　　When He appeared in flesh ;
Glad tidings rang throughout the earth,
　　And joy sprang up afresh.

The wise men journeyed on their way,
　　And lightly trod the ground ;
Until the star was seen to stay
　　O'er where the child was found.

Though many years have passed us by,
　　Since that eventful day ;
Another, shining brilliantly,
　　Again may light our way,

And lead to where the children are
Who, innocent and gay,
Convey instruction, through the "The Star,"
To light the youthful way.

Fifth Month 3rd, 1848.

TO GEORGE HATTON.

On the Death of his Wife.

GOOD is the Lord, and good his gifts to man—
   Tho', in his wisdom, He should take away
The earthly prop, leaning on which he ran
The race before him, as *she* smoothed the way :
But *this* to try his faith, to test his love,
That his firm hold on Heaven, He thus may prove.
Shall man distrust, and cast away his shield,
As though with oil he had not been anointed ;
While called to labor in the harvest field,
And seeing plain the work to him appointed?
Ah, no ! dear brother ! Help Divine is near,
And in the flaming bush God *does* appear.
His voice thou knowest, when in language sweet,
He calls thee forth to preach his glorious word,
On holy ground thou stands ; from off thy feet
Go put thy shoes ; again gird on "the sword"—
That powerful weapon which lops sin away,
And gains the passport to eternal day.
Sinners are made to tremble when they hear
The solemn truths which instruments declare :
How glorious do the feet of these appear
To those who would for peace and rest prepare.

Then gird on strength ; let gladness clear thy brow ;
As valiant once, so valiant be thou now.
And in thy turn, when all thy work is done,
When from thy labor thou art called to rest,
No sorrow, sighing, grief shall then be known,
But joy and gladness—blest, forever blest,
Thy soul immortal—freed from bonds of clay—
Shall wing its flight to everlasting day.

First Month 19th, 1850.

STANZAS.

Found, on a paper used as a marker, in the Bible of M. S. L.

WE ask, Who shall ascend on High,
        To scan the world of spirits?
To see the glory—majesty—
        Each ransomed soul inherits?

No eye untouched—with healing salve—
        By God's own finger, e'er
Can see the brilliant crowns they have
        Who dwell forever there.

The vulture's eye beholdeth not,
        The lion's whelp ne'er treads
The path—that consecrated spot—
        In which *his* spirit leads.

The eye of Faith discerns the way
        Emmanuel's sons have trod ;
Which, bright'ning to the perfect day,
        Ends in the House of God.

Ninth Month 21st, 1857.

Mary S. Lippincott.

LIFE.

HOW short is life! Alas, how soon
    The morning verges into noon,
      The noon to sombre night;
But sweet the noon, and bright the day,
To those who walk in wisdom's way
      Loved children of the Light.

Though morn and noon have passed you by,
And evening's shades are drawing nigh,
      The night will bring you rest:
For not in vain, your lives were given;
To aid the needy you have striven,
      And such are ever blest.

Through straits and trials we must go
Along our pathway here below;
      For 'tis the lot of all;
Sinner and saint temptations have,
But God is ever near to save
      Those who upon Him call.

A *beacon light* is placed within,
To show the right, to warn from sin—
      And he that will obey,
Can journey on with faith preserved
In God, whom he has loved and served—
      To lead him on his way.

ON THE DEATH OF MY HUSBAND.

OH, what a blank ! A sad and aching void !
　　Yet do I feel a sweetness, everywhere,
In contemplation of the past, the happy years
We passed together : he a partner kind,
My staff, my armor-bearer : how he loved
The truths held dear by me ; how paved my way
For the fulfilment of some work required.

Death came, not unexpected. Long he looked,
And waited long in quietude and patience,
Till that hour when the final call should come,
The voice be heard—"Come to the marriage feast."
With joy he hailed the messenger ; with calm
And smiling face he looked upon us all
Even in agony, was much conveyed
(Though power to speak had failed him) of the strength,
Support and fortitude with which he bore
The wearing out of that which mortal was ;
His trust was in Jehovah. To *his* care
He looked, in Him reposed all faith and hope ;
On Him relied to bear him safely through
The gates of death, and lift his soul to life.

Fifth Month 16th, 1858.

MY DEPARTED HUSBAND.

AH ! know'st thou, dear departed, how I fare ;
　　Alone, retired, with none my griefs to share ?
For, by my side, I thee no more behold,
But sad and lone, my weary arms I fold.

Mary S. Lippincott. '

No mortal knows, or can, the widow's state ;
Left, like a dove, to mourn her missing mate—
Did not Kind Providence design our good,
In being left to dwell in solitude?
Did I not view it so, could I sustain
The load of grief assigned, and not complain?
But, as it is, my soul contritely gives
To God the glory, and his love receives.

As late I walked beside thy narrow grave,
    And felt that all was gone which made earth dea
To God, alone, I looked, my soul to save,
    And strengthen me, my weight of grief to bear.

Third Month 27th, 1859.

APPENDIX.

Extracts from the "Scrap Book" of Mary S. Hallowell.

A LETTER FROM JOHN MOTT.

Dearly Beloved Children of Westtown Family:—After attending meeting to-day at this place, in which we were once more favored with the ownings of Israel's Shepherd, I felt a salutation of love to you, as dear children of the family of our Heavenly Father, whom I love in the Truth. The encouraging language which arises in my mind to address you with is, "The righteous also shall hold on his way, and he that hath clean hands shall grow stronger and stronger." Hold on your way, dear children, *that way* which many of you have been favored to see. Although it is a way of self-denial and the daily cross, wherein we have to deny ourselves all things which we believe to be wrong, yet I have a testimony in my heart, obtained by living experience, that it's a way of pleasantness, a path of substantial peace. Hold on then, in this blessed way, I entreat you, as a father that loves you, that those good desires which many of you feel in your minds may be strengthened, your hands being washed in innocency from the defilements and spots of this world's spirit, so that you may acceptably compass the altar of your God.

Accept this little tribute of my affectionate regard, and be sure, dear children, above all things keep in remembrance your Creator, in the days of your youth, and believe me, the observance of this counsel (which I trust is imparted through the flowings of the love of God) is not a vain thing unto you. Farewell!

JOHN MOTT.

"Ancient Memoranda."

[Sources, except of the first, not given by M. S H.]

I.

" Be it remembered that on the 12th day of First Month, in the
year 1670, in the dwelling-house of Thomas Camm, of Cammgill, within
the County of Westmoreland, was present Matthew Jepson of Lancaster, and Rebecca Camm, of the aforesaid Cammgill, when and
where the said Matthew Jepson did, voluntarily and publicly, marry
and take to wife the said Rebecca Camm, and hereof we whose names
are underwritten, amongst many others are witnesses.

Thomas Camm, John Strong, Thomas Green, and sixteen other
Friends."

A true copy, taken by H. H., from the original, which was on
a piece of paper four inches broad, and six inches long, in the possession of M. Jepson of Lancaster.

II.

"At a Monthly Meeting held at Falmouth, this second of Eleventh
Month, 1673, Friends having met together in the fear of the Lord,
found all things well and in order, and so departed in love, giving
God the glory—who is blessed forever."

III.

" Twentieth of Ninth Month, 1688.   It is concluded that the
Friends appointed in every Particular Meeting, shall give notice publicly in the meeting, that cross-pockets before men's coats, side slopes,
broad hems on cravats, and over full skirted coats, are not allowed
by Friends."

IV.

" Seventeenth of Ninth Month, 1691.   It being discovered that
the common excess of smoking Tobacco is inconsistent with our holy
profession, this meeting adviseth that such as have occasion to make
use of it, take it privately, neither in their labor nor employment, nor
by the highway, nor [at] ale-houses, nor elsewhere, too publicly."

V.

"First of Fifth Month, 1693. Minute seventh before a Query offered to the Quarterly Meeting, concerning Friends making, ordering, or selling striped cloths, silks or stuffs, or any sort of flowered, figured things of different coulars ; it is the judgement of the Quarterly Meeting that Friends ought to stand clear of such things."

SOME ACCOUNT OF THE CONVERSION OF A DEIST.

BY JACOB GREAVES.

On my way home from Baltimore Yearly Meeting, I fell in company with Jacob Hocket, from Wabash, Indiana. In the course of conversation he gave me the following account of a man that had been a confirmed deist, many years. One morning he said, " I am sixty years old to-day : I will go to Quaker Meeting ! " He accordingly went to one which Priscilla Hunt attended. After the meeting was gathered and still, she arose and spoke thus : " I am sixty years old to-day. I will go to Quaker Meeting." These words I believe were spoken this morning by one that is present, whose mind is in a dreadful situation. I know not who it is. She then described his condition, and said that as arguments would arise in his mind she would confute them as pointedly as if she heard him speak them (to which he since owns), till he was entirely disarmed of them all. She then sat down, but in a few moments rose again, and asserted that she had gained her point ; that he was divested of his false arguments ; and unless he should again solicit the revival of them, he might live in that way which would lead to peace and salvation.

On the next meeting day he attended again, when Priscilla kneeled in supplication ; he also kneeled, which very much astonished those present.

After meeting he made known the state of his mind, and soon after requested to be received into membership with Friends, since which time he has lived the life of a steady, sober, religious Friend— that is to say for two years.

MISCELLANEOUS PAPERS.

A JOURNEY TO OHIO.

Eighth Month 24th, 1854.—We left home about eight o'clock, A. M., met our friends in Philadelphia, took lunch, and before one P. M., were on the "lightning train," bound for Wheeling, *via* Baltimore. In fifty-two minutes we were in Wilmington, and in time proportionate at Havre de Grace. The weather being warm, and the road dusty, the change from car to boat, though for a short time, was delightful. The cool and gentle breeze from the water was exhilarating, and the undulating motion of the boat caused the sunbeams to play prettily on the surface. The prospect on either side of the river was pleasing, and the country through which we passed, though somewhat dry, indicated for the most part a favorable season, thus presenting a scene cheering to the eye of the beholder, and gladdening to the heart of the industrious husbandman. Nature seemed to smile as we viewed her in her varied aspects.

Evidences of man's ingenuity and perseverance are presented, travel where we may. Evidences, too, that if he will not be provident and labor for his sustenance, he must pay the penalty for his negligence, by suffering from want and misery.

We arrived in Baltimore about five o'clock. We took supper at a tavern, where we were supplied by a girl in her teens, who also took the place of bar-tender, and handed out the poisonous cup to the sterner sex. Poor girl! It grieved us to see one who, under right tuition, might rise to eminence, or at least move in a sphere more creditable to her womanhood, exposed to such degradation. But she was probably under the influence of parents whose lives reflect dishonor upon themselves, and bring misery upon their helpless offspring. We left her with a sigh, and again pursued our journey. We were comfortably accommodated in the ladies' saloon-car, and our only companion in the apartment was a lone woman bound for St. Louis.

The evening was fine, and our spirits were buoyant enough to enjoy the prospect so far as it should be visible after night-fall. We passed swiftly along from place to place, observing with interest the exhibition of the freaks of nature and the ingenuity of man. As the shades of night gathered around us, the prospect ahead, and the danger attendant upon midnight travel by railroad, through a mountainous region, caused serious reflections ; but with me all fears were hushed by the remembrance of the recommendation to trust in the care of Providence.

> " The Lord my pasture shall prepare,
> And lead me with a Shepherd's care ;
> His presence shall my wants supply,
> And guard me with a watchful eye.
> My noonday walks He shall attend
> And all my midnight hours defend "

We ascended the eastern slope of the Blue Mountains by a zig-zag course, and on our way met a long train of cars loaded with stone, passing rapidly by us, while our locomotive seemed to be jerking, and frequently stopping and starting. We observed that great precaution against accidents was taken, by way of lighting the track, watching the rails, testing the wheels of the cars, &c. In the tunnels, and at many of the curves, were stationary lamps of great brilliancy. The latter enabled us to see portions of the country through which we were wending our way. People work early and late, indoors and outdoors, each at his calling. At a late hour we saw a man plying his needle, perhaps to fulfill a promise and thus be true to his word, or possibly to provide for his wife and hopeful progeny the necessaries of life. It was near one A. M. when we neared Martinsburg, and heard the ringing of bells, the sound of music, and the voices of the multitude. The colored people, male and female, were hilarious as they " toated " their refreshments from car to car and offered them to the sleepy passengers. I told J. A. that many slaves were here, and repeated, in a loud whisper, some lines from my favorite Cowper :

> " I would not have a slave to till my ground,
> To carry me, to fan me while I sleep,
> And tremble when I wake, for all the wealth
> That sinews bought and sold have ever earned."

Perhaps this quotation, or else the supposition that we were "Quakers," drew around us our colored friends, from those of sombre shade to some who were almost white. One bright youth especially attracted me, for I thought that it only needed the skilful

18

artist to bring a choice piece of sculpture out of that stone—a man of eminence might be evolved from this boy of mirth.

As our train sped away, we enjoyed looking at the firmament, for the clear atmosphere enabled us to see the stars in all their brilliancy. Before reaching the Alleghenies the day dawned upon us, and as we ascended them the sun arose in all his brightness. Our way lay up giddy heights, while on one side of us were fearful precipices and on the other huge rocks or high lands with tall forest trees rising one above another. We looked down on the tops of tall trees, and yet were far beneath the roots of those on the other hand. Though dangerous to appearance, yet safe was our journey, and very extensive the grand panorama spread out before us.

At Oakland, a neat little village near the summit of the mountain, we had a comfortable breakfast, and were allowed sufficient time to take it without any haste.

We passed through several tunnels, one of which was 3,400 feet long. The darkness, though relieved by many lights, the coolness of the air, and the reverberated sound of bell and the different noises made by the train, produced a feeling of solemnity which must be *experienced* before it can be appreciated. It is exalting in its character, and it leads—as mighty works of nature, and wondrous feats of art always do lead—to an adoration of the First Cause of all.

In Western Virginia we began to see evidences of a parching drought, and the lively green of summer was changed to the dull yellow of autumn. There was a gentle breeze, and though clear above us, fog and floating white clouds were on the mountain side beneath.

About one P. M. we reached Wheeling, a place of considerable business, and enveloped in a cloud of smoke. Near the city are iron foundries, from the huge chimneys of which issues smoke ; and as the coal used is bituminous the smoke is very dark-colored, thick and oppressive. After an attempt to get rid of the coal dust, we left Wheeling in a vehicle called a hack, the manager of which rode on horseback, leaving Isaac to take the reins. We wound around the highlands on a plank road, on the verge, in many places, of precipices. We crossed the Ohio, and then went by a road so curving at one place, as nearly to form an O. A journey of five miles brought us to the home of Friend W., where we were cordially welcomed. The house is so elevated as to command an extensive prospect of hill and valley, timber-land and cleared farms. It is a fine agricultural country, and many of the farms do credit to their owners. Next morning we left this comfortable and hospitable abode, and were taken by I. W. six miles to meeting at Mount Pleasant. After meeting went to Samuel Griffith's, which is to be our home during the time of the Yearly Meeting.

Our hearts were saddened by the sight of the withering effects of the long continued drought. The ears of corn are shriveled, and the fields of withered pasture are brown and dusty. Flowers in door-yards are withered and fading in early bloom. The water supply is insufficient to satisfy the thirst of the cattle, which is increased by the prevalence of dust. There are many cases of dysentery in the different neighborhoods, and some Friends have been deterred from coming to Yearly Meeting on account of its reported prevalence. We have not found serious indisposition anywhere, and we ourselves, have been favored to keep remarkably well, notwithstanding the heat and drought.

Almost daily, gathering clouds were seen, but they would disperse before evening, and afford brilliant sunsets. So it continued during the week—hot, dry, and very dusty. The dependent farmer has to wait, not being able to command the clouds to distill the rain or to descend in gentle and refreshing dew.

On Third-day we dined at the home of E. Griffith, Samuel's mother. Her grandfather was a brother to John Woolman. On Fourth-day we were at Aaron Packer's, and on Fifth-day, at the close of the meeting, we went to Ann Packer's. Twenty-five Friends supped, lodged and breakfasted there.

Next morning started on our way to Salem. Stopped at Reason Baker's to dine. There is the same general aspect of drought, but it is relieved by strips of country that have been visited by refreshing showers. Before night-fall we arrived at Harlem Springs, where we passed the night at a comfortable hotel. It is a place of summer resort. Met a number of Friends going to their Yearly Meeting, of the other branch. Eleven of them, and the same number of us, passed the evening together very pleasantly. From the Springs we journeyed on, via Mechanicstown, &c., toward Salem. The drought, or the evidences of it, more distressing than any that we have heretofore seen. Cattle, sheep and swine look hungry, thirsty and hot; the trees have been stripped of their boughs, as far up as the cattle

could reach, and many large forest trees are about to die for want
of nutriment from the soil.

Our axle-tree broke, but we were kindly aided in getting it
repaired ; and while we were waiting in the barn, the wife of the
carpenter who lived at the place, and who had rendered such timely
aid, came out and invited us to dinner. She would take no denial,
so we went in, and were made very welcome. Their home had the
appearance of comfort and plenty.

We went on to William Reader's (in Samuel McLain's carriage)
and arrived there before night, fatigued, warm and dusty. William
and his wife Lydia, have an interesting family of children. Next
morning attended Sandy Spring Meeting, and went to David Batton's
to dine, and went thence over a very hilly road to Salem. The
gardens are parched, and water is too scarce to admit of its being
taken to irrigate them. Salem is a pretty place, even in this dry
season. We stopped with Samuel and Fanny Trip, and next day
rode out in a buggy to Samuel French's. After visiting at S. Hunt's
and calling on some other Friends, we left for home.

MOORESTOWN BOARDING SCHOOL.

This institution was so closely associated with the life of our
subject, that it seems worthy of a passing note.

It was established by Isaac and Mary S. Lippincott, and was
opened for the reception of pupils in the spring of 1842.

When Isaac purchased the property there was an old stone
dwelling-house on it, that had stood at the time of the Revolution.
To this he built an addition before the opening of the school, and
some years later another, both of which were of frame. The building,
composed of these three parts, stood until after the property had been
sold by M. S. L., at whose request the new owner called it " Rosamond." After the removal of a part of the building, and alterations
in the remaining parts, it was fitted up for a summer boarding-house,
under the name of " Rosamond Inn." It was thus used for several
seasons, but latterly it has remained closed all the year.

The Boarding School was continued from 1842 to 1879, and the
Day school one year longer, the latter being abandoned in Sixth
Month, 1880.

Of the teachers Ellen Thomas had the longest term, having taught in the school from 1848 to 1880—thirty-two years; Rebecca W. Oakford taught thirteen years; Mary Emma Satterthwaite, ten years; Susan Roberts, nine years; Abigail Woolman, five years; and Edith Newlin, Susan M. Chalfonte and several others were teachers there for short periods.

The largest number of pupils at any time was ninety, and the average for many years was from seventy to eighty.

The health of the pupils was generally very good, but in cases of illness, Dr. Woolman, while he continued to practice, and after his retiring, the two Drs. Stokes were the attending physicians. The professional services of these were very satisfactory to the Principal of the School, who felt the weight of her responsibility in caring for the sick, when they were far away from home and parents.

Daniel P. Lippincott, Isaac's only son who lived to the age of manhood, died some years before his father, so that at the time of Isaac's death, the one to take his place in business matters, and in the charge of the family, was his oldest grandson, Isaac L. Woolman. He came to live with Mary and her daughters, and took the place of a son and a brother. He transacted the business, took charge of the farm, and proved himself a devoted caretaker. About five years he occupied this position, and to the end of her life, Mary looked to him for advice and assistance, as she would have done to her own child. She appreciated his business ability, and felt grateful for his kindness to herself and daughters.

Daniel P. Lippincott, Jr., after he was fifteen years old, was also a member of the family, and though much of his time was passed at boarding schools, yet grandmother's house was his home.

Among the pupils were found quite a number of the second, and possibly, of the third generation. It would be interesting to hear mother and daughter comparing experience of the happy days passed at the Moorestown home, and of the many pleasant memories associated with the place. But whatever changes time had made, however different might be the surroundings, there was one point that remained fixed, one condition that did not change, and that was the never-failing kindness of "Aunt Mary." In all her writings, with the frequent allusion to school and to family, she does not once, in all those thirty-eight years, speak of having an undesirable pupil or teacher in the institution. Is not this strong *negative* testimony, confirmed by much, very much, that is positive, to prove her fitness for being at the head of a boarding-school? It is probable that not a few of her pupils bade her farewell with subdued emotion, and with the good resolution which they carried out, and of which they are now receiving the benefit.

> " We will treasure up thy precepts,
> They may be, in future years,
> Balm to soothe our saddened spirits,
> Strength to banish doubts and fears."

Brief Reminiscences.

One winter some cases of varioloid having occurred in the large family of Mary S. Lippincott, it caused a suspension of intercourse with the neighbors. After several weeks of this isolation, two of her friends (they were elderly men, and probably had been inoculated in the old-fashioned way), who had no fear of the contagion, came to make her a visit. Great indeed was her surprise, and no less her gratification, on meeting these valued friends, who had come so far to see her and to encourage her. They dined, and remained several hours in the house, and when they bade her farewell, she said, in the fullness of her heart, *I now feel as if I could stand a fast of forty days.* The friends were Samuel Willits of New York city, and Samuel J. Underhill, of Jericho, L. I.

A visitor gives the following :—It was my privilege, at different times, to be a guest at the Moorestown home of Mary S. Lippincott, and hence to know what it was to receive her cordial welcome and to enjoy her hospitality. It seemed to be one, among the many, of her gifts, to lead the conversation from that which was cheerful and even sprightly, to themes of graver import, and thus to introduce the serious and all-important subject of religion without any seeming violation of the social courtesies, or of that deep sense of *reverence* which she was so careful to preserve in herself and to cherish in those who were under her care.

Once when I was there, at sunset, she called attention to the brilliancy of the Western sky, and then quoted from her favorite poet, Cowper :

> " Scenes must be beautiful which daily viewed
> Please daily, and whose novelty survives
> Long knowledge and the scrutiny of years ;
> Praise justly due to those which I describe."

When the hour for retiring came, the guests were invited to accompany her into the large school-room, and to attend the evening collection. One of these occasions is vividly remembered after the lapse of nearly thirty-five years. It was on a Seventh-day evening, and the social mingling in the parlor had been not only pleasant, but unusually sprightly. At the appointed time we repaired to the school-room, and after we had taken our seats there was a solemn pause of suitable length for all to feel the weightiness of the occasion. Then, Mary opened the large Family Bible, and read the fortieth chapter of Isaiah with such reverence and such pathos as seemed to give an unction to the words as they flowed from her lips. The dignity of her presence, the gravity of her manner, and the benignity of her countenance could scarcely have failed to have a solemnizing effect upon the pupils, whose solid deportment was their silent response to the reading, and the seal of their appreciation of the deference due to the Book.

Once, when attending a Yearly Meeting of Ministers and Elders, our friend expressed a concern for these members, as they are looked upon as the heads of their meetings. The concern had reference to the example which they should set of *weightiness of manner and of appearance* in our religious meetings.

She referred to the Scriptural account of the Queen of Sheba, who in her admiration of the beautiful order in Solomon's household, did not fail to notice the sitting of his servants.

A young minister who was present on the occasion, was much impressed with her concern, and with the effect of it upon the meeting. It is to this (then) young man, that we are indebted for the account of that exercise.

An Appointed Meeting at Millville, New Jersey.

[The Friend who was present, and who gives the account of this meeting, does not remember the year.]

Our dear friend, Mary S. Lippincott, had an evening meeting appointed at her request, in the Presbyterian place of worship at Mill-ville, New Jersey.

The assembly was large, and was made up almost entirely of those who were but little acquainted with Friends or with their principles. She seemed to be wonderfully strengthened by Divine power to explain some of the main doctrines that we as a Society own. She dwelt largely on the light within, or the power of God unto salvation, by and through Jesus Christ, our Lord, establishing the Sonship between God the Father and his children, by and through the living Christ, which would ever lead away from the perishing things of this lower world, up to the things that pertain to a higher life. She also called all, in a powerful and feeling manner, to let go of the idea that man could save his brother, or give to God a ransom for his soul. She felt that, with some that were present, there was too much of a dependence upon man, instead of looking up to a Higher Power.

It was a favored opportunity, and we seemed to be dipped into fellowship and love together, under the power of Christ, through this dedicated servant.

Two men, both of whom were ministers, came to Mary after the close of the meeting, and told her that they had come there partly out of curiosity to hear a *woman preach ;* but that they had been both instructed and edified, for her explanation of the *light within*, or the power of God unto salvation, was the most satisfactory they had ever heard.

First-day Schools.

At one of the last meetings (perhaps *the* last) of the Representative Committee of Philadelphia Yearly Meeting, that Mary S. Lippincott ever attended, she was much exercised on the subject of First-day schools. Notwithstanding the interest that she had formerly taken in this work, she seemed now to have grave apprehensions lest these schools might absorb the interest which should be felt in our religious meetings ; adding emphatically, *If it is so, do let the First-day schools go.* She impressed upon the members of the committee the importance of the matter, and wished them to take it home with them, and to consider it weightily.

She expressed the same apprehension to a Friend who visited her a few weeks before her death, and found her exercised on account of the state of the Society.

My first acquaintance with Mary S. Lippincott was soon after her removal to Camden, in the year 1881. From this date until the end of her life, I was often called to see her professionally, and I came to regard her as an interesting and somewhat remarkable character. The unclouded intellect at her time of life, the interest manifested in current events, the patience in suffering, and the deep, religious trust, all combined to render her a good example of one green in old age.

The last time that I saw her was only about half an hour before her close. Even at that late period her mind was clear, still showing that remarkable force of character and Christian faith so characteristic of her long and well-spent life.

ALEXANDER M. MECRAY, M. D.

THE SCHUMACHER OR SHOEMAKER FAMILY.

The earliest information we have of the Shoemaker family, is that obtained from "Besse's Sufferings of Friends." From this it appears, that in the year 1657, William Ames and George Rolfe, English Friends, visited Kreisheim, now Kriegsheim, a small village situated on the right bank of the Rhine, in the Palatinate, whose inhabitants were mostly farmers. Among these simple-minded people, these Ministers made many converts to their faith, who soon began to suffer persecution. In 1663 a fine of five shillings was imposed on each person, every time they assembled for worship; to collect it, their cattle and household goods were seized, and sold, they declining voluntarily to pay the same. Among those whose names appear the oftenest are, George and Peter Schumacher. A few years ago Professor Seidensticker, of Philadelphia, hoping to get earlier data of them, visited Kriegsheim, but learned that a fire, in 1848, had destroyed the church records, so that nothing further could be obtained.

In 1680, William Penn learned of the persecutions they were undergoing, and visited them, inviting them to join him in the Province he was then founding, now the great State of Pennsylvania. This they gladly accepted, and it led to the formation of the Frankford Company, who secured 5,350 acres, about six miles north of Philadelphia. On this spot they located. The first to arrive came in 1683; among them was Jacob Schumacher. There is no way now of knowing positively, but most likely he was a brother of George and Peter, and being single, apparently, he probably acted as a pioneer, to report the kind of place it was.

The ground on which the Friends' Meeting House stands, Germantown Ave. and Coulter St., was given by him for the purpose. We find the following in the Borough and Court Records of Germantown : "1692, the 29th day of 9th Month. John Silans (upon Jacob Schumacher's complaint) promised before this Court to finish the said Jacob Schumacher's barn within four weeks next coming."

How primitive this now appears to us; there were no fines or penalties attached for nonfulfillment, but simply the delinquent's promise exacted. The late Joseph S. Paxson was much interested in his Shoemaker genealogy, which he worked back to Jacob and Margaret, but could not discover satisfactorily who Jacob was. After investigation, I became convinced, and I think he did too, that it was this Jacob, who removed in 1714–15 from Abington to Philadelphia (Germantown Meeting Records were kept at Abington at this time), with his wife, two sons, and daughter Susannah. His wife was Margaret Gove, but the date of their marriage is not known.

Jacob's Will is dated 9 Mo. 22nd, 1722, by which he leaves to his son-in-law, John Breintwall (no doubt Susannah's husband) five shillings; to his wife Margaret the remainder, to be divided at her death between his three sons, George, Thomas and Jacob. Jacob married Elizabeth Roberts, and had three sons—Thomas, and David and Jonathan, twins. From Jonathan, who married Sarah Lownes, comes what I may term the Paxson-Hathway-Pickering line.

Jacob's report to those of his kin must have been favorable, as the following shows: "The Francis & Dorothy from London, Richard Bridgeman, Commander, arrived in Phila. 10 Mo. 12th, 1685. Among the passengers were Peter Schumacher and Peter his sonn, Sarah his Cosen, and Frances and Gertrude his daughters." Peter seems to have taken an active part in the affairs of the new town, as his name is mentioned in various capacities. In the Records of Abington Meeting, appears the marriage of Peter, Jr., to Margaret Op den Graeff, daughter of Herman Op den Graeff, 2nd Mo. 6th, 1697. The two fathers are among the witnesses.

Peter, Jr., and Margaret Shoemaker had ten children, and no doubt there are numerous descendants, but I have never come across them. Elwood Michener, of Toughkenamon, Pa., has a genealogical tree of their descendants, prepared by his father, the late Dr. Ezra Michener.

The next of the family to come, are of more interest to us, as from them the most of those bearing the name are descended. They were George, Sarah his wife, and their seven children; George, Jr., 23 years of age; Barbary, 20; Abraham, 19; Isaac, 17; Susanna, 13; Elizabeth, 11, and Benjamin, 10. They sailed in the ship Jefferies, Thomas Arnold, Master, from London, landing at Chester 3 Mo.

20th, 1686.* They did not, however, all reach here, as the father
died at sea, of small-pox ; but the widow and her children came on
to what their English neighbors then called the German Town. Of
their early struggles we have no account, but they were, no doubt,
severe. The first of the children to enter matrimony was Isaac, who
married Sarah, daughter of Gerhard Hendricks, a prominent Friend,
and one of the signers of the first Protest against Slavery, as will
appear later. Hendricks had drawn lot No. 8 in the Pastorius division of the town, which extended from the Main St. to the Bristol
Township Line. His house he built about a quarter of a mile from
the Main St., on the Wingohocking Creek, the Lane leading back
being known until the last few years as Shoemakers' Lane, and of
course now being built up. The house stood until torn down in 1840
(by a person named Mehl), and from its passing to Isaac, through his
wife, became known as Shoemakers' house ; see its picture in Wat-
son's Annals. On a large rock, forming a cliff, close to the house,
William Penn preached to the people assembled below in the meadow.
On the Rock itself a house still stands, known as the "Rock House,"
and probably used originally for tenants or work people.

The old Hendricks' Bible is now in the possession of the widow
of Samuel M. Shoemaker, of Baltimore. It was printed in Zurich,
A. D. 1538, by C. Fronschover, and has a number of Shoemaker
records in it. Isaac was a tanner by profession, his yard being located
on the Main St. above Shoemakers' Lane, about where Harkinson's
stores now stand. On the north corner of the Lane and Main St., he
built, somewhere about 1725, a long two-story house of stone. After
the manner of the old country, its main entrance was from the rear,
but a doorway from the Main St. gave the appearance of a three-story
dwelling. After the battle of Germantown, the British used it as a
hospital, under the charge of Dr. Moore, whose patients filled every
room. It remained in the family until purchased by the late George
G. Thompson, who tore it down in 1843, and erected on its site Cot-
tage Row.

Benjamin, a son of Isaac and Sarah, was invited to a seat in the
Provincial Assembly, at the same time as James Hamilton ; after considering two months, he determined to accept, and was qualified
2 Mo. 4th, 1745–6. He was mayor of Phila. in 1743, 1751 and 1760,

* There is an apparent discrepancy of dates, owing to "Old and New
Style."

and from 1751 until his death in 1761, City Treasurer. His son Samuel, on the father's death, succeeded him as Treasurer. He was also Mayor two years, 1769 and 1771, and served two terms in the Assembly, 1771 and 1773. He likewise had other positions of trust. Like most Friends he disapproved of the Revolutionary War, and as a consequence his property was confiscated. He went to New York, where he was of much service to American prisoners during the war. A portion of the time he spent in England, and while there, had an interview with George III, under the auspices of his friend Benjamin West. The King asked him, "why the Province of Pennsylvania improved more than the neighboring Provinces, some of which had been earlier settled?" Samuel politely replied to this German King, "it was principally due to the Germans;" and the King as politely rejoined, "that the improvement was principally due to the Quakers." The King was pleased that he could speak German, and the Queen wept when he spoke of the death of his children. Samuel concluded that so kind a husband, and considerate a man, could not be a tyrant. He returned to this country in 1789, and got back a portion of his property, which was secured to him by the Treaty of Peace of 1783. He died in 1800. During his residence in Philadelphia, he built a fine country-seat in Germantown, on Main St. above Washington Lane. This was erected about 1760. During the Revolutionary War it was filled with tailors and shoemakers, employed in making goods for the army. Of latter years it was known as "Pomona," and belonged to Amos R. Little.

A writer speaking of this period says, "There are no names more cherished at home, and more deservedly known abroad, than those of Wister, Shoemaker, Muhlenberg, etc." The late Samuel M. Shoemaker, of Baltimore, who stood very high in the community, and was extensively engaged in commercial enterprises, was a grandson of Samuel, the Mayor. From this line of Isaac and Sarah, descend what is known as the Shoemaker–Rawle–Morris–Pennington branch. For a fuller account of them, see Keith's "Provincial Councillors." Isaac's sister Susanna, married on the 4th day of 1st Month, 1696, at the house of Richard Wall, according to the good order of Friends, Isaac, son of Phillip Price.

Witnesses present—William Jenkins, Richard Wall, Richard Townsend, Jon. Roberts, Robert Owen, with many others. From this line came the late Eli K. Price, who in a little volume called

"The Family," has traced out their branch. George Shoemaker, the eldest of the emigrant children, did not marry until he had been in this country eight years (probably the burden of supporting his fatherless brothers and sisters came on him), and when he did, his selection was Sarah, granddaughter and only heir of Richard Wall. The venerable old marriage certificate is still owned by a descendant, and is dated 12 Mo. 14th, 1694. It commences thus : "Whereas, George Shoemaker and Sarah Wall, both of the township of Cheltenham, in the county of phylladelfia, having declared theyre Intentions of taking each other as husband and wife before several publique meetings of the people of God called Quakers, according to the good order and use Amongst them, whose proceedings," etc.

George signs it in his native German script, while Sarah attaches her new name, in English, in a bold, clear hand, spelling it Shewmaker, a curious variation from the mode in which her numerous descendants spell the now wide-spread name.

Richard Wall, as a direct ancestor of the Shoemaker family, and from the prominent position he held, is worthy of mention. He was an English Friend, who, according to the Records at Harrisburg, had several tracts granted to him in the years 1682, 1683, and 1684, in Phila. County, on the Quesenoming, now called Tacony Creek. It consisted of 600 acres of land, most beautifully situated, in what is now the heart of Chelton Hills, and covered with many of the handsomest country-seats around Philadelphia.

I have little question, that his house, which was of stone, still stands, and forms the back building, or rear, of Joseph Bosler's dwelling. It was quite customary in those days, when Meeting Houses were not plentiful, to use a private dwelling for the purpose of worshipping in. This was done with his house ; the meeting being afterward known as Abington Meeting ; though at the early period in question, called Dublin Meeting. So closely identified were these, our ancestors, with a noteworthy historical incident, that it must be an excuse for placing it here in full. It was the first Protest against Slavery issued in this country. The original is in the possession of Friends at 4th & Arch Sts.

"This is to the Monthly Meeting held at Rigerts Worrels.* These are the reasons why we are against the traffick of mens-body as fol-

Richard Wall's.

loweth : Is there any that would be done or handled at this manner? viz : to be sold or made a slave for all time of his life? How fearfull & fainthearted are so many on sea, when they see a strange vessel, being afraid it should be a Turck, and they should be tacken and sold for slaves in Turckey. Now what is better done as Turcks doe? yea is it worse for them, wch say they are Christians, for we hear, that ye most part of such Negers are brought heither against their will & consent, and that many of them are stollen. Now, tho' they are black, we cannot conceive there is more liberty to have them slaves, as it is to have other white ones. There is a saying, that we shall doe to all men, licke as we will be done ourselves : macking no difference of what generation, descent, or Colour they are.

"And those who steal or robb men, and those who buy or purchase them, are they not all alicke. Here is liberty of Conscience, wch is right & reasonable, here ought to be lickewise liberty of ye body, except of evildoers, wch is an other case. But to bring men hither, or to robb and sell them against their will, we stand against. In Europe there are many oppressed for Conscience sacke ; here there are many oppressed wch are of a black Colour. And we, who know, that men must not commit adultery, some doe committ adultery in others, separating wifes from husbands, and giving them to others, and some sell the children of those poor creatures to other men. Oh ! doe consider well this things, you who doe it, if you would be done at this manner? and if it is done according Christianity? you surpass Holland & Germany in this thing. This mackes an ill report in all those Countries of Europe, where they hear off, that ye Quakers doe here handle men, Licke they handle there ye Cattle ; and for that reason some have no mind or inclination to come hither. And who shall maintaine this your cause, or plaid for it? Truely we can not do so, except you shall inform us better hereoff, viz : that christians have liberty to practise this thing. Pray ! What thing in the world can be worse towarts us then if men robb or steal us away & sell us for slaves to strange Countries, separating housband from their wife and children. Being now this not done at that manner we will be done at, therefore we contradict & are against this traffick of men body. And we profess that it is not lawfull to steal, must lickewise avoid to purchase such things as are stolen, but rather help to stop this robbing and stealing if possible, and such men ought to be delivered out of ye hands of ye Robbers, and set free as well as in Europe.

"Then is Pensilvania to have a good report, in stead it hath now a bad one for this sacke in other Countries. Especially whereas ye Europeans are desirous to know in what manner ye Quakers doe rule in their Province, & most of them doe loock upon us with an envious eye. But if this is done well, what shall we say, is done evil? If once these slaves (wch they say are so wicked and stubborn men) should joint themselves, fight for their freedom, and handel their masters & mastrisses, as they did handel them before; will these masters & mastrisses tacke the sword at hand & warr against these poor slaves, licke, we believe, some will not refuse to doe? or have these negers not as much right to fight for their freedom, as you have to keep them slaves?

"Now consider well this thing, if it is good or bad? and in case you find it to be good, to handle these blacks at that manner, we desire & require you hereby lovingly that you may inform us herein, which at this time never was done, Viz : that Christians have liberty to do so, to the end we shall be satisfied in this point, & satisfie likewise our good friends and acquaintances in our natif Country, to whose it is a terrour or fairfull thing, that men should be handled so in Pensilvania.

"This is from our meeting at Germantown, hold ye 18 of the 2 month, 1688, to be delivered to the monthly meeting at Richard Warrel's [Richard Wall's].

gerret hendericks,*

derick op de graeff,†

Francis daniell Pastorius,‡

Abraham op den graef." ‖

The Germantown Friends having thus discharged the burden of this concern, the missive shortly came before the Monthly Meeting, held at the house of Richard Wall. The disposition which this made of it is as follows :

"At our monthly meeting at Dublin, ye 30, 2 mo., 1688, we having inspected ye matter above mentioned & considered it, we finde it so weighty, that we think it not Expedient for us to meddle with it here, but do rather committ it to ye consideration of ye Quarterly meeting, ye tennor of it being nearly related to ye truth.

On behalf of ye monthly meeting. signed, pr. Jo. Hart."

* Gerhard Hendrick. † Dirck Op den Graeff. ‡ Francis Daniel Pastorius. ‖ Abraham Op den Graeff.

It then passed to their next higher meeting, as follows :

" This above mentioned was Read in our Quarterly meeting at Philadelphia, the 4th of y° 4 mo., '88, and was from thence recommended to the Yearly Meeting, and the above-said Derick and the other two mentioned therein, to present the same to y° above-said meeting, it being a thing of too great a weight for this meeting to determine.

Signed by order of y° Meeting,
Anthony Morris."

At the Yearly Meeting held at Burlington the 5 day of 7 mo., 1688, "A paper being presented by some German Friends, Concerning the Lawfulness and Unlawfulness of buying and Keeping Negroes, It was adjudged not to be so proper for this Meeting to give a positive Judgement in the case, It having so general a relation to many other Parts, and, therefor, at present they forbear it."

It is not strange that these simple-hearted people, who had sacrificed so much in order to secure freedom and religious toleration, should have viewed with sorrow the wrong done their colored brethern ; and they deserve great credit for the effort made against an evil that baffled all attempts at its remedy by our greatest statesmen, for nearly two centuries.

A few years after the marriage of his granddaughter, Richard Wall found his health failing, and made his Will as follows :

" In the name of God, Amen, the fifteenth day of the first month, Anno Domini 1697–8, I, Richard Wall, being weak in body, but of perfect mind and memory, thanks be the Lord for it, do hereby make and ordain this my last Will and Testament, that is to say, Principally and first of all, I recommend my soul and spirit unto the hands of our faithful Creator and Saviour, my body to be buried in a Christian like and decent manner, at the discretion of my dear wife, and executrix, and as to touching such worldly estate, wherewith it hath pleased God to bless me in this wilderness, I dispose of the same in the following way and form. Imprimis, &c.

One bequest is the following :

" Item. I freely give and bequeath unto Friends of Cheltenham Meeting a certain tract of land containing about six acres, lying and being at the South West end of the S' my plantation, and this piece of land I give for a burying place, and for the only and sole use of

friends of the now mentioned Cheltenham Meeting. And I do here-
with constitute, make and ordain the above said my granddaughter,
Sarah Shoemaker, my only Executor, requiring that this my last will
and testament may in all points be accomplished and fulfilled. In
witness whereof I have hereunto set my hand and seal."

I have been unable to find any record which furnishes the date
of Richard's death ; but my reason for thinking it was soon after his
Will was made, is from the fact that he makes his mark, which would
indicate extreme weakness, and the close proximity of death, as I have
little question a man of his standing knew how to write.

The Burying Ground thus provided for, is beautifully located on
Cheltenham Ave., or as the country folks called it in times past,
" Grave Yard Lane." About half an acre is enclosed with a stone
wall, and all is in excellent order ; owing much of latter time to the
care and attention bestowed on it by Robert Shoemaker. Almost in
the middle are two large box-bushes, under which, tradition says,
lie the bodies of Richard Wall and his wife.

It is said a Log Meeting House at one time stood alongside of
the ground ; if this was so, all traces, even of the foundation, have
gone ; so it cannot be verified. The Ground has always gone by the
name of " Shoemaker Burying Ground ; " but as we have seen in the
Will, it is not strictly a family one, though as a matter of fact, the
majority of those interred there bear the name of Shoemaker, or are
allied to it by marriage. About a 150 years ago, Cheltenham Meeting was absorbed by Abington Meeting, and since that time this
burial place has been held by Trustees (Special), appointed by the
Meeting. Of late, few interments have taken place within its limits.
The earliest stone is that of Isaac, dated 8 Mo. 23d, 1741. Friends
in those days did not approve of marking the last resting place of the
departed, so that there are comparatively few stones. For the following list of those named Shoemaker, interred here, I am indebted to
Robert Shoemaker :

8 Mo. 23d, 1741, Isaac, son of George & Sarah Shoemaker,
aged 41.

1758, Elizabeth, wife of Isaac. (Not the Isaac above.)

1762, Amy, Widow of Abraham.

1764, George, " of Cheltenham."

1764, Dorothy, widow of Isaac who died in 1741.

1764, Isaac.

1765, Elizabeth, daughter of Isaac.

1775, Benjamin, son of Isaac.

1775, Arnold.

1779, Isaac, son of John & Elizabeth, aged 24.

1782, Susanna, wife of William.

1783, Elizabeth, daughter of Jonathan.

1783, Sarah, daughter of George.

1793, 3 Mo. 17th, Mary, wife of Benjamin. (Grandmother of M. S. L.)

1793, 10 Mo. 22nd, Benjamin, Jr.

1793, 11 Mo. 14th, Mary Allen Shoemaker.

1793, 11 Mo. 15th, Mary, wife of Thomas. (The writer's great-grandmother.)

1795, 5 Mo. 30th, Elizabeth, wife of John.

1811, Benjamin. (His wife was a Comly & died in 1793, see above.)

1826, 8 Mo. 12th, Mary, daughter of Thomas & Hannah, aged 20 years.

1827, Hannah, wife of Thomas.

1837, 2 Mo. 11th, Thomas (Husband of Mary who died 1793). Aged 74.

1841, 11 Mo., Ellis C., aged 21 years.

1843, Comly, son of Benjamin & Mary, aged 68.

1845, Sarah, widow of Comly.

1849, 12 Mo. 23d, Martha, widow of Robert, aged 90. (Grandmother of Robert & Benjamin ; her husband died of Yellow Fever in 1795, and was interred at 4th & Arch Sts.)

1852, 6 Mo. 12th, Margaret, widow of Thomas. (He had three wives.)

There were other interments, not noted, but which we are almost sure took place, as for instance, George, and his wife, Sarah Wall Shoemaker, etc.

After the death of Richard Wall the place began to be known as Shoemaker's, and as a little village grew up, it naturally took on the name of Shoemakertown.

*   *   *   *   *   *   *

A small number of the family of George and Sarah Wall Shoemaker remain around the old site at Shoemakertown, many have located in the neighboring counties, a few drifted back to the first

home of the family in Germantown, while others again have wandered
to the remotest parts of the country.   It is, however, a little remarkable, that so many have remained true to the *faith* for which their
ancestors sacrificed their home and country, settling in a wilderness,
in order to enjoy religious toleration.

Thos. H. Shoemaker.

Germantown, Ninth Month 8th, 1892.

[The above is the *early part* of an elaborate account, prepared by T. H.
S., of these worthy ancestors, and their numerous descendants.   In the remaining portion he traces the different lines down to the present day, and gives
a number of incidents and anecdotes—some recorded, and some traditional—
which, taken in their several connections, form a history of great interest to the
family, and one which would be valuable to the Society of Friends.--Ed.]

www.ingramcontent.com/pod-product-compliance
Lightning Source LLC
Chambersburg PA
CBHW021046030726
47496CB00006B/1708